THE ANNIVERSARY

SARAH K. STEPHENS

Print ISBN 978-1-913419-37-0

ALSO BY SARAH K. STEPHENS

It Was Always You

To my children, whose stories inspire me

PROLOGUE

A sluice of fear shoves itself down my throat. I start to shout out a name, to call for help, but my words are cut off as fingers wrap around my neck. I put my hands around both wrists, gripping at the arms that surround me and flailing my feet as I try to get traction against the soft ground.

The gash in my leg keeps pumping blood, and my heartbeat pounds in my ears.

I can't breathe.

I can't move.

Starbursts flood my eyes. All I can think about, as darkness begins to saturate the color around me, is how the last image I'll ever see is someone I love wanting me to die just a little faster.

1

The cabin sits at the bottom of a ravine, at the end of a long and winding gravel drive. There's no mailbox. No sign. We only find the turn-off because the owner gave Jackson GPS coordinates to input into his phone for directions.

By the time we pull up at the spot my husband chose for our honeymoon, we haven't seen another living soul for miles.

There's a stream running through the valley where the cabin sits, the dried riverbank around it suggesting the water is usually much deeper than the gentle flow twinkling in the sunlight. Driving to the cabin, we have to cross a crescent-shaped bridge that arcs from bank to bank, looking like something out of a storybook.

The cabin matches its surroundings perfectly, and taking it in with my eyes leaves me with that deep pit in my stomach I used to get when I'd ask my mother to read me a bedtime story. The roof of the cabin is painted red, with shingles that curve underneath the gutters. Each window is flanked by green shutters with hearts carved in the middle, and there's a long, wide porch facing the gravel drive, strewn with a scattering of rocking

3

chairs and an unfinished checker game on an antique-looking barrel.

Bright red geraniums burst out into the sunlight from their flowerbox beds lining the porch.

It looks like someone's version of heaven.

"Do you like it?" Jackson asks as we pull in.

He parks the car in the gravel lot next to the cabin, and the air is perfectly still as we step out of the car, broken only by the bright call of a bird flying across the blue sky through the treetops.

My husband and I both jump out and rush up to the porch. We can unpack later.

"I love it," I tell him, because there's nothing else I can say.

There's a lockbox on the door, and Jackson checks his phone to get the proper code to let us in. Inside, the cabin is just as picturesque as it is outside. Pale wood paneling covers the floor, walls, and ceiling, making me feel like I'm in Geppetto's workshop. The furniture in the living room consists of a slick faux-leather sofa in a muted brown, and two soft recliners nestled in front of the fireplace.

"Where's the bedroom?" Jackson asks, coming up from behind and wrapping his arms around me.

I lean into him. A patch of stubble has grown up on his chin over the three days since he's come home, and I ignore the scratch of it against my cheek as I turn around and kiss him.

"Who needs a bedroom," I say.

Even with everything that happened after he left, my need to be near him, to touch his body and feel his weight on me, is undeniable. Here, in this cabin he's chosen just for us, on our honeymoon that should have happened nine months ago, the certainty that we're meant to be together––that nobody could feel this much desire for another person if it wasn't meant to be––tries to settle over me. I want it so badly to be true.

4

His eyes fix on mine, and our breathing joins together in quick gasps. I curse myself for wearing a shirt with buttons. Jackson fumbles with the eyelets, and I take over undoing them. Just as I'm about to get it off, and unveil the new red lace bra I bought during my emergency shopping trip with Dani the day before Jackson flew home from Australia, my husband pauses. He looks at me, his gaze moving up and down over my body like he's stroking my skin.

"Not yet."

My mouth makes a small sound––somewhere between a bleat and a pop––and my confidence in the two of us crumbles like shortbread in my pocket. I move away from him. When Jackson laughs, I have the urge to turn around and slap him.

And I could, I realize. No one would hear it. No one can see what either of us will do to each other in this cabin.

A shiver runs up my spine.

Dani's words from our phone call yesterday, while I packed for this impromptu honeymoon, spring to the front of my mind. "You barely know him," my best friend told me, in that voice of hers reserved for reasoning with rude customers at our store and disciplining overly friendly dogs. Stern yet loving, anxiety peering in at the edges.

I'd laughed when she brought it up. "He's my husband," I reminded her. As if that justified everything.

"Honey, I don't mean not now," Jackson says. "I just mean, not yet."

But I'm not listening.

I've headed back out to the car to gather the rest of our bags, my cheeks flaming with embarrassment at Jackson's lack of interest in me as much as my own lack of self-control. Desire, mistrust, love, guilt, pain, longing. There is a toxic cyclone inside me that's been building for the last nine months while Jackson was busy halfway across the world, and if I don't get it under control I will ruin everything. I just need a few moments to calm down.

My shirt is still unbuttoned, and it flaps in the breeze as I take the steps down the porch to the open trunk of our car. The air on my skin, sweaty from our near-romp and the heat of the day, makes little goose pimples rise on my stomach and chest, so I wrap my arms around my waist, holding my shirt closed like some suburban mom's robe as she rushes her children off to school from the front door.

We didn't exactly pack lightly for our trip. Both Jackson and I have a suitcase each, plus the grocery bags full of food and provisions we bought at the supply store, and a few other sundries we've brought from the apartment.

I stare up into the trees, and wonder what the hell I'm doing with my life.

My mother has a treatment later this week that Dani is going to take her to. Maybe I should just leave––drive back and be there with her, instead of being patted here in a platonic way by my husband.

I take a deep breath and remind myself that there's no grace in self-pity. I have made choices, and now I need to live with them. I know that.

It's just that I also think I'm justified, after all the time I've spent wishing my brand-new husband home, that he be categorically, insurmountably desperate to put his hands on me.

All anyone really wants is to feel wanted.

My mother taught me that.

I should call her. The thought cuts in unexpectedly, and it feels good knowing that I can call my mother. That she's a part of my life again.

But before I can pull out my phone there are footsteps behind me, and I turn to see Jackson all pink in the cheeks and bashful.

I've left my shirt to swing free again as I haul a suitcase from the car, followed by a bag of groceries capped with a baguette and leafy greens spilling out the sides. It reminds me of a print Dani has framed in her apartment, with a Parisian street in black and white and a bicycle leant against a doorway, a basket at the front overflowing with flowers and fresh bread.

If this were Paris, I think, *my husband would be fucking me right now*.

"Mary, come on. You misunderstood me."

"Let's just get settled in."

I start to roll the suitcase across the gravel, but a wheel catches on the stones below and twists out of my grasp. My left breast spills out of the––perhaps in hindsight––one-size-too-small basque bra I'd bought from Victoria's Secret, despite Dani's warnings. At the time, I'd pictured it as the perfect accent to the bright yellow and red dresses my best friend helped me pick out for Jackson's arrival at the airport, and the welcome-home party she'd helped me plan. Now, though, it just feels wrong.

"Stop. Just stop for one second."

I ignore him and keep rolling across the gravel, like a granola-loving Lady Godiva.

"It's fine, Jackson." I bite down hard on his name. "It's not a big deal."

"Clearly it is," he says, more than a little exasperated at this point. "What's wrong with us having a little slow burn this time?"

Something in what he says makes me stop. Finally.

Because he's right. There's nothing wrong with that.

We've had plenty of hot, immediate sex over the three days since he's come back from Australia. At this point, making love might as well be our favorite pastime. But I've spent the first almost-year of my married life living like a spinster with a

pretend husband, and everything Jackson did––or didn't do––
while he was gone setting up a new satellite office in Sydney for
the financial firm he works for throbs like an open wound.

Having him take one look at my half-naked body and decide
he could wait was just the last straw. Vulnerable isn't a good look
on anybody.

I should tell him this. He's my husband, after all. We're
supposed to share our secrets with each other. Instead, I tuck it
away along with all the others I'm keeping from him.

"You're right. I love a good, slow burn." I quirk the corner of
my mouth up into what I hope is a sexy-ish smile.

Jackson stubs the toe of his shoe into the gravel, worrying a
large round piece of limestone. "Do you?" he asks.

"Look, I'm sorry," I tell him. I let go of the suitcases and start
to button up my shirt. "I think I'm just hungry. Hangry. You
know how I get."

I ignore the little voice at the back of my head that says,
"Maybe he doesn't."

"I'm sorry too." Jackson puts his hands over mine and pulls
them away from my buttons. "Can I make it up to you?"

He kisses that spot on my neck that sends electricity
straight through my body and out, well, you know where. It's
like an ignition button to my endorphin system. God's little gift
to me.

I mold my spine into the curve of his torso, and his hands
slip below the waistband of my jeans.

"Hold on," he whispers into my ear. "Just wait a second."

I bristle instantly, anticipating an encore performance of our
fight.

Jackson slides his hands from my waist and down my arm,
giving a firm tug away from the porch.

"There's a hot tub," he says.

"I didn't bring a swimsuit."

8

He turns back as he pulls me along and gives me a smile. "Neither did I."

We met during one of those summer downpours that promises to be over in a few minutes, but ends up taking the sunlight hostage for most of the afternoon. Customer traffic in the store Dani and I share, Kitchen Kabinet, was as ambivalent as the weather, with only a few people stopping in for most of the day. Dani went out to run errands, so I stayed behind the counter, ready to hold the ship steady during the flood. I stood on a stepladder, dusting the hard-to-reach objects that were up high because they were either terribly expensive or terribly unpopular. Sometimes both.

The bell dinged, Jackson stepped in, all raindrops and cheek bones, shaking the rain off of his coat, and my life divided itself right then and there.

Before Jackson.

And after.

Jackson scanned the store, clearly looking for something in particular. I waited, holding my breath, wishing and dreading the moment his eyes found me. He was just too gorgeous to be real.

When he spotted me—*finally*, it seemed—he rushed over and crooked his neck up to meet my eyes.

"Do you have any olive oil that will impress someone who knows about olive oil?"

Those were the first words Jackson said to me. Maybe not the most earth-shattering, granted, but good enough, apparently.

I climbed down the ladder, glad that I'd worn my slim black pencil skirt that day, along with the tights *without* the run in them, and Jackson told me about his boss, the foodie banker, who was getting married.

We had fun picking out a bottle of plain Portuguese olive oil (extra virgin) and another with hints of basil. He kept asking if I needed help bringing bottles down from the shelves, and seemed nervous whenever our eyes met, although I caught him staring at me a few times while I tried to answer his very specific questions about the differences between refined and virgin.

It occurred to me, with all the subtlety of a cake being smashed in my face, that this beautiful man was flirting with me.

When he asked for my number after I'd gift-wrapped the bottles of olive oil to within an inch of their lives, I didn't hesitate. I wrote it down on his receipt, like some saucy heroine out of a black-and-white movie. Our hands brushed for a moment as I passed it to him across the store counter, and I would swear that it wasn't just me who was trembling as we touched. It felt important, I think, to both of us. Like life was happening.

Jackson called the very next day, and after talking on the phone for longer than is appropriate for anyone over the age of thirteen and past the year 1998, we settled on a date that coming Friday at a little Italian restaurant around the corner from the store. After we hung up, my phone rang again immediately, and without even looking at the number I picked up, certain that it was Jackson calling back, just because.

But it wasn't Jackson. It was my mother.

Seven years of waiting. Seven years of devoting part of my mind to the constant ticker tape of everything I'd done wrong. And then, just like that, she was back.

For a moment, it felt like the happiest week of my life.

Until my mother explained that she was dying.

I follow Jackson as he leads me to the side of the cabin, my eyes fixed for more than a moment on the back of his neck. The place where the collar of his shirt meets his skin is like a trapdoor that I fall through every time. For some people, it's a firm bicep, a smooth breast, a rippled torso. But not for me. For me, it's the edge that beckons, not the reveal. Anticipation has always been my weakest link, and right now, watching the tanned skin of my husband's neck flex as he turns to make sure I'm following him, every worry and irritation of the last few minutes––several months––drops away, and I think I just might die from wanting him so much.

I force myself to look away.

Jackson steps along a cobblestone path carved into the grounds, winding around the side of the building, both his feet and mine brushing up against the pink petunias and bright yellow marigolds planted along the edges as we walk.

As we move around the cabin, the shape of its rooms becomes clearer. There's a shed out back, stocked with fresh firewood, and the structure of the cabin itself seems to consist of two long rectangles, one clearly an addition to the other original building, given the different shades of wood used to build each. The windows sit prettily in the walls, with flower boxes underneath and gauzy white curtains floating around inside the cabin. The hot tub is tucked around the side of the screened-in back porch, nestled in between the corner of the original cabin and the newer addition.

We trot over to it like children heading out to recess after a long morning, hands reaching out for each other and little bursts of laughter streaking through the sunshine. As we pull up to it, though, I find there's a cover on top with a lock holding the lift mechanism down. I peer over at the hot tub dubiously.

"Are we allowed to use it?"

"Of course we are." Jackson lets go of me and sets to the lock, punching in a numerical code he reads off an email from the rental agency on his phone. The lock pops open with a satis-fying click. "The owners keep it locked for when no one is around. It'll just take a minute to get it fired up."

He pushes a few buttons and the pumps inside the tub whir to life. Bubbles break on the surface, and blue lights march along the sides of the tub. After a few seconds, Jackson puts his hand into the water, and tests the temperature.

"Perfect."

My husband turns and looks at me, his hazel eyes locked on mine. "Perfect," he says again.

We trade matching grins, our earlier miscommunication forgotten with the anticipation of something new and slightly scandalous dangling in front of us.

"After you." I gesture with my hand for Jackson to lead the way. His shirt and shorts are off in a flash, and he climbs into the hot tub without a shred of embarrassment. I watch his toned legs, his carved hipbones and rippled back descend into the water until the lower half of his body is camouflaged by the bubbles.

"You're sure there's no one around?" My impulsiveness in the cabin has transformed into a slight awkwardness. It's a different feeling, being naked out in the open instead of within the secu-rity and privacy of four walls. Jackson and I have only ever made love indoors, with no prospect of being spotted by anyone or anything else.

A flash of fear flies through me. *Are there bears in the Pocono mountains? And do they like hot tubs?*

I start to voice my worry, my earlier certainty of our alone-ness now gone, but Jackson interrupts me. "We are as remote as you can get––don't worry. Once we crossed the river, we're the only cabin for miles and miles." He wiggles his eyebrows at me, his cheeks flushing from the heat of the water and, I hope, other enticements. "That's why they call this cabin the honeymooner."

I respond by taking a deep breath, which I hope Jackson doesn't notice, and whipping my shirt off, twirling it cowgirl style over my head before releasing it somewhere into the far edge of the gardens.

Jackson puts his hands to his mouth and lets out a loud wolf whistle.

I decide to keep the red bra on, and in another set of swift motions I've similarly slipped out of my pants and, adjusting my matching red panties so they lay flat against my hips rather than bunching into a lacy knot, start to descend the stairs of the hot tub. Jackson swims over to me––the hot tub is huge, and could probably seat at least ten people at full capacity––and buries his head into the skin just below my navel. He tugs playfully at the edge of my panties with his teeth.

I take a moment to look over his shoulder and around at the surrounding forest. Jackson's right, I can't see another building anywhere. The only sounds are the hum of the hot tub, my husband's quickening breath, and my pulse, tenderly beating in my ears.

We float over to one of the seats in the hot tub, and Jackson fixes himself on the seat and pulls me so that I'm astride him. I feel his hardness against the inside of my thigh, and his excitement sends a pulse of confidence through my body.

"Do you like what you see?" I ask him, and press my mouth hard onto his. I reach down and start to stroke him, and my husband moans with pleasure.

He grabs my breasts in his hands and the strength of his grip sends another lightning bolt through me. Jackson reaches behind me and fiddles with the clasp of my bra, eventually tugging at it until one of the metal hooks gives way.

I'm still playing with him, and he tenses as I reach lower and start a gentle massage. Another gasp escapes his mouth, and I match it with my own as he moves his hands lower on my body, teasing the other spot God gave to us women for pure enjoyment. I offer a silent prayer that I married a man who actually knows what the clitoris is.

Finally, when both of us are caving into the need for each other, to be as close as possible, Jackson tips me back, slips my panties to the side, and guides himself into me. As his body joins with mine, I forget our fight. I forget my fears that we rushed into this marriage. I forget all those times I've been told by the people I love that I'm worthless.

Instead, I sink into the delicious pleasure of having a beautiful man love me.

2

Jackson's relaxed into a post-coital nap and I can't move because my arm is pinned slightly underneath my naked husband's leg. How men can just drop off after sex remains a mystery to me––based on what Dani tells me, there seems to be a switch inside their brains that just flips afterwards into a state of total relaxation, and Jackson is no exception. I, on the other hand, always seem to come crashing back down and my mind gets muddled with every fear I've ever had, jumbled into one big ball of nerves. Sometimes I feel so grateful that I actually like sex, given how my mind tends to twist itself into coils afterwards. Dani told me once that it's like getting hives from shopping––this post-sex anxiety of mine.

Which, of course, is why I'm thinking of Dani.

I don't understand why you're heading out of town so soon. Two nights ago, Dani's voice had trickled into my ear as I balanced the phone against my shoulder, rushing around my bedroom searching for clean socks, underwear, scarves to pack into my duffel bag.

Our bedroom, I remember correcting myself. Jackson's and mine.

After waking up just slightly hungover from buy-one-get-one-free margaritas at his welcome-home party, Jackson surprised me with a much-delayed honeymoon in the Poconos. "Honeymoon capital of the Northeast," he'd crowed, before tickling me under the sheets.

"Because Jackson wants to spend some quality time together; just the two of us," I told my best friend. "And we can celebrate my birthday and our anniversary all together."

I didn't tell Dani what else I was thinking. That it would give me a chance to explain to Jackson what would happen after my birthday. How turning twenty-five in two days will mean more than just another candle on my cake.

"Your wedding anniversary isn't for another three months." Dani does deadpan better than anybody.

"The anniversary of when we first met," I clarified.

"What's that sound?"

Dani has the ears of a hawk. Or a mouse. Whichever has better hearing. Jackson was whisking something in a metal bowl, and the scraping sounds rattled the air of *our* apartment. He had been in the kitchen, whipping something up for dinner for the two of us.

Apparently, he did a lot of cooking when he was in Australia.

"And you'll check in on my mother, right?" I said, ignoring her question.

The line went quiet for a few beats.

"Of course I will," Dani replied. She's not the biggest fan of my mother. "She'll be fine. You deserve a break, you know."

I nodded.

"Stop nodding, and just say okay," Dani reminded me. And then she said something else.

"Have a good time. Don't die of happiness."

We both paused. I know Dani is happy for me. I know she wants me to be happy. But she also hasn't had a relationship for a long time. Hook-ups and a few second dates––yeah. Plenty of those. But commitment has never been her strong suit. For boyfriends at least.

"I love you," I reminded her.

"Love you too," she replied. And then she hung up.

Just then Jackson had walked in wearing an apron that said *Kiss the Cook*, frying pan in hand.

"Was that your mother?"

"No," I said, tension pitching my voice higher. He knows my mother and I'm not quite back to *I love you* terms at the end of phone calls. "Why?"

"I'm just wondering who my gorgeous wife is saying 'I love you' to." He smiled, but there was something behind his eyes that made me stop for a moment.

"It was just Dani," I told him. "She says hello, by the way."

Which she didn't, but sometimes lying is the only way to deal with my husband.

I tug at my arm, trying to move it from underneath Jackson, and he gives a slight murmur that sounds more than a little satisfied (if I say so myself) and rolls over slightly. He pulls his right arm from where he's tucked it underneath his thigh and wraps it around my shoulders, squeezing me in tighter than is comfortable.

His eyes are still shut, but he murmurs something again.

I lean my head closer, trying to catch what he's saying. He doesn't usually talk in his sleep. Then again, he's still been coming back from his Australian-born jet lag. I've woken up the last few nights to find his side of the bed cool, the sheets barely rumpled. One time I got up, and found Jackson staring out the window of our living room, like he was in a trance.

That night, I could have gone over to him, wrapped my arms around his chest, and leaned my chin into the soft hollow of his neck.

But I didn't.

He looked like a stranger in my apartment. I saw his reflection in the window, his eyes sunken with dark crescents that would somehow be gone by morning. His hair had tousled itself into a flurry of dark curls on his head that gave him a manic energy, despite how late it was. He was shirtless, and something about the light made him seem ferocious. Like his arms and chest were clenched for battle. I had to actually swallow a scream when I first spotted him in the dark. I barely recognized him.

It's been hard, adjusting to him being home. To being married.

So I turned around as silently as possible and crept back into bed. In the morning––the morning of Jackson's homecoming party––we both went about our newly settling routine, and I didn't ask him about what was keeping him up at night. I just acted like everything was fine.

And now he's mumbling in his sleep, and my mind is sprinting through everything that could be wrong, because that's what I do when I feel amazing, apparently. Is he saying another woman's name? Some woman in Australia who kept him up at night and made him not return my phone calls and emails and Facetimes?

I glance at his face, and just then his mouth twitches up into a half-smirk.

She's probably some impossibly tall, blond model who surfs at dawn and eats only organic produce. Her name's Sheila, or Cassidy, or something else equally earthy and sporty at the same time.

My husband is still talking in his sleep, but the damn

bubbles in the hot tub are making it impossible to hear the name of the woman he fell in love with in Australia. Maybe.

Why else would he avoid me almost entirely for nine months after begging to marry me just three weeks after our first date?

Why? Because he regrets his decision.

Because he doesn't want to be married anymore.

I lean closer still, trying to read his lips.

There's definitely an S, and maybe a T coming through.

Stella? Is he wishing I were someone named Stella?

Has he taken me out to the woods, alone, in order to let me down easy? Maybe he's figuring he can prime me with a week's worth of amazing sex, and then explain that it's just not going to work out for us and that he wants an annulment.

What is he saying?

I must have said that last part out loud because his eyes pop open.

"I'm saying, stop worrying."

Jackson fixes me with a look that makes my heart stop, just for a split second.

"I can feel the tension literally vibrating off of you. I just wish you'd relax a little. Everything is fine. We're on our honeymoon, at a beautiful cabin, in a hot tub for Christ's sake. There's nothing to worry about."

I shrink away to the other side of the hot tub.

"Come on," Jackson calls over to me. "I didn't mean to embarrass you. I just know how you get up in your head sometimes after, well, you know." He gives me a grin. "And I want this trip to be relaxing, for both of us."

I almost say it. I almost tell him that I can't relax, because we barely know each other and he's spent the beginning of our marriage several continents away ignoring me while he posts happy pictures of himself eating delicious food and hanging out at barbecues with his posh bosses from the office and chronicling every single fun thing he did without me. And because he married a version of me that I created, during those three weeks after we met. The wife he married isn't the woman sitting in the hot tub with him.

But I don't tell him that. Instead, I swim back over.

"There's something we can do to keep me from worrying," I tell my new husband.

Jackson doesn't hesitate. He pulls me into him, harder than the first time.

"You know, sex in a hot tub is a cliché, right?" I give a nibble to Jackson's chest as we lie wrapped in each other's arms, half submerged in the water, trying to recover. My thighs already have a throbbing ache to them that I know will only intensify as the day goes on.

There's always that thin line between pain and pleasure.

He has his eyes closed, and he chuckles at my teasing.

"Cliché or not, that was amazing."

"Or maybe it's that you can't get pregnant in a hot tub." Dani had explained this to me once, maybe two years ago, over coffee at some fancy café in town when she was recounting her prior evening's entertainment with her latest 'hook-up' (her words, not mine). She'd leaned back in her chair, adjusted the bow on the new blouse I'd seen in the window at the boutique down the street just a few days before, and proclaimed that the heat of the water killed off any chances of a mishap. As inexperienced as I was, I hadn't believed the adage then and I still don't buy it now. Though, granted, Dani's never had a pregnancy scare, so perhaps there's some power in her positive thinking––if you believe something hard enough, it just might come true.

"What a shame," Jackson says lazily, sinking an inch deeper into the water.

I pause, unsure of what to say to that. We've talked about children, but only in the most superficial and starry-eyed of ways. We both want kids. That's fairly clear for both of us, but the other wh- questions related to starting a family haven't really come up.

When. Where. Why.

An image of my mother, birthday cake spilled onto the floor and a crumpled letter discarded on the table, flashes in front of me. People have children for all sorts of reasons, but people seem to stop wanting them for the same one.

A small snore breaks into the quiet buzzing of the hot tub. I turn my head up from Jackson's chest to confirm. My husband has fallen asleep. Again.

I try not to move, urging myself to be content to sit in the water and relax. To enjoy being married to this gorgeous man, dammit.

It's just that everything happened in such a fizzy rush after we met. Our first date led to a whole lot of firsts––kisses, nights and then mornings together, 'I love yous'––which all burst into one firebomb of happiness when Jackson proposed at the fountain in the center of downtown, right in front of the public library.

We'd only known each other for three weeks.

At first I told him to stand up and stop being ridiculous. I think I may have suggested we go get ice cream. But Jackson stayed where he was, his knee bent on the sidewalk, pinning a flaming red maple leaf. I remember trying to keep my thoughts from collapsing in on themselves by mentally tracing the curves of the leaf as it branched into points, while Jackson explained that he'd had an offer from his investment firm to go to Australia for nine months.

He'd have to leave in just a little over four weeks.

He'd said he wanted me to come with him, but he also understood my situation. That my mother had just been diagnosed with cancer and that she needed me here. Jackson didn't know the entire truth about my mother and me––he still doesn't––but he knew enough to understand that having my mother back in my life was a big turning point for me. I couldn't just move halfway across the world, not when my mother needed my help.

"This is such a great opportunity for me, Mary. For *us*," Jackson said, still bent on the sidewalk, his hands reaching out to grab hold of mine. I let him take them, and the feel of his rough palms over my fingers was like water smoothing over a stone. "It could really set me to the next level in the firm, and it'll help establish me for years to come. Better salary. Benefits. Everything a family needs."

We'd had one conversation about children, over a big bottle of red wine one night back at my apartment, but it was just pie-in-the-sky fun. It was the kind of conversation you have when everything is going great at the start of a relationship.

Not that I have a ton of experience with that.

I tried to consider what he was saying, but the only thought going through my head seemed to be, *He's leaving!*

That was when I should have told him about my family. Just laid everything out for him––everything that happened. And how everything could change when I turned twenty-five later that year. But Jackson kept talking, and what he said next was something I couldn't risk him taking back.

"I just want to have you to come back to."

Jackson held my gaze as he finally stood up and shifted towards me. His forehead pressed down into mine, and the pressure of his body connecting to me sent a surge of adrenaline through my chest. I've never done drugs, but from what Dani's told me I was pretty sure that that's what it would feel like.

And more than part of me wanted that for the rest of my life.

All of me wanted it.

So I said yes.

And now here I am, with this naked half-stranger asleep next to me.

I glance down at my bare skin, and suddenly my nakedness seems like a vulnerability I can't risk for one more second. I lean gently over Jackson's bare torso and reach for the button to turn the jets on, hoping to obliterate the contours of my body with the bubbles.

As I'm reaching out, my hand gently brushing against that tanned skin of Jackson's shoulder––all those weekends spent surfing on an Australian beach I'll never get to see, I think––my eye is caught by something moving in the forest.

I instantly tense, and swing my eyes over to the corner of the cabin, on the far side of the screened-in porch, where I saw the movement. Ready to stare into the eyes of some woodland creature, remembering stories of big cats traipsing through Pennsylvania for hundreds of miles.

But it's not an animal I see. I catch the edge of a shoulder, the fleck of a checkered shirt.

Someone is out in the woods.

3

I sink down further into the water. Jackson gives a sigh, his breathing deep and steady, as I reposition my body and shove my hands into his shoulder.

"Someone's out there," I whisper to him.

But even as I say it, I only see the bright leaves of the trees, the streaming rays of sunshine, and an empty forest surrounding us.

Jackson rouses himself and a satisfied smile curls his lips. He instinctively reaches out to me, and his hands wrap around my waist.

"Was I asleep?" He sounds bewildered, and just a shade close to drunk if I didn't know better.

"I think I saw someone, out there." I point towards the corner of the cabin.

"What?" Jackson rubs at his eyes and wipes a hand over his mouth and jaw. He nuzzles close into my neck, not reading the fear radiating off my body. Or simply ignoring it. "That was amazing, by the way."

I blink my eyes and stare at the spot again. *What did I see?*

"I thought I saw someone, in dark jeans and a checkered shirt."

Jackson's more awake now, but far from what I would call alert or alarmed. He releases his grip on me and leans back against the edge of the hot tub. "Really? Are you sure?"

His nonchalance seems to infect me with doubt, partly because I don't want him to think I'm looking for reasons to ruin our honeymoon, and partly because I know myself. Sometimes I see what I want to see.

But does that mean I want an excuse to leave? To go back to the routine of normal life, where I can ignore my feelings about my marriage more easily?

I look again at the spot in the woods, adjacent to the edge of the cabin. The branches of the trees, the texture of the logs that make up the cabin's walls, and the litter of grass and leaves on the floor all mix together into a palette of greens and browns and––yes, maybe––reds and even darkish black shadows.

No, I'm not sure. It could easily have been a trick of the light or just my imagination ramping up. My post-coital anxiety playing out in new and interesting ways. And Jackson said that there aren't any other cabins or camps nearby.

I glance back at my husband, and Jackson's face is a blank. He doesn't say anything, but he's the furthest he's been from me since we came into the hot tub together.

I involuntarily fold my arms over my chest, and the movement of my body seems to prick something in Jackson because his expression shifts to a tense knot. He glances at his watch, the waterproof James Bond-looking timepiece Dani helped me pick out as a wedding gift. I had a special inscription engraved on the inside plate, a message that at the time had seemed poignant and sweet, but now seems perhaps a little on the nose. *Only fools rush in*, it says. After his proposal Jackson and I would joke with each other, about how people might say that we were impulsive, that we were crazy to get married so soon, but that we both really knew what they were feeling.

Jealous. They were all jealous of how in love we were, how certain we were of our future together. And then Jackson would start singing the lines from that old Elvis song to me, about fools rushing in. About how he couldn't help falling in love with me.

He hasn't sung it since he left for Australia, and the jokes we made have trickled away into awkward pauses, so that now those memories seem far away. Like they're coming from a different couple, and Jackson and I just happened to be there, watching.

"It was probably just my mind playing tricks on me." I shrug, willing myself to believe what I'm saying.

Jackson's forehead creases. Droplets of water bead on his cheeks and chin. "Maybe it was a hiker who was lost?"

"Yeah, maybe," I tell him. "Or maybe it was nothing at all."

"Are you okay?" He doesn't reach out to touch me.

I press my palm to my forehead. "I'm fine."

"Maybe you're just hungry? I seem to recall you getting a little irritable earlier." He doesn't look at me as he talks. My stomach does a flip, and I know I need to fix things.

"I'm sure you're right." I cast a smile at him and hoist myself out of the water, over the steps, and onto the soft grass below.

Shivering despite the warmth of the air, I start to gather my clothes.

"Next time we'll bring towels with us." I laugh a little too loud, and wonder if there will be a next time. Whether either of us will want one.

"Let's get warm inside," Jackson says, pulling himself out and rushing like I did to gather his own clothes. "I'll make dinner."

"I like the sound of that." It's a peace offering, and Jackson seems to take it. The tension in his shoulders that's built up over the last several minutes seeps away.

We half run, half walk to the front of the cabin, our clothes flapping in the breeze at first and then clinging to our wet bodies. By the time we reach the steps of the porch both of us are prickled with goosebumps.

I'd like to think it was from the cold, and not from the feeling that, as my husband and I run naked into our honeymoon cabin, something was very, very wrong.

4

Inside the cabin, and fully clothed again, Jackson sets to making dinner as I sit and sip on a glass of wine. He heats a pan with a little garlic and olive oil, rips two chicken breasts from their package to sear, and heats water for pasta.

"I can make a salad," I offer, taking another sip of the wine and enjoying the sensation of ease spread over my body as the alcohol hits my bloodstream. It's delicious.

I tell myself again, silently, that I didn't see anything. Or anyone.

And that it didn't matter that Jackson thought I was imagining things.

I simply ignore the fact that my fear made my husband suspicious, rather than protective.

"Are you sure about that?" Jackson eyes me cautiously, but his voice is playful.

On our fourth date I'd tried to impress him by making dinner. Dani had given me detailed instructions about how to cook the lamb, fluff the couscous, and wilt the greens. It's just that she hadn't specified which greens to use. Sitting at the table I'd set with hand-hewn silverware and organic cotton fair trade napkins Dani had brought over as probationary new items for us to sell at our store, I'd set the plate down expectantly in front of Jackson.

He'd eaten every bite, exclaiming over how tender the lamb was and how, ahem, fluffy and flavorful the couscous tasted. I'd been a little too nervous to really enjoy my food––it was Jackson's first time back at my apartment, and I was wearing a complicated lingerie set that was more buckles and straps than actual fabric––so when Jackson held up a forkful of the veggies, swallowed, and said, "Is this chard?" I took a bite of the greens and realized Dani's instructions had led to me sautéing an entire head of romaine lettuce until it was a gloopy, stringy mess.

"I don't understand," I told Jackson over that candlelit dinner in my apartment. "I followed Dani's instructions, just like she told me."

"Don't get me wrong––I really appreciate such a wonderful home-cooked meal," Jackson had said. He leaned over the table conspiratorially. "I just think next time you might want to keep the lettuce off the stove."

I stared at him for a second, and he must have thought I was going to cry or something, because he started to put on that concerned face he has and backpedal his reaction to the limpy lettuce. Before he could insist that he loved limpy lettuce, it's the best, he'd eat it every day if he could, I cut him off with the loudest bubble of laughter I'd had in a while prior to that. Ever since then, I've been the one on salad duty. And every time, he's reminded me how lettuce really is best wilted.

Watching my husband cook dinner for us now, an ember of warmth burns cool and bright inside my chest. It feels good to trade inside jokes with each other, a subtle proof that our lives have knitted together enough to have stories in our shared past that are worth retelling.

Jackson turns off the stove and starts to mix the chicken and pasta together into a delicious sauce. The aroma of garlic and tomatoes fills the room.

Abandoning my salad-making duties, I step around the small counter into the kitchen, and eye Jackson with my best come-hither stare. I wait to see if he'll protest that his dinner will get cold, but he doesn't. He kisses me, hard, and we move out of the area with hot pans and cooling burners.

We hadn't taken time to explore the cabin fully, and so moving into the living room area near the front door I bump into a small end table and an antler lamp, not having really registered their existence when Jackson and I first came in and made a beeline to the kitchen.

I start to pull Jackson towards the nearest flat surface––the couch––and just as we're about to tip over onto it my eyes catch on something long and hard in the corner of my eye.

No, not what you're thinking.

Nestled in the corner of the living room, in a shadow along the edge of the fireplace, is a gun. Not a small gun. It's a large gun, with two barrels and a wide handle made from a deep red wood. The gun looks like it could be an antique design, but every part of it shines as if it had been used and cleaned this morning.

I gasp at the sight of it––I've never seen a gun in person, actually––and Jackson misinterprets it to mean that he should bear down on his intentions. He presses his face into mine, deepening his kiss until our teeth click against each other.

The stubble on his chin scratches against my face until it becomes a fierce clash against my skin.

I push Jackson off me instinctively. After all, there's a gun. In the room.

"What the hell?" Jackson falls off the couch onto the floor with a thud. "What are you doing?"

I peel my eyes away from the gun for a moment and catch

Jackson looking at me with a lethal mixture of disappointment and annoyance.

"There's. . ." I begin, but Jackson isn't interested in hearing what I have to say as an explanation.

"There's what?" he asks. "There's someone following us in the woods? There's something wrong with me kissing my wife? Why are you acting like you don't want me––is there something else you'd rather be doing than spending the day here with me?"

I don't know what to say to him. The sudden shift between where we were just a few moments ago and where we are now is giving me whiplash. I could just tell him why I pushed him away, that it had nothing to do with him, but something he said gnaws at the words rising in my throat: *acting like you don't want me*.

He had exactly two seconds of feeling that way.

So I don't correct him.

"I don't want to do this right now," I tell him, which earns me a little huff and a searing glare.

"I'm going to go eat something. I think we've been spending too much time together." He sweeps his hand across the room, as if he's capturing all the hours we've collected since he returned from Australia. "Clearly, that's what you think, too."

Even though I'd provoked it, the bitterness in his voice clamps around my throat and I regret that I didn't explain, the misunderstanding registers almost instantly. I could have just told him that there's a firearm inside the house, and that having something in our honeymoon cabin designed with the sole purpose of killing makes me more than a little uncomfortable–– but instead I had to get my dig in. Because why would I talk to my husband about how hurt I am that, when he was in Australia, he wasn't just away. He was gone.

Clearly, passive-aggressive jabs are so much better.

Everything is going wrong. It's all my fault.

Jackson clatters silverware out of a drawer that he's violently pulled open, and the scrape of a plate cuts through the still air of the cabin as he dishes out the chicken and pasta for himself. I'm crumpled on the couch, head in my hands as I try to control the groundswell of feelings rippling through me.

Without a word, Jackson moves through the kitchen and down the hallway towards the bedroom. I hear the distinctive creak of a screen door open and the rattle of it closing.

It's the first night of my honeymoon, and I am alone on a faux-leather couch crying for the person I've become over the last nine months––needy, jealous, insecure––while my husband eats the dinner he's made for us alone.

A deep sob hurls its way up my throat.

I wipe my eyes with the sleeve of my shirt and push my hair behind my ears. I want to go into the porch, and explain everything to Jackson, but I also know that trying to make up before he's calmed down will just lead to more arguing. I paid that price enough while he was away.

Being a newlywed without your husband is not something I would recommend to anyone. I essentially spent the months Jackson was gone making a beeline from my apartment to the gym, to our store, to my mother's to check on her, and then home again. The only thing that would change my routine would be escorting my mother to her doctor, or if Dani insisted that we go out to dinner.

"You used to love trying new restaurants," she'd say. "Just think, you can take Jackson there when he gets back, and recommend the best dishes to try. But that means you have to go out with *me* tonight."

Luckily, Dani wasn't worried about having company at the bars she'd go to after our dinners out. How she managed to show up to work, bright and early, dressed impeccably with a shiny blow-dry, I'll never know. Some mornings she'd already be there by the time I arrived––and I got there seriously early, at least until I started needing to check on my mother in the mornings. Dani might already be working at the computer in our back office or straightening up display items before we opened for the day.

And her hard work, combined with mine, manifested. Having so much of my time to devote to the store seemed to show, and our business thrived during the months Jackson was away. That part of my life was the opposite of fraught, at least. Dani's reports of sales at the end of each month were so exciting to see, with the graphs she printed out always showing lines going up, up, up. We'd be able to pay off our small business loan in just a few more months, and then we'd be entirely in the black. It was small consolation, but I'll take what I can get.

For someone with only a high school diploma––correction, for two people who only finished high school, because Dani got her General Education Diploma a year after she should have graduated, and didn't go to college either––we're doing pretty well for ourselves.

Most nights I'd sit around waiting for Jackson to call. Sometimes I'd end up having to wait a couple of nights, especially if I'd used our last conversation as an opportunity to explain how lonely I was and how I wished he'd respond to my messages more often. Later on, I'd spend my evenings scrolling through Instagram, looking to see if Jackson had posted anything new about his life across the world.

I sent packages to him. There were the care packages that I put together, and then spent a mint shipping over to Australia for him. At first I sent his favorite snacks––Cheetos and Hershey's chocolate, along with a few sexy pics I'd taken of myself and printed out on our home printer––but I stopped doing that after the packages were delayed in customs and one of them showed up at Jackson's apartment partially opened, with the photos of me visible for all his neighbors to see.

Eventually, I learned that criticizing your husband wasn't the way to keep him interested in you. And that my husband, especially, seemed to need his space.

However difficult it might be, I need to wait out this disagreement until Jackson decides it's time to make up. Otherwise, it'll just be another case where I become more and more desperate, and the person I love becomes more and more distant.

I shake my head, hoping to clear my thoughts, and decide that I should eat something. Maybe I can blame some of my distress over the amount of wine I've drunk, which isn't much, but the wine we bought at the little store outside the park must be stronger than most, because I already feel a bit wobbly on my feet.

I make myself a plate of the dinner Jackson prepared, without the salad I'd promised but never delivered on, and after pausing in the hopes that the sound of my plate scraping its way out of the cupboard would bring Jackson back over to me, I sit down at the table and start to eat.

I've opted for a glass of water in lieu of more wine, and take a sip as I settle into my chair and survey the rest of the cabin. I notice a card sticking out of a large bouquet of flowers set on top of the hallway cupboard, which seems to be the storage place for well-worn paperback novels and board games. The scent of the lilies had given the cabin a fresh and welcome scent when we first arrived, but I'd dismissed the bouquet as a pretty but impersonal arrangement, and hadn't examined it further until just now. I eat my dinner quickly and mechanically, too nervous about Jackson's insistence on avoiding me and the looming prospect of three more days spent together to enjoy any of the flavors. After I finish, I listen for any signs that Jackson is coming back.

When I don't hear anything, I decide to check out the note on the bouquet as a helpful distraction. Jackson picked out the cabin himself, and I'm hoping that the note is from the owners. It'd be nice to learn a little bit more about the place we're staying at. After whatever it is I saw––or thought I saw––out in the hot tub earlier, reading a note from the normal, reasonable people who rent the cabin out regularly would help make this place feel less isolated.

I glance over my shoulder at the shotgun in the corner.

And less dangerous, I think.

The flower arrangement is a combination of yellow tulips, red roses, and white lilies. None of them are my favorite flow-ers––personally, I'm a carnation girl myself––but all the colors combined are pleasing nonetheless.

I pick up the card.

When Jackson and I got married, it was mostly my family, although a few aunts and uncles had shown up from Jackson's side, along with two or three friends from his college dorm days. His Aunt Rachel was there, of course. We'd only met at the rehearsal dinner the night before, but as would prove true to form, she'd come over and promptly wrapped me up in an embrace after the ceremony, followed by a kiss on the cheek so emphatic that her waxy lipstick imprint seemed indelible. Before we posed for photos, standing in front of the two large vases of lilies my mother had insisted on ordering as decora-tions, Jackson had to rub my face with a handkerchief so hard it almost hurt.

"Lilies are more for funerals," I'd mentioned cautiously when my mother suggested them, as I drove her to one of her doctor's appointments.

My mother pursed her lips. Even from the corner of my eye I could see her expression shift.

"Well, I *am* dying, you know," she'd said.

That had shut me up.

And now there are lilies on my honeymoon.

When I open the card, I'm probably more surprised than I should have been.

Dear Mary, it reads.

Wishing you a wonderful birthday. You are the best daughter a mother could ever ask for.

Love, Mom.

The card starts to tremble in my hand. I'm sure my mother didn't mean to upset me.

I put the note down and slowly make my way over to the couch, studiously avoiding the long-limbed shadow of the shotgun in the corner.

In the months following my father's death, my mother's birthday was a bright light on the horizon for me. She'd said she didn't want to celebrate it, but I was certain that if I found the perfect gift she would be pleased. My mother loved––still loves––things.

And if I could find just the right present to add to her collection, I thought that she might re-emerge back to herself, if only in some small way. I wanted Dani to go with me to the store, but she was off on some outward-bound hiking trip her mother had signed her up for.

I took the bus over to the mall and, despite all my forethought, had no clue what to get my mother. After browsing around aimlessly from store to store, rejecting every option as too tacky or too expensive, I found myself in the kitchenware section of one of the big department stores flanking the center of the mall.

Neither of us had been cooking much since the accident,

although I'd made some attempt at a beef stew one night, which had been floury and overcooked. My mother thanked me, but picked at her plate until she thought I wasn't looking as I started to clean up, and poured the bulk of her helping discretely into the trash.

Under the harsh industrial store lighting, even the smooth porcelain of the crème brûlée casserole dishes looked overdone. I was just about to turn around and leave, when a saleswoman approached.

"Are you looking for something in particular?" a woman with jet black hair, straight as a ruler and cut chin-length, asked me. There was a slight lilt to her voice, and her name tag read, *Francesca*. She had a red handkerchief tied at her neck, as though she were in a French film.

"I'm looking for a birthday present, for my mother."

She nodded her head enthusiastically. "What does she like?"

My first instinct was to tell the truth: not much. "She likes things that are well made. Things that are. . ." I searched for the word. "Elegant," was the best I could come up with. My foot tapped nervously on the floor while I waited for Francesca to give me some clues as to what a woman like my mother might like.

"I see." She was thoughtful for a moment, and then with a sudden exclamation she rushed over to an aisle just a few yards from where I was looking and handed over a box after removing a sticker from its side. "Every woman should have a good set of knives," she declared.

I eyed her dubiously. The box was nice enough, and the knives were a German brand. The sticker she'd removed had left a slight gluey tab on the side of the cardboard container, and I rubbed at it with my thumb.

"She doesn't really cook."

"Of course she doesn't. If you don't have a good set of knives at home, why bother? An elegant woman can't enjoy the kitchen without the proper tools." She leaned in conspiratorially. "Trust me. The right tools make all the difference, and home cooking is so popular right now. Everyone is becoming their own personal chef."

I thought of my mother's thumb, throbbing with blood after she'd tried to slice a lemon for her tea the other night with our dull knives. My father's knives.

"I'll take them," I said.

"You won't regret it." Francesca swept me over to the cash register to ring them up.

After I'd paid, the gift nestled in its bag, I felt a bit brazen. As though I might fit in with women like Francesca, and my mother.

"Are you from France?" I asked, in the basic French I'd learned over the last four years of high school.

Francesca gave a little laugh and replied with something in French that I didn't understand.

I smiled and nodded at her, and it was only as I was walking away that a word rose from my memory.

Mistake. She'd said something about a mistake.

It's the same word echoing through my mind as I try to understand my mother's message.

She wouldn't do that on purpose, I tell myself over and over again. I stare out the cabin window into the deepening night covering the woods. *She just wanted to wish me a happy birthday. She wants me to be happy.*

I'll be twenty-five years old in two days.

And before then I need to tell Jackson the truth.

5

After my mother called to tell me she had Stage 3 breast cancer, I met her at 525 Eden Place, my childhood home. Pulling into the driveway that day was surreal. I couldn't stop thinking about the last time I'd been allowed to come, not that long after my father's accident, and how my mother had just stood there on the front porch and demanded that I stay in my car, a sheaf of papers waving in her hand like a misplaced surrender. I shouldn't get out, she said. I should turn around. I should find somewhere else to call home.

She needed her space.

It was just too painful for her to look at me.

She would get better if we were apart.

She had a mixed assortment of explanations. Caramels and nougats and lemon creams.

There's a creak from the direction of the cabin's porch door, and I stand to start cleaning up the kitchen. I've been sitting on the couch for far too long, staring out into the oncoming night and ignoring everything else around me. I don't want Jackson to find a messy kitchen waiting for him.

I run the water in the sink, and the soft scent of dish detergent calms me. Cleaning has always been a solace of mine, which is partly why it seems to always fall on me, and not Dani, to tidy up the dusty corners of our store whenever needed. Dani does the numbers, and I do the displays. We're two halves of a whole in that way.

Which reminds me––I need to call her.

I listen for footsteps coming down the hallway from the bedroom of the cabin, but aside from the swinging door of the porch, I don't hear anything.

"Jackson," I call out. No answer.

I fill the sink with bubbles and start scrubbing away at the dirty pots and dishes left from dinner. I'll add Jackson's once he decides to come back to me.

The day I saw my mother again, after many years apart, she was on the porch, just like before, her arms crossed over her chest against the eyes of neighbors and passers-by who might catch a glimpse of our reunion.

Without a word, she turned and we headed into the house.

She'd defrosted little petit fours from an Entenmann's package, and had them displayed on a plate alongside a pot of freshly-brewed tea.

"I made them myself this morning," my mother told me as we sat down, and we both played along and pretended that she'd risen early to bake and ice these small cakes for me, her daughter. It's better that way. To sometimes just go along with my mother.

And I want her in my life. Every child wants their mother.

I'm not delusional. I know my mother is selfish, and difficult. But she's the only mother I'll ever have, and the only family I have left. She's the only person who shares so many of my same memories of Dad. I need her, and I also think she needs me.

I don't know if I can say the same for Jackson. *Does he need me?* He seemed to do just fine without me, heading into the Australian bush and climbing the corporate ladder.

I scrub harder at the dish in my hand. Sometimes I surprise myself with how bitter I can be, and how easily I can convince myself that, if I just try hard enough, all those feelings will just go away.

Do I need him? Maybe that's the better question.

That day, at my childhood home, my mother announced her illness like someone would announce they were starting a new job. Or trying a new diet.

"I'm on the keto diet now."

"I'll be working in customer relations."

"I have cancer." My mother's never been one for embellishment. I remember, just as she said it, I took a bite of still-frozen mini-cake. I couldn't decide whether to swallow or spit it out.

She was dressed in a black sheath dress with penny loafers and dark tights, despite the unseasonable warmth for the day. It was strange to think about this disease eating away at her body, because even after so many years she'd managed to look exactly the same. Her green eyes were bright and agile, flitting from my face to other objects in the room when our eyes met. Her hands were still creamy white as she poured my tea. She looked a bit thinner than before, but that could have also been the way her dress hung on her.

When I asked her what I could do to help, I'd made the mistake of reaching out my hand to touch hers. Her skin was cool and smooth––she'd always felt like a statue to me when I was growing up and I'd been allowed to hug her––and I saw her retreat back just a hair's breadth as our hands met. But she recovered herself.

"I'm sorry," she said. "I'm just so used to being alone."

"It's going to be okay, Mom." By this point, I'd retreated back to my chair and held my cup of tea in between my hands, like a mug of cocoa.

"You don't know that, Mary."

And I'd thought we'd leave it at that, but then my mother kept talking.

"I've wasted so much time," she said, and I'm ashamed to admit it, but my heart did a little flip, because all that hope I'd buried for seven years was pushing up inside of me, ready to burst. "After your father died, I couldn't. . . I couldn't cope with the world. I'm sorry that included you."

"I'm just glad we're together now," I replied. I took a sip of my tea in order to stop myself from doing anything else I might regret.

And then I excused myself to the bathroom where, as soon as I closed the door, I buried my face in the pink towels with the embroidered flowers that'd hung there for guests to use for the last twenty years, like an emblem to another dynasty, and burst into tears.

I'm drying the dishes because there is nothing left to do, and if I don't have something to keep my hands busy I will march right over to that porch and tell Jackson exactly how ridiculous it is for him to throw this temper tantrum.

Or maybe I'd march over there and apologize.

I'm just about to roll the emotional dice and head over to Jackson's little hideaway––I haven't even ventured into the bedroom yet, let alone the porch––when there's a knock on the front door of the cabin. My blood instantly freezes in my veins.

I think about a red and black checkered shirt. I glance over at the gun, leaning hard and blank against the dark edge of the fireplace.

Jackson said we were all alone out here.

I tiptoe over to the hallway and whisper-shout my husband's name, but there's no response.

There's another series of knocks on the door, louder and more insistent than the first. I see the frame of the door shaking at the impact, and dust motes fly out from the wood in the streams of sunlight coming in through the windows as the sun sets.

It'll be dark soon, I realize.

"Jackson," I call again, louder this time, but he doesn't reply. I peer round the corner and see that the door to the screened-in porch is closed. I'm about to rush over and open it when the banging starts again, only to be replaced by the soft metal churr of the doorknob as whoever is on the other side tries to force it open. I can't remember if either of us locked the deadbolt, which at this moment strikes me as ridiculous given that I'd thought I saw someone lurking around the cabin, and any normal person would have thrown the deadbolt as soon as they were inside. I did put on the little chain lock, at least, and as the door swings open––unlocked, it seems––I follow the animal instinct building in my gut and lunge for the gun. I don't know if it's loaded or not, but I figure a large shotgun pointed at anybody will be a good deterrent to robbery or assault or whatever this invader wants to do to us.

Before I can snag my fingers around the body of the gun, though, the door opens with one big shudder, as if it doesn't quite fit into the frame of the cabin, and the chain lock on the door snaps in two. In the descending darkness I see a shadowy figure backlit by the setting sun. My body is throbbing with adrenaline, but my mind feels clear and crisp. I'm defending us from this maniac. I'm protecting my marriage.

The sound of footsteps comes from the hallway, and I shout out to my husband to stay back as the figure in the doorway takes a step forward. I can't strip my eyes away from the front door, and my fingers keep sliding on the slick surface of the gun barrel, as if it's just been oiled, and I can't find any purchase on the casement or gun itself. The shadows in the room play mean tricks on my vision, and one stretch of darkness seems to move further back in the cabin as if it's retreating, just as the other shadow in the door diminishes to show me a familiar face.

"Jackson," I say, bewildered by my husband standing at the front door to our cabin.

I glance back over to the hallway, but there's nothing there, shadows or otherwise.

What is happening to me?

"Mary, what the fuck?" Jackson says.

I look at my husband. I've had more practice recognizing the signs since Jackson came home, but it still takes me a few moments to understand what I'm seeing.

My husband is angry. Angry with me.

He lunges for the gun, and even as I let the smooth metal and wood slip through my hands and into my husband's, my mind conjures a memory that hums with neon-yellow and streamers and a little boy with chocolate smearing his face, and I wonder just how much Jackson already knows.

6

"What were you thinking?" Jackson asks, holding the gun in his arms like a wounded deer.

I don't answer him. I can't. My thoughts are scrabbling at the edge of something, desperate to gain some purchase.

It was two days ago. We were at a party store around the corner from our apartment, and the aisles were crammed with plastic beads, frilly doilies, and cheap table ornaments for every Marvel Comic ever published. Jackson and I were making a little date of it––his suggestion––and picking up decorations for the welcome-home party Dani had insisted I throw for him.

I'd wanted to get just a few party essentials. But that day, in the party store, Jackson was like a kid in the candy aisle, eyes glazed over with the abundance of choices. And I'd wanted to scream, because I was using this shopping trip as yet another excuse to avoid talking to my husband about what was really on my mind.

"What's that?" he'd asked, reaching for a package of SpongeBob SquarePants tablecloths. "Do you think I'm too old for these? Maybe I could get them and be ironic, you know? Like a hipster thing."

"I already have a start on the beard," he added. "Maybe my homecoming present could be a fedora?"

I gave a non-committal laugh and stared at a life-size cardboard replica of Spider-Man.

In retaliation, Jackson proceeded to load our cart with five packets of My Little Pony napkins. "Or do you think six?" he'd asked.

I laughed.

This was how it'd been since he came home. Up and down. Connect and disconnect.

Staring at all the cheap junk sold in the store, part of me wondered if Dani had suggested the party as a way to get me to consider her push for Kitchen Kabinet to sell more upscale party goods and other luxury items. I wouldn't put it past Dani––she's always been good at reading a room.

And so I was distracted, thinking about my business and my best friend.

"Why don't we just offer to pay for the meal for everyone, instead of worrying about these ridiculous party favors?" I suggested. As soon as the words were out of my mouth, though, I knew I'd made a big misstep.

"Why would you offer to do that?" Jackson cornered me in the aisle.

"We can't just leave this stuff in the cart," I started to say, moving to put the items back, but he held onto the cart so I couldn't move it.

A mom with two toddlers and Lululemon leggings, with a distinctive smear of chocolate on the thigh, rushed between us to snatch two Incredible Hulk streamers, which gave me a moment to think about how to salvage this situation. The little boy holding her hand reached out and let another trail of chocolate bar run off in his wake along the aisle's merchandise.

Jackson lowered his voice. "I'm talking about offering to pay for dinner at a fancy restaurant for twenty people. We can't afford that."

"I—I'm sorry," I stammered. "I just thought it would be easier."

Jackson gave me a strange look.

"Easier?" The corner of his mouth quirked up, his eyes pinched with irritation. "How would it be easier to spend money we don't have?"

He drew out the last bit of his question, like he was testing the words. Or waiting for me to jump in and correct him.

But I didn't.

And now I'm standing in our honeymoon cabin, with my husband breaking down doors and holding a shotgun. Miles away from anyone I could turn to for help.

"What were you thinking?" Jackson repeats, and his voice booms around the walls of the cabin.

The open front door creaks as a cool breeze whips into the room, banging the door against the frame and then shooting it back out. The crack of the wood against the metal guard at the bottom of the doorway jars me, and my shoulders jerk up instinctively.

I don't know if it's the damaged door, or the accusatory look on Jackson's face, or both, but I finally lose it. I jump up and slam the door closed, shooting the still-functioning deadbolt into its lock, and then I turn towards my husband.

I have a few things to answer for, but so does Jackson.

Like a pressure valve turning, I tell my husband exactly what's been on my mind.

"What was *I* thinking?" I shout at him, flailing my arms wildly, not caring that he's still holding the gun. This has been a long time coming.

Nine months coming.

"Oh, I don't know. I guess I was thinking that my husband

47

had left me––again––and that he wasn't coming back, and that there was someone trying to break into the cabin and that I needed to protect myself. Just like I've done for the entirety of our marriage while you were halfway across the world, making time to post pictures of your favorite meals and beaches and new friends."

My teeth bite into my words. I may or may not spit a little, and I take the sleeve of my flannel shirt and wipe it across my mouth like a barmaid. I'm in full swing now.

Jackson looks horrified, and in the deepest corners of my body I am glad. Glad, glad, glad that he is feeling something, finally, about the way he's treated me while he was gone. And also glad that, perhaps, I'm diverting both our attentions from what might be on his mind. That I'm keeping important pieces of my life from him.

"But you couldn't stand to call, or text, or write. Not more than was absolutely necessary. You couldn't bear to let your *wife* know you cared about her."

I see his mouth open and close, trying to protest what I'm saying, but I don't let him. I talk above whatever he's trying to offer as his explanation for what he did.

I ignore the fiery tendrils working their way through my heart that are telling me I'm being unfair. That I've done things that have hurt Jackson. That maybe I deserved for him to abandon me.

"I was so lonely. Thinking that you didn't want me anymore."

"I did want you," Jackson says, and both of us prick up at the past tense of *did*.

I start to cry. This is not how I ever imagined my honeymoon would be.

"I *do* want you," Jackson corrects as he moves towards me, but he's still holding that fucking gun, and he can't reach out to touch me.

"Put it away," I tell him, swiping my hand at the air between us. "Get rid of it."

He shifts away, and I watch as my husband expertly disassembles the shotgun to reveal two neon orange shells inside the twin chambers.

A chill goes up my spine.

I really don't know the man I married.

Jackson tilts the shells out into the palm of his hand, and a small blip of relief tracks its way over my chest. He clicks the barrel back into place and asks me where I want him to store it.

"How did you know to do that?" Even though I try to keep my voice from sounding accusatory, the strain echoes through the room and I watch Jackson flinch at my words. My tears are drying themselves out, and my mouth feels full of cotton.

Where did Jackson learn to do that?

Growing up, the nearest I got to a gun was the water Super Soakers we'd take down to the community pool. My father wasn't a hunter, and my mother had no interest in the outdoors, or in self-protection beyond our suburban security system and a can of dusty pepper spray clunking around in her purse.

My house wouldn't have been a good place for guns, either before or after my father died.

"I grew up on a farm," Jackson tells me, setting the gun on top of the dining table in the center of the room. He wraps his fingers around the shells and swiftly puts them into the pocket of his jeans. He won't look at me, and I don't know if it's because he's avoiding our fight, or because he can't stand to look at me, or because he's thinking about the secrets he might have discovered I've been keeping from him.

I stumble back a bit and manage to knock over one of the dining table chairs as I move into the kitchen to get a glass of water. I need something to do to keep my hands busy, and when

I spot the bottle of wine Jackson brought out earlier, I decide to pour a glass of that instead.

"I thought you grew up in Pittsburgh," I reply. I rack through my brain, searching for some missed memory where I forget that my husband is a country boy. My slicked-up, pocket-square-wearing, banker husband. And I come up with nothing.

Jackson gives me an inscrutable look.

"Well, yeah, but Pittsburgh has a lot of farmland around it."

I shake my head.

"But you took me to your neighborhood when we went to visit. It was in the suburbs. You showed me where your house used to be, and ended up being torn down for developers to put up a condo development." I force myself to take another sip of wine.

Nothing to see here. Everything is fine.

We went back to where Jackson grew up, partly because I wanted to know more about his past. Jackson doesn't talk about his family much. His parents were drug addicts who died from simultaneous overdoses when he was a teenager. All he's really told me about his childhood, pre-foster care and Aunt Rachel, was that his parents were never really meant to be parents. The way that he said it made it clear that I didn't want to press for more from him. Not then, at least.

But after he proposed, and we fast-tracked the wedding, I figured seeing some of the places where he grew up would be a good, and gentle, start.

Jackson absentmindedly reaches into his pocket and starts fiddling with the two shells he put there.

"I spent a lot of my childhood outdoors. It was a means to get away from everything happening in my house."

I can't believe what has happened in the last five minutes.

Guns and farms and misplaced childhoods.

Looking at the door, not at me, he says, "I accidently locked myself out of the porch. I went outside to look around the spot where you thought you saw someone. I couldn't get back in. And then I heard you shouting inside––calling my name. I thought someone was in the cabin, trying to hurt you. So I broke the door in."

Something dissolves in my chest, and I rush over to him and wrap my hands around his waist from behind.

"Thank you," I mumble into his back. And I mean it. *Thank you for looking. Thank you for believing me. Thank you for coming to save me when you thought I needed you.*

I'm suddenly so very tired. All I can think about is climbing underneath soft covers and drifting off to sleep, where I could forget about everything we've just said to each other.

It takes a moment, but Jackson reaches up and puts his hands on mine. He gives them a squeeze, and we let go of each other.

"It's been a long day," he says, like he's reading my mind. "Let's go to bed early. We'll start fresh in the morning."

I follow him into the bedroom, neither of us daring to touch each other again.

I wake up in the middle of the night, and the sheets next to me are cool when I reach my hand out. I get up silently and tiptoe over to the living room, but Jackson isn't there. I hear the scrape of the porch door, and realize he must be up and outside.

In the haze of my sleep, I stumble back into the bedroom and peer through the doorway into the porch. My husband is standing in the moonlight, staring out into the night, his phone clenched in his hand. I can't see his face, but something about his posture keeps me from going to him. Or maybe it's our unresolved fight from earlier.

Either way, I start to turn back to bed, hoping he won't notice me, when I hear the distinctive ping of a text message arriving. I watch as my husband pulls his phone closer and starts tapping away at the screen.

His hand drops back to his side after he sends his message back, and I can almost feel the shift in his body after he hits send.

His shoulders ease, and he leans his arm and hip up against the frame of the window.

He seems relaxed. Soothed.

He looks like a man should look on his honeymoon.

I can't watch my husband anymore. It hurts too much.

As I slip back into bed as quietly as possible, certain that sleep won't come back to me anytime soon, I realize something else.

I didn't see the gun on the table when I was in the living room.

I don't know where it is.

7

DAY 2

I wake up at dawn, the sunrise streaming through the gauzy white curtains of the cabin's bedroom. Reds and pinks and deep oranges glaze the bed, my arms, with Jackson's taut and creviced torso peeking out from the sheets. I watch as the light slides slowly upwards, until the bright yellow of the sun catches at Jackson's chin. He murmurs in his sleep and turns over, his arm slipping out from around my waist and freeing me from where it found me sometime in the middle of the night, once he came back to bed.

That's when I finally get up and make my way to the kitchen.

The options for breakfast are far too numerous to decide on only one thing to make for my husband. Because that's what I'm going to do.

I didn't sleep most of the night, although I pretended to be asleep when Jackson came back to bed a little while after I saw him at the window on the porch. I spent those hours, drifting between half consciousness and actual rest, thinking over what happened yesterday between Jackson and me. And the months and months before that.

I came to a decision.

I can fix my marriage. I *want* to fix my marriage.

And the first step to that is making breakfast for my new husband.

The second step is to stop pretending and tell him the truth.

Since he's arrived home, Jackson has insisted on cooking for me almost for every meal. Pancakes and roast chicken, carne asada burritos and Caesar salads.

One of the consistent things Jackson did while he was away was to post pictures of the food he was buying, making and eating. In one of the few actual conversations we'd had while he was in Australia, he'd promised to have an entire catalogue of new meals for me when he got back. And he has.

Which is why his new-found cooking obsession is so comforting. It means that, yes, he was spending a lot of his time away learning how to sear a salmon filet or braise a beet.

But today I am going to cook for him, even if scanning over the contents of our cabin's fridge makes me feel almost instantaneously overwhelmed.

When I'm not trying to impress my new gorgeous boyfriend with wilted lettuce, I'm a basic cook. I can fry up eggs, cook pasta and sauce from the jar, and have been known to make a cake or two. It's a little odd, since I co-own a kitchen store, but it makes sense to me. I love to eat. I love trying new foods. I love digging into new restaurant recommendations. And I'm lucky that the people around me love to cook, Dani and Jackson included.

Growing up, my father was always the cook in the family.

When I think of my father, I often picture him standing in front of the stove on a Saturday morning, flipping pancakes with the smell of frying bacon wafting over the entire house. Even when his hands shook and his voice was sloppy he was the master of our kitchen.

I shift my gaze from the counter strewn with fruit back to the refrigerator behind me. My heart cracks down the middle, and I promise myself again that I'm going to tell Jackson everything.

Everything about my father, that is.

Cool air wafts over my thighs, and I realize I'm staring at the half gallon of milk we bought at the store on the way into town.

I can't remember if we bought any bacon.

As I turn round, my eyes catch the empty corner where the shotgun was propped up yesterday. For a second I swear I can see the negative image of it against my field of vision, the lightness of its sleek barrel and embossed handle stark against the shadows of the room. But then I blink and it's gone.

I tell myself it doesn't matter that it disappeared from the table last night; Jackson must have put it somewhere. I'm safe.

We're safe.

I've finally managed to find a small packet of bacon in the meat drawer, and I start to fry it up in one of the small pans I find in the kitchen cabinets. As the bacon heats to a sizzle, I crack a few eggs and start toast in the spotless toaster oven on the counter.

Coffee, I think. We stopped by a general store just outside the park for groceries, plus a few cheap paperbacks, along with a copy of the local paper with a trail map insert, but we'd forgotten to get filters for the coffee maker.

As I'm rummaging around in our pantry, hoping that some other guest remembered to buy filters, I see my phone where I've set it on the counter.

I should call Dani. I promised I would call her when we got here.

I hope she isn't too worried.

But I wasn't about to call her last night. Not with Jackson and I already picking at each other's soft spots. We'd had a disagreement on the drive down here, after I'd asked for the address of the cabin. He told me he'd already texted my mother with the information––just in case she needed to get in touch and reception was bad––and I'd wanted the details of the cabin to text to Dani, too, with regards to her request. Which was when Jackson pointed out that even though Dani is my best friend, we both know she's a little much sometimes, and that if she knew where we were, she'd end up driving down and interrupting our getaway with some emotional emergency she'd found herself in.

Your best friend shows up drunk and weeping at your door at 2am one time––three, okay, three times––and your husband thinks she's high maintenance.

Which is why Jackson wouldn't give me the address of the cabin, although he'd tried to play it off as a joke.

"It's a secret cabin," Jackson had told me, revving the engine to overtake a bright yellow convertible on the highway. I'd gripped the handle of my door, wishing Jackson wouldn't speed so much.

"Secret from me?" I'd asked, trying to settle into the passenger seat.

I thought I'd kept the edge of my voice flirty, but Jackson sped up and passed another car. Not looking at me, he said, "Especially from you."

So I'd let it drop. Jackson had slowed down, and we made it to the cabin.

I pick up my phone and click Dani's name from the recent calls list. It rings for a second and Dani picks up almost instantly, but before I can say hello back the call drops. I dial again, but my screen sits there, trying to make a connection and coming up empty. I check the reception icon in the upper left corner, and see what I'd already assumed when the call was disconnected: I have one bar, and then no bars. And then two. And then none.

My phone rings, the shrill sound of the call breaking through the quiet air of the cabin, and of course it's Dani calling me back. I pick up and move towards the front door in the hopes of getting better reception, but when I try to talk to Dani all I get is static and then silence.

I compose a quick text, letting her know we're fine and that the cabin is great and we're having a fabulous time––because I don't want her worrying, and also because I don't want Jackson reading through my messages again and finding something incriminating, like the one time, just a few days before the wedding, when he used my old passcode to check on dinner reservations and saw the messages I'd exchanged with Dani about how annoyed I was with his insistence on being abstinent in the lead-up to the wedding. At the time, four days of my future husband refusing my come-ons felt like eternity.

That was before Australia, and months and months of fever-dream celibacy.

At the last minute I also type out the address for the cabin that I'd found written on the information sheet in the kitchen utility drawer, because I know Dani will feel better if she has it. After I send, I wait a few beats while the message spins, and then it lights up in green with a small *delivered* underneath the message box.

I feel a sudden surge of relief, the guilt at not having remembered to call her lifting off me.

When I try to send a second message, asking if she's checked in on my mother yet, an error comes up and it won't deliver. Which is exactly when I smell smoke, and the shriek of the smoke detector starts to pummel my ears.

The bacon.

The pan where I was frying the bacon and eggs is spitting grease, and flames burst out of the pan, nearly licking the hood of the stove.

I rush over and put a lid on the pan, extinguishing the flames, but the damage is already done.

Jackson is awake, standing in the kitchen looking foggy and

still clinging to sleep, and the breakfast I wanted to make for the two of us is ruined. The air in the cabin is so dense with smoke that both of us start coughing simultaneously, and I have to rush around and open the windows to vent out the putrid smell of bacon grease and burnt animal fat.

Once the air clears, I see that I've also managed to burn the toast to a bright black crisp. I notice Jackson laughing.

"What's so funny?" I wipe a strand of hair out of my eye.

Jackson comes closer to me and wraps his strong arms around my shoulders.

"You are gorgeous in the morning, do you know that?" he murmurs into my ear, ignoring the chaos around us. His breath smells faintly of toothpaste. He kisses me deep on the mouth, and presses his hips against mine, which are balancing along the edge of the counter.

Who were you messaging last night? What are you hiding from me?

The thoughts invade my mind and I flinch away from Jackson's touch for the briefest second. If Jackson notices, though, he doesn't say anything. He lets go of my hips and makes his way over to the stove, moving the covered pan off the heat. "I'll finish breakfast. You go sit down."

There's a shade of annoyance in his voice, and so I go and sit at the table in the living room.

A few minutes later, breakfast is on the table, steaming and looking perfect. Two bright yellow yolks, crisp bacon, and two slices of buttered toast alongside a cup of dark coffee with just a touch of cream. I remember reading somewhere that true love is someone knowing just how you take your eggs and coffee in the morning.

In the wake of everything that's happened this year, good and bad, seeing how easily Jackson remembers this small part of who I am––sunny side up with coffee dark enough that you can't see the bottom of your cup––is perhaps more reassuring than it should be. It's just breakfast after all. But still it's something.

He sits down across from me––over easy, with coffee that's more sugar than is appropriate for a grown man––and we start to eat in the first companionable silence since we've arrived. The clatter of our forks and knives on the dishes rings through the cabin, and light pours in with an insistence that seems to beckon us outside.

The air smells more of warm bread and fresh coffee now, rather than my disastrous attempt at breakfast.

"I've missed you," Jackson says. He's looking over the rim of his coffee cup, his light eyes stormy and serious. "I missed you so much."

There's something different in his voice as he says it. Something rougher, and more durable. I want to swim around in those words. I want to live in the way he's looking at me, in just this moment.

But then I remember that he doesn't know who I really am.

"Mary, I need to tell you something," Jackson says suddenly, pre-empting me. He leans over the table and takes my hand. Something flickers inside my head. I squeeze his hand back, but my palms are already sweating.

I knew it was all too good to be true.

"I know I let you down while I was gone. I know I wasn't there for you as much as I should have been." Jackson's voice sounds choked, and his fingers clasp my hand harder. He isn't crying, but he looks like he's just on the verge of tears.

Instead of feeling compassion for my husband, though, I feel the pricks of something knotted and sharp growing inside of me.

"I was just working so much, you know," he tells me, his voice deeper than usual. "After I met you, and I had this opportunity in Australia, I felt like I had to do everything I could to make our life as stable as possible. I wanted to build a future for us. I took every opportunity I had over there, working evenings and weekends. Whatever it took to impress my bosses. And I'm sorry it meant that I wasn't there for you as much as I should have been."

He picks his gaze up from our entwined hands and looks at me. I don't want to touch him anymore, and pull my arm back from his.

I think about that glowing screen, lighting up my husband's face late last night. I wonder where Jackson's phone is, and whether or not I can get into it.

Because I don't buy it. The near tears. The heartfelt remorse. *It's too much. Too easy.*

I'm certain my husband is putting on a show. I'm just not sure why.

"I just need you to know that I was doing it for us. For our future. For our children, when they come along." A glimmer of a smile tugs at the corner of his mouth. I don't smile back, and Jackson breaks into an even wider grin, which fades as our eyes lock on each other.

"I want to make sure I'm contributing to our life together," he goes on, his words not matching his body, which has gone stiff and hollow. Jackson's eyes have shifted from me to the corner of the cabin.

"How long have you known?" I say, but Jackson speaks over me, his alarm dominating my quiet resignation.

"Where'd you put the gun?" he asks.

8

The night my father died started out the same as most nights did in our household back then.

With my parents silently seething at each other over yet another wholesome dinner of meat, potatoes and vegetables, the three of us ate in almost total silence, save for the scraping of forks against plates and the tinkling of ice in the glass of my father's drink. It was either the second or third glass of whiskey for him that night.

By this point in my parents' marriage, my father's ritual drink in the evening had expanded to five or six large tumblers by the time he fell asleep in his lounge chair.

My parents hadn't shared a bedroom for years, although the last few weeks before my father died had been like a rebirth. Almost. I'd come home a few times from Dani's house to find my parents emerging from what was once their bedroom, and had recently become only my mother's, with rosy splotches on their necks and cheeks and wild hair. It had given me a little bubble of hope in my stomach, like I could float away on the promise of my parents falling in love again. A bubble that would burst whenever they were near each other outside their bedroom.

After dinner, my mother would retire for her own nightly ritual of a long soak in the bath with a few glasses of wine, while my father and I would clean up the kitchen.

He really was a good father. He was just a better drunk.

That night, like most nights, he washed the dishes. I took them from his soapy hands to dry, and we chatted about my day. Our rhythm would pause every so often so Dad could reach out and get a sip from his drink.

By the time his glass was drained, so was the sink.

The night he died, my father wrapped his arm around my shoulder after we'd finished, and gave me a squeeze. "I'm so proud of you," he said.

It wasn't unusual for him to say this to me, especially not after a certain point in the evening. He wasn't the kind of man who refused to offer compliments. He often told me how lucky he was to have me for a daughter.

Which meant, however, that his sweet statement rolled off me that night like all the others. I smiled and nodded, and probably gave some little murmur of thanks, but that was it.

I'm certain I didn't tell my father I loved him, or that I was glad he was my dad.

I just put away the last dish in the cabinet and headed to my room to finish my homework.

As I was heading out of the kitchen, I remember my mother walked over to my father with the phone in her hand. She must have come straight from the bath, because she was wearing her bathrobe with her hair wrapped up in a towel. I can picture it perfectly in my mind, as I watch my husband's face contort into something fierce and strange across the breakfast table in our honeymoon cabin, how she put her hand on my father's arm.

It was the first time in a long time that I'd seen my parents actually touch each other. Whatever my mother said to him as she leaned in and whispered in his ear was enough to drain the color from my father's face.

When I asked what was wrong, neither of them answered.

Instead, my mother continued to hold the phone out to my father, but he pushed it away. I watched as she shrugged her shoulders and clicked the end call button. She dropped the phone into her pocket.

"Nothing's wrong," he told me, running his hand over his jaw like he'd had a sudden toothache. It was a nervous habit of his. "I just need to go out for a few minutes. I need to go to the store to get a few things."

My mother and father locked eyes, and in that moment I felt something crack open between them, and blossom. My father smiled.

Even though he drank, he only did so at home––as far as I knew, granted––and he never drank if he needed to drive somewhere in the evening.

I reached out to take the empty glass in his hand, but my father shifted out of my reach. When I looked up, my mother's gaze caught mine.

"I'll make some coffee," she said, not missing a beat.

My father cupped his hand around my mother's face, the gesture so unexpected and so tender between the two of them that I had to look away.

Ten minutes later, my father was on the road to the store, while my mother returned to her bath and I waited in my room.

Thirty minutes after that, the call came from the police.

A week later, we'd buried my father.

The week after that, they buried the young woman he'd killed.

And then, I can't say exactly when, but soon after that, my problems started.

It'd take another three months for my mother to get the restraining order against me.

And then, another seven years for her to want me back.

But Jackson doesn't know any of that, except for the skeletal details I've had to tell him: My father died in a car accident. My mother and I were estranged.

It's what came after—what's coming—that I think he's figured out somehow, and for now I'm not sure what to do with this hunch of mine.

"How long have you known?" I repeat after Jackson asks me where the gun is, as though my mouth is on autopilot. It takes a few moments to register what he just said.

"Known what?" Jackson sounds agitated, and he starts pacing around the kitchen, opening and closing the larger cupboards and looking on top of shelves as he continues. "Known that you hid the gun somewhere? Because you don't trust me to keep you safe?"

I could press on, and force him to talk about the pieces of my past that he's conjured together, somehow, but his insistence that the gun is missing distracts me.

"What do you mean?" I counter. My mind whirls back to the night before. I remember him taking the gun apart, putting the shells in his pocket, and then our discussion about why he knew how to do that.

I also remember the tension that crept in when I started asking him about his childhood, and my attempt to smooth it over.

I remember waking up in the middle of the night and seeing the empty place in the living room where the hard body of the gun had been left gleaming in the moonlight through the window.

I don't know where the shotgun is, because Jackson does.

"I didn't do anything with it. It was on the table when we

went to bed. And then. . ." I pause, catching myself before I reveal that I was up in the middle of the night, not wanting Jackson to know what I'd seen. "And then when I woke up this morning it was gone."

Dani and I once took a class through the local business bureau about de-escalation and better communication in the workplace. A few expensive items had gone missing, and we'd had to fire one of our part-time employees after Dani notified me that she'd caught them stealing a high-end Moroccan salad bowl. The seminar instructors kept emphasizing that to defuse a conflict you couldn't bear down on what you thought was right and insist on the other person agreeing with you. That would only inflame the situation more.

So I don't emphasize that I fell asleep before Jackson, or that he knows more about guns and had the ability to stow it somewhere while I was sleeping. I don't tell him that I know, with absolute certainty, that I did not move the gun.

Instead, I ask him a question.

"When did you last see it?"

It lets him know we're on the same team, trying to figure this issue out together. At least, that's what the dusty seminar booklet residing in the bottom drawer of my office desk would say.

Jackson seems to calm down a bit at my question, and he stops pacing to look at me.

"It was right here." He gestures to the table.

"That's where I remember it too," I tell him.

We eye each other cautiously. Jackson's gaze darts from the table, to the hallway leading to the bedroom, and back again. He suddenly looks more concerned than confused. And then a trace of defensiveness creeps into his jaw. "I took the shells out of it."

"Yeah, I remember that," I tell him. I've risen from my chair, and Jackson and I stand facing each other, the dining table between us like a wall. "You put them in the pocket of your jeans."

"What?" He glances around the room, distracted. "Yeah, I did, but then I put the shells on the dresser in the bedroom after I changed into my boxers for bed."

I rush from the table, my chair clattering on the floor behind me as I knock it over on my way to the bedroom. If we find the shells, at least it means the gun isn't loaded. We haven't found any more casings of ammunition.

I need to get to those shells before my husband does.

Jackson is right behind me, but even though I arrive in the bedroom first, my search proves fruitless. I scan the dresser, but its pale wood only holds a decorative lamp, a small jumble of receipts from Jackson's pocket, the local paper we picked up at the store, folded into quarters where Jackson had been reading it, and our wedding rings, matched perfectly next to each other. We both take them off before bed and put them back on in the morning.

Or at least that's the habit I've formed in the months since our wedding, and Jackson seems to have followed suit since returning from Australia. When he returned home, there was no tan line from his wedding ring on his finger.

I check the floor around the dresser, the nightstands next to each of our bedsides, and even pull up the quilt and sheets of the bed itself, just in case the bullets somehow became caught within the fabric.

There are no fluorescent orange shotgun shells anywhere.

Jackson follows me in, but doesn't help me search. Instead, he stands in the doorway to the bedroom, leaning his long body against the door frame, and the tension he'd shown earlier drained away.

"I can't find them," I say. "They aren't where you said you left them."

He moves towards me, his hands raised in what is either a surrender or a gesture of solidarity.

"They have to be here somewhere." Jackson leans in to try to plant a kiss on my mouth. Like he didn't just accuse me of hiding a gun from him.

The hairs on the back of my neck stand up, and even though my mind is working at a thousand miles per second and nowhere in the vicinity of wanting my husband to touch me, I lean into his kiss.

I feel his shoulders relax, and his hands start to pull at the waist of my flannel pajama bottoms, but then they stop suddenly.

He scans the room, just as I did a few minutes ago, but doesn't move to overturn any of the furniture, or check the pockets of our suitcases. Instead, he reaches out to put his hands on my shoulders, pressing the weight of his muscle and bone into me.

Sometimes I forget how much bigger he is than me.

I'm alone with Jackson in the woods, with no reliable way to call for help, and with a missing gun. I'm too scared to not give him what he wants.

"I'll go check in the bathroom," he says as he breaks his hold on me. Luckily, he doesn't wait for me to answer. In the next few moments while he's in the bathroom I move over to his suitcase, which he's stored in the closet and covered in a disarray of his clothes from yesterday. I have a hunch and I'm hoping I can carry it out before he comes back. I reach inside his discarded jeans from the day before, and instantly feel the two hard bodies of the shells before I see them.

I pull my hand out and start to shove the shells into the pocket of my sweatshirt, but Jackson is already back.

"What are you doing?" he asks.

I have a split second to decide what to do.

I thrust my hand triumphantly towards my husband.

"I found them. They were in your pocket!" I say, just a hair's breadth away from sounding manic. As if finding the shells was the best part of our honeymoon yet.

I take a few steps towards the hallway leading back to the kitchen, and Jackson doesn't seem to notice.

Jackson looks at the twin casings in my hand as a dark ribbon passes over his mouth, moving from his jaw to his temple. I hold my breath.

"I distinctly remember putting them on the night table."

I pause for a second. "It doesn't matter, really."

"No, I guess not," Jackson says. He shrugs. "Now that you've found them, are you going to tell me where you put the gun?" He won't look at me as he says it.

I can't believe he's still trying this on.

"I didn't put it anywhere," I remind him. I take another step away from him. "Maybe you put it somewhere and just don't remember doing so?"

I'm keeping my tone conciliatory, but I'm reaching my limits.

Jackson moves towards me and swipes his hand across the dresser, knocking off our rings and the receipts and the newspaper. A flush is rising up his neck.

"Don't patronize me, Mary." His voice is so quiet in contrast to what he's just done that I freeze on the spot. I know, rationally, that I should leave the room. I've never seen him so angry. But my feet stay rooted to the floor, as though I'm watching a movie unfold in front of me. As if this isn't my real life. "How could I just forget something as important as moving a fucking shotgun on our honeymoon?"

He leans in towards me, and I stifle a whimper when he gets closer, but he's only bending down to pick up the items that he's knocked on the floor. As the sound leaves my mouth, I watch my husband with the alertness of an animal cornered, and as I do a thought occurs to me.

He's scared, I think. Maybe he isn't trying to manipulate me. Maybe something or someone has frightened my husband.

I don't let myself wonder if that someone is me.

Instead, I bend down and start helping Jackson pick up the papers off the floor. I find my wedding ring and slip it on, and then snatch at the newspaper, which has come unfolded to a center page. The headline catches my eye, and as I read it a lead weight drops in the pit of my stomach.

"Jackson," I say, holding the paper in my hand. "Have you read this?"

He glances up, worry lines creasing his forehead. He pulls the paper from my hands, and folds it up neatly again. "I was hoping you wouldn't see that."

But I have done, and even with the words tucked safely away underneath other pieces of news, the headline burns in front of me.

Same Individual Suspected in Hiking Trail Sabotage.

"Let me read the article," I say firmly, and he hands it back over. I scan the write-up which tells me about the different incidents in the Poconos so far. Tree limbs falling unexpectedly, with cuts in the branches. A small suspension bridge with damage done to the lines. The article quotes a park ranger, who wants to assure everyone that the string of state parks situated in the Poconos are all safe, but to always be alert to suspicious activity and to report it to the Park Services Office and local law enforcement. It's suspected that these incidents are the actions of one individual, given their timing and spacing.

I think about the person I thought I saw yesterday, lurking in the woods beyond the cabin.

My eyes meet Jackson's, and I realize now where his fear is coming from. And why he was so insistent that I moved the gun.

Because if he didn't remember moving it, and I didn't either, then someone else must have come into our cabin in the night and moved it. Someone who shouldn't be here, with us, alone in the woods.

"Oh my God. Jackson, what's happening?"

We are crouched down on the floor, our bodies angled away from each other. I try to lean closer to him, to read the way he's holding himself for clues as to what he's thinking, but my knee catches on a swath of blanket billowing out from the bed and I lurch to the side.

Jackson doesn't say anything. He just reaches out silently, and steadies me with his huge palm.

And then he moves out of the bedroom and into the living room of the cabin. He crouches down beside the fireplace and seems to examine the corners around the plinth at the bottom, as if the gun could hide itself inside the stone. I move to the opening of the hearth and reach up underneath, feeling for the flue and finding a solid ledge inside the fireplace, tucked inside the chimney. I push my hand up, feeling for anything hidden but finding only smooth, flat edges.

Our eyes meet across the flagstones, which are mostly gray, but with hints of rose swirled in sections like a violent storm. I don't know why he has us checking over the fireplace, as if the gun might be hiding in plain sight instead of having been secreted away by some intruder.

"Shouldn't we leave?" I ask, trying to keep the panic from my voice.

"Not yet," is all Jackson replies, and he keeps his eyes focused on his search of the cabin.

We both work ourselves around the fireplace, trading places with each other silently after we've exhausted our own. Once Jackson finishes inspecting the hollow of the fireplace, he abruptly stands up and trots to the outer door, and then switches direction, only to head further into the cabin, back towards the bedroom.

"Where are you going?" I call out to him. I'm feeling more and more desperate by the minute. I pull my phone from my pocket, but there's still no reception.

I follow him back towards the bedroom and am just behind him when he turns. We are so close to each other again that my forehead almost crashes into his chest. He dips his chin down and nuzzles his mouth against my neck.

I'm so caught off guard that I don't do anything for a moment. I just listen to his breathing in my ear, shallower than I've ever heard it before.

"I remember now," he says, his voice muffled as his lips move against the curve of my neck.

"Remember what?" I sound frantic, because nothing that has happened in the last fifteen minutes makes any sense. "I don't understand," I tell him.

And there's that look again crossing Jackson's face. The one he had when he lashed out and knocked everything over, and as I watch it cover his features again, I realize exactly what it is.

Shame.

"I took it outside, to the woodshed in the back," my husband tells me. "I could tell you weren't comfortable with it in the cabin, and I went outside and took care of it after you fell asleep."

I move back, and Jackson runs out of the cabin to the shed. I follow behind him, and as I approach I see my husband, waving the gun in his hand like some triumphant suburban warrior.

As I get closer, I start to ask Jackson where it was, but before I can get any words out he sets the gun carefully along the wall of the shed and reaches out to kiss me again, the fear that pulsed through him a few minutes ago replaced with happy relief. I push away from him.

"What is going on? Why couldn't you remember something that just happened last night?"

I am exasperated, and the words flow out of me as I reach my hands into the air and shake them in frustration and confusion and disbelief. I can't keep my mind straight.

Something shatters around the edges of my husband, and now he's really crying.

"What?" I ask, all irritation and no comfort. I was thinking it was just the same as before, when he was trying to make up for abandoning me while he was away. Tears that are all show and no substance.

Tears that will help him get what he wants from me.

But then he goes on.

"I had trouble sleeping last night, and I had to take a few of my pills before I went to bed. Sometimes they make me foggy in the morning, and sometimes I have trouble remembering what I did the night before."

I shake my head.

"I didn't know you had trouble sleeping," I say. I picture him staring out the window last night, and wonder again about what he was doing, who he was messaging.

"It's no big deal. Not really," Jackson says, wiping his hand over his nose and swallowing hard. He laughs, and takes a hard little breath. "Well, until I end up misplacing a--at least unloaded--shotgun."

He goes on. "I'm ashamed. I'm sorry I didn't tell you. It's just that, when I was in Australia, so much was happening and I was under so much pressure that I started having difficulty turning my brain off at night. The doctor suggested I try some medicine to help. It took a few tries to find a dosage that actually worked, and we had to increase it a few times. Eventually, we found something that helped me sleep. But, like I said, sometimes I feel the effects the next day. Still, it's better than not sleeping."

He moves his hand through his hair.

It hits me, like an avalanche overtaking my body, how little Jackson and I really know each other.

"I'm glad they help," I say quickly. "And I'm glad I know about them now. Just in case I'd ever need to help you with. . ." I trail off, not really sure where I'm going with what I'm saying. "Thank you for telling me," I add lamely.

"I don't want to keep secrets from you," he says.

"No more secrets," I reply, my hand in my pocket, feeling the smooth casing of the shotgun shells.

It isn't the first time Jackson's lied to me.

And it isn't the last time I'll lie to him.

9

After making our way back to the cabin and double-checking the locks on the doors and windows, Jackson says he's going to take a shower and I wander onto the screened-in porch at the back of the cabin. I'm hoping I might be able to get a few bars of reception out here. *Like Jackson did last night.* I push away the thought, and hold my phone up in the air, like some early noughties actress in a romantic comedy. A few bars appear. A voicemail dings into my inbox, and when I click into the list of messages I see that it's from Dani.

I click on the call to play back the message Dani left, the timestamp saying it was just after I tried calling her and the connection dropped out, but the reception in the cabin is too spotty, and it won't play. I don't bother typing out a text message, because I assume it won't send. Instead, I dial Dani and sit on the slightly damp cushions of the porch's wicker couch, fingers crossed that I'll get to talk to my best friend.

There's a weighted pause on the line, then miraculously I hear ringing, and then Dani's voice.

"Mary? Is everything okay?"

"I'm so sorry. The reception here is awful, and I couldn't get through again earlier. You haven't been worrying, right?"

A wave of guilt creeps up my chest. I wait.

"No, no, it's fine. I just wanted to make sure you got there safely." Dani's voice sounds cheerful enough, but there's an edge to it that I recognize.

"What's happened?" I ask.

I think about yesterday morning, and the guy I saw Dani with.

I'd gone into the store early for a few office to-dos, hoping to cross them off my list before heading out for the week, and before we officially opened at 9am.

I'd let myself in through the back door, and after checking to make sure the *Closed!* sign was in place up front, started organizing the display for the newest celebrity cookbook, which featured a jaunty picture of a waifish actress gnawing on a huge turkey leg and declaring the book was dedicated to *home-cooking made simple again.* The books were set out next to our expensive olive oils and Instagram-influencer-approved chinaware Dani had insisted we start carrying.

"It's made from mud taken from the river bottom of the Amazon," Dani had explained, although I still wasn't convinced it was anything special. Or that anyone would pay that much for a salad bowl.

I was back in our shared office, checking the receipts for the special Amazon crockery and writing a note to Dani to check the numbers, because they didn't seem to add up, when I heard a car pull up outside the back door I'd left cracked open. The emptiness of the store and the street outside prompted me to go and pull the door closed––there'd been a few robberies last year at some of the stores nearby––which is when I spotted Dani, talking to a man. Dark, slicked-back hair. Well-cut suit.

The two of them were talking intensely, Dani's head tilted up towards the man, who was at least a foot taller than her. They didn't touch. At one point, I saw Dani nod her head twice as the man reached out, like he wanted to touch her arm, only to decide against it and drop it back along his side. I'd headed back inside after that, watching Dani without her knowing I was there.

There didn't seem to be anything romantic between them, but still it seemed there was something electric and pulled tight with the way they didn't look at each other.

Hearing Dani's voice on the phone, I realized that maybe they had slept together.

"Well. . ." Dani draws the word out to twice its normal length.

I love my best friend, but her life can be a hot mess sometimes. Ever since we were teenagers, she's looked for love in the wrong places and trusted the wrong people. My mother used to say it was an impulse control problem, which I have to admit makes sense. Dani lives with her heart outside her chest, for better or for worse.

I'm also not surprised my mother sees it that way. She lives her life with her heart under lock and key. Or she has, especially since my father died, although if I'm honest with my memories I could see the signs even before Dad's accident. Which is all the more reason I'm grateful for these last several months with her.

Baby steps, I tell myself.

"Baby steps," I tell Dani. "Just start at the beginning."

"It's really not that long a story," Dani says. "I met someone at a bar the other night, and we hit it off and I ended up spending the night. Or at least I thought I was going to."

So this isn't about the guy at the store, I think. A squeal comes through the wall, and the far-off sound of rushing water intensifies. I know I'm hearing Jackson in the bathroom, taking a shower, but the thinness of the walls still unnerves me. I move a little further into the porch, towards the open wall of windows and away from the shared wall between with the bathroom. The sun is bright outside, and nothing––not even my own reflection––stares back at me.

"Why didn't you?"

"Well, around 3am I wake up to feel someone shaking me. And it's Mark."

At least she knows his name, I think.

And then I immediately feel chastened. Dani deserves better, from me and from the men she lets into her life.

"He's shouting at me to get up and get out. He says that his wife's coming home early from her shift at the hospital. I was so humiliated."

"It's not your fault," I tell her, my skin prickling just at the thought of this guy taking advantage of my best friend. "How were you supposed to know he was married?"

"He wasn't wearing a ring, and he didn't talk about his wife or his kids."

"Kids?" I ask, trying very hard to keep any hint of judgment out of my voice. I know Dani would never hurt a family, not after what she went through when she was in high school.

There's a small gasp, and I hear Dani crying. My heart lurches. I think again about how she deserves so much better than this, and a hot flash of anger surges in my chest.

"When he was shoving me out of his house, I passed by their bedroom doors. They had the name-tag signs on the outside, in those colorful letters, you know? One said Sadie and one said Carter."

Which means this sleazebag's kids were asleep when he brought my best friend home, to have sex in the bed he shares with his wife.

"I'm a terrible person," Dani says between a mixture of hiccups and sobs.

"Oh, sweetheart, no you're not."

"I don't think about the consequences of my actions. I don't think things through."

"You're a wonderful person, Dani. You're a brilliant business-woman, and the best friend anyone could ever ask for."

"Really?" she asks.

My arms start to reach out instinctively, just as if I were about to hug her. Muscle memory. And I tell her as much, that I wish I could hug her right now.

"I just wish I was as level-headed as you are," Dani says. "You always seem to make the right choices."

An image floats to me of reaching for the shotgun, just as the cabin door was flung open by my husband. On our honeymoon.

It comes out of my mouth before I can think about what I'm saying.

"Well, I'm the only one of us married to someone I barely know."

I laugh, but it comes out too loud and warped from my throat, so that it sounds more like a yelp.

"What happened?" The tension streams down the line with Dani's voice.

I'm quick to quell her worry. "Nothing. Seriously, nothing happened. I'm just in a weird mood. Things are a little off, out here in the middle of nowhere. I don't like being so far away from civilization."

"I can come and get you, right now," Dani says.

I don't bother to tell her that the cabin is too hard to find, or to point out that she has my mother's treatment appointment today.

"Jackson and I got into a fight," I begin, and then stop. I realize I'm too embarrassed to tell Dani about seeing a shadowy figure in the woods, and the lost and found gun, and suspecting

Jackson married me for some ulterior motive other than loving me. So I tell part of the truth.

"He apologized for being so distant while he was in Australia, and I didn't quite believe his explanation, and it sort of blew up into a whole big thing," I finish lamely, my voice trailing off.

"That's awful," Dani says. "He should be begging you to forgive him. It shouldn't just be some *I'm sorry, I was just so busy with work* excuse."

"That's exactly what he said." I think back to breakfast, and Jackson's tears. It's not enough. Nine months of feeling thrown away followed by a twenty-second *mea culpa* is not enough. Not when you love someone. I tell Dani just as much.

There's a shudder in the wall of the porch, and I hear the taps shutting off as Jackson finishes his shower.

"Are you going to talk to him about it?" Dani asks me, and as I think about her question a certainty works its way up the back of my neck.

"I think I have to," I tell her.

There's a pause.

"Don't tell him everything," Dani says. "He doesn't need to know everything."

I swallow hard. Because Dani isn't talking about my father, or my birthday, even though she knows the details of my inheritance almost as well as I do. After I left my mother's house, Dani was the only person I could really talk to about this burden—and that's what it really feels like, sometimes. A life raft and a burden. For me, for whoever I love.

Because I'm certain she's talking about what I did while Jackson was gone.

I nod, and Dani admonishes me. "Stop nodding your head, and say okay."

We both laugh; just a little flicker of brightness that rises out from the worries we both have.

"Okay," I say.

We start to say our goodbyes, Dani promising to call and update me on my mother's appointment later today, and me thanking her again for helping out while I'm away. We're about to hang up when Dani says something.

"You're locking your door, right? On the cabin?"

"Yes. Why?" I sound more at ease than I feel.

I don't tell Dani that the chain lock is already broken––or that it was Jackson who snapped it when he forced himself through the front door. I remind myself that the deadbolt still works.

"There was a news story I saw, something about someone sabotaging the trails for hikers in the Poconos. A few hikers have been hurt this season, I guess, and that doesn't usually happen. I'm sure it's nothing really, but just promise you'll be careful, okay?"

"I saw it too," I tell Dani. "It was in the local paper here."

"Promise," Dani repeats.

"I promise," I say. My mind thinks of the shotgun, now sitting empty in the shed. That glimpse of red and black checker cloth I thought I spotted out by the hot tub.

We say our goodbyes, and I walk into the bedroom.

Jackson is there, lying naked across the bed.

"Come over here," he commands.

But I don't. I just stand there, wishing Dani were on her way over here, right now, to save me from my husband.

10

I didn't plan on cheating on my husband. I wouldn't have even been out if it hadn't been for Dani.

It'd been a great week for the store. Record sales––Dani showed me the numbers, just before we closed. She had convinced me to come out after watching me obsessively check my phone for the entire afternoon, hoping to see a response from Jackson. I hadn't heard from him in four days. Although, as I told Dani more than once as the hours at the store ticked by, he'd managed to post three new photos of his adventures on Instagram. The club we were at was known for its cheap drinks, frenetic deejays, and reasonably-clean bathrooms. The walls of the building were so thin you could hear the music pumping from down the block by the bus stop, which we arrived at after Dani and I had ridden in a bus from her apartment.

When we got inside, we found the dance floor packed and the strobe lights turned on across the room, making everyone seem to move slower than normal. The deejay had a soul patch and a dingy-looking hoodie, but the beat was ripping through the crowd nonetheless, and I followed Dani as she made a beeline for the bar. She ordered us both something called a Sex Dream which, when I took a sip, turned out to taste like a mixture of lighter fluid and Kool-Aid.

Something buzzed in Dani's purse, and I watched as she took out her phone.

"Who is it?" I asked, partly worried that she'd received a text from a guy and was about to leave me alone at the club. Not that she'd ever done that to me, but everything that had happened with Jackson had left me feeling sensitive, if not a little paranoid.

But Dani's face as she looked down at the screen wasn't excited or giddy. It was tense.

She swiped her hand over the bottom of her screen to dismiss the call.

"Stupid telemarketers. I swear I get like twenty robocalls a day," she said.

I didn't get a chance to ask her more, or to find out whether she was really upset about something a guy had sent to her and was just putting on a brave face, because my best friend grabbed my hand and pulled me towards the dance floor.

"C'mon, let's dance!" she called over her shoulder as I followed behind.

The Sex Dream cocktail on top of the shots Dani and I had had at her apartment on the way to the club were mixing badly with my empty stomach, and the lights of the dance floor started to blend with the music around me. I don't usually drink, and that night I'd already had more alcohol than I'd had in the last three months combined. My head swirled as dizziness clamped down hard. I instantly regretted wearing a pair of Dani's sky-high heels. When I reached out to steady myself on Dani, I misjudged how close she was and quickly found myself grasping onto thin air. I fell, face first, onto the dance floor.

A group of greasy guys descended on me, their hands scrabbling around my body, trying to find some purchase to hoist me up. Or that's how they wanted it to appear, maybe.

I slapped their hands away and managed to pick myself up.

The air in the club was suddenly suffocating. I needed to get out of there, but I couldn't find Dani. To the right of me was a glowing exit sign, and I started to make my way over there, thinking that maybe she'd also gone outside to get a breath of fresh air.

Stepping into the frigid air was a shock to my system, but the coolness felt welcome on my clammy skin. I scanned around the back alley, which was surprisingly clean, but didn't see Dani anywhere. The alley connected to a side street, which was empty except for the lit sign of a parking garage.

Just as I was about to go back inside, one of the guys who'd attempted to pick me up from the floor came through the door. "Great idea," he said to me, coming closer than I was comfortable with. He reached out to grab my hips. "We can be alone out here."

He was so close that I could smell the mixture of Red Bull, vodka, and mints on his breath. He was very, very drunk.

"Leave me alone," I said, and tried to move past him back into the club.

"Hey, hey, why're you leaving so soon? I just got here." He reached out and grabbed my wrist. Although he'd seemed short in the club, out here, alone with him, he loomed over me.

An icy gust of wind blew through the alley, and my skin burst into goosebumps.

"I'm just looking for my friend," I said, wrenching my arm from his grip.

But he yanked back.

"I said, why leaving so soon?" he repeated, his voice turning rough. He stared down at me, his pupils dilated in the mercury light hung above the club's door and his mouth drooping at one corner as he lurched towards me.

I wished I'd never come with Dani. I wished I'd just stayed home.

I wished Jackson were here with me.

And then a hot anger pulsed through me at being left alone by my husband. While he posted his weekends away about the second most beautiful beach in Australia on Instagram, but couldn't return any of his wife's calls.

"Get away from me," I said, and shoved back against the sleazy guy's chest with both hands.

He stumbled and fell back. "You fucking bitch!" he roared. "You fucking whore!"

He reached back, ready to grab my hair, but something stopped him.

"What the fuck's your problem, man?" a deep voice rumbled from the shadow outside of the circle of light cast by the door. Moving out of the darkness, a tall man, older than Dani and me by a few years, in a checkered shirt and jeans, came into view, his large hand wrapped around the other guy's arm.

Matched up to each other, he made the greasy-haired club kid look like a middle-schooler.

"Leave her alone. Didn't you hear her say that the first time?" He grabbed the drunk guy and shoved him towards the door of the club. "Get out of here." Once the guy was back inside, the man stepped in front of the gap in the door and covered it with his broad back.

"Are you okay?" he asked.

"I'm fine. I was just looking for my friend."

"Are you sure?" He scanned around the alleyway, as if there were more drunk assholes waiting in the darkness. For all I knew, maybe there were.

I nodded. "I just want to go home."

"Here, let me help get you a cab." He looked down at me and smiled. "Or, I was just walking to the diner on the corner. Are you hungry?" He gave me a quick glance up and down. "It looks like you should be."

He was handsome. Not the way Jackson is handsome––this man was rougher, with his faded shirt and jeans, his stubble and long hair pulled back into a ponytail. But he had kind eyes and a warm smile that he gave me just then.

"I promise not all of us are like that," he said.

I can't explain what I did next, except to say that I was lonely, and he was being so sweet to me, and I really wanted to feel safe and loved in that moment. I had so much emptiness filling me up, and he looked so full of life, and warmth, and desire.

I stepped up to him and kissed him. Hard. So hard that I had to catch my breath for a moment. So hard that I could feel his tight torso against my thin dress, his hands wrapping around my waist.

So hard that I wanted to take him inside me right then and there, without even knowing his name, because maybe he could fill up my emptiness.

"Mary!" The voice came from behind me. I swiveled around.

Dani was standing in the cracked doorway of the club, her mouth open and her eyes wide from drink and panic. And something else, maybe.

I stepped back from the man.

"I'm sorry," I said, and ran back to Dani and disappeared inside the club, ignoring his requests to just hold on a moment.

Dani and I didn't say a word to each other on the bus ride back to her apartment.

The next morning, I still didn't have any messages from Jackson.

SARAH K. STEPHENS

And now Jackson is lying on the bed in this luxurious cabin of ours, expecting me to jump at the chance to link our bodies together again, because we've fought and made up, and he's apologized and confessed his big secret of having sleep problems.

But, like I said earlier, it's not enough. It was almost better before he apologized, because then I could convince myself that Jackson didn't realize what he was doing. I could tell myself that he believed the way he acted during his time in Australia was fine, even normal. I can't do that anymore, though.

He knows that he hurt me. And his expectation that I would just forget about it because he gave me his little dance of an apology has left me with a deep pit in my stomach that I just can't shake.

I look over at him and watch his expectant face light up at the thought of me slipping in beside him, but as soon as he sees my face he must know that something is off, because I watch the anticipation fall off him like an ill-fitting coat.

"What's wrong? What's happened?" he asks, standing up from the bed and whipping on a pair of boxers.

I have to fight the urge to slap him. He moves around the bed towards me, but I put my hands up as a barrier and he stops.

"I need some fresh air," I tell him, and quickstep out of the room. It's a gorgeous day outside, and I can't stand to be indoors any longer. I need to clear my head, and figure out just what the hell I'm doing.

"Is Dani okay?" Jackson asks, following me into the living room like a frazzled puppy. *Where was all this attention while you were gone?* I want to scream. *What do you want?*

Of course, I need to ask myself the same question.

"She's fine," I nip back at him. "I just need some space. You know, like you did last night at dinner?" I can't keep the sneer out of my voice, and Jackson stops dead in his tracks.

I glance up as I'm putting on my shoes, and see the slump in his shoulders and the furrows in his forehead. He suddenly looks worn around the edges, and I wonder whether the medicine he's taking is actually helping him to sleep.

"I'll be back soon," I add, trying to smooth the edges of my voice, although I'm still seething inside. "I'm just going to walk around the property. I won't go far."

We lock eyes for a moment, and a silent message passes between us.

Both of us seem to understand that when I come back our marriage might be over.

"I'll be right here," Jackson calls out to me as I head through the door. I can't decide if his words are a comfort or a concern.

Being outside is a relief after the stifling confines of the cabin, and I take even strides towards the tree-line around the property, my skin soaking in the sunshine. There's a copse of rhododendrons near the driveway, and I hear the chatter of chickadees calling out their distinctive song, providing the woods with a feeling of lush sound around me.

Chicka-dee-dee-dee. Chicka-dee-dee-dee.

I walk in the opposite direction, not wanting to disturb the wild creatures in the woods, and follow the paving stones around the back towards the hot tub. I spot a trail winding into the forest just beyond the corner of the cabin, and my mind goes back to yesterday, when I thought I'd seen someone in the woods. It occurs to me that I might have been right––that I simply spotted a hiker following along this trail.

But when I get to the opening, it's clear that this is just a path carved into the woods around the cabin, and that no one looking for a trailhead would stumble across this. The sun goes behind a cloud and darkness spills over the ground for a few seconds, giving me enough time to glance back at the cabin and spot Jackson's figure watching me from the window in the kitchen.

I start walking down the pathway. I don't think about sabotaged trails or shadowy figures in the woods. I just think about how it will feel to have some privacy to sit with my own thoughts, away from my husband.

The path is clear, with shifting spots of leaf litter intermixed with vibrant green plots of grass poking out from the floor of the woods. The trees are starting to leaf out, and the sunshine dims the further I get into the horseshoe-curved pathway. I don't have to go far before I can see why the path is cut into the woods. A creek bed appears ahead of me, probably one of the tributaries of the larger stream we crossed on our way down to the cabin, with a bench placed underneath a huge oak tree.

It seems as good a place as any. I turn round, making sure that Jackson hasn't followed me, and sit down on the bench, letting the soft trickle of the running water fill my head.

I pull out my phone, partly to check the time and partly to see if Dani or my mother has called to update me about the appointment. When I glance at the time, though, I realize that my mother's appointment isn't for another few hours. I also see that there's no better reception out here than at the cabin itself.

I wonder how my mother will manage with the treatment today. At first, she wasn't able to tell me much beyond the stage the cancer was at, but her oncologist, Dr. Bradbury, has been more than solicitous in answering the myriad questions I had as I attended my mother's initial consultation, and then treatments, with her. He's been there for us every step of the way.

He's really been a godsend, and I couldn't imagine going through my mother's chemotherapy treatments without his soothing presence there to assure us that everything will be okay.

He's a gorgeous man, with a huge shock of sandy blond hair, combed up and back like a 1950s movie star. Dr. Bradbury is the type of person that triggers some strange conditioned response that makes you delve into the recesses of your memory, searching for a shared connection. He's an incredible doctor, although sometimes I find myself wondering how he can manage to be so attentive at his job, and work such long hours. The first time we were in his office for my mother's consultation I didn't see any personal items except for one photograph. It was of a little girl with pigtails, sitting on a horse and smiling at the camera.

I remember feeling guilty, looking at the picture, because I was certain that Dr. Bradbury's devotion to his patients had a trade-off, and that his daughter probably didn't get to see him as much as she would like.

Daughters are a tricky business.

The sun finds its way through the treetops as I sit on the bench by this little stream, and I pick up my phone and dial my mother, but the call drops instantly without connecting. The small corner of my screen reads *no reception*.

I check the time again and realize she wouldn't be able to talk to me even if I could get through. My mother volunteers twice a week at Westerly Prep Elementary School, and she's just wrapping up her shift now. Even when her treatment started in earnest, she refused to give up her volunteer position. "The children need me," she'd explained, and I'd be lying if I said her commitment to children she barely knew didn't leave my heart more than a little bruised.

She had her reasons for asking me to move out, I remind myself. To stay away from her.

Which brings my thoughts back to Jackson. He doesn't know about any of that.

There's so much my husband doesn't know about me. When we got married, it didn't seem important. We were in love; we were happy. The past didn't seem to matter.

Now, nine months into not being happy, those notions all seem so quaint. I was so stupid to think that love conquers all. Or that you can have love without trust.

Is that what happened when Jackson left? Did he find out that I'd hidden the truth from him, and decided to punish me for it? There would have been public records, probate documents he could have used to target me. Or, a small voice inside my head says, maybe my mother told him. And now he's just trying to stick around until he can get his share.

On the day of our wedding, my mother had pulled me aside to ask if I'd told Jackson about my inheritance. How, when I turn twenty-five in just a few months, I'll inherit all the money my father had stockpiled away during his lifetime. Almost two million dollars.

He'd left almost nothing for my mother.

I remember how fragile her fingers felt, wrapped around my shoulder as she leaned in towards me. It was only a few weeks into her treatment regimen, but already I could see the signs of her body flagging under the chemotherapy's effects. Dark circles peered out from a layer of makeup she'd applied under her eyes, and her collarbones jutted from above the neckline of her slim black dress.

Jackson didn't know about my inheritance, and when I told my mother this, she'd explained how relieved she was. "With this rush of a wedding, and Jackson being such an exceptional young man, and him then rushing off to Australia for nine months right after the wedding––I was worried that perhaps he was marrying you for your money."

It isn't the cruelest thing my mother's ever said to me. But it came close.

Even so, I knew she was right. I hadn't told Jackson about my inheritance because I didn't want it to influence his feelings towards me.

I'm turning twenty-five tomorrow.

What am I going to do?

11

"Where did you go just now?" Jackson asks when I return to the cabin.

I'm still clutching my phone in my hand. Absentmindedly, I set it on the cabinet in the hallway, and the soft petals of the flowers my mother sent brush against my skin. I move away from their fragrant scent. "There's a path, out behind the back of the cabin. It leads to a little stream. I went and sat there for a while."

Jackson purses his lips. He won't look at me.

I've made my decision.

"I'm going to head home," I tell him, which is the coward's way of saying, *I don't think we should be married anymore.* "I'll bring the car back with Dani later today, and you can drive back when you feel like it, but I'm not staying here with you any longer."

Jackson's body goes rigid as my words register. All the color drains from his face, and I ask myself whether this is his reaction to losing me, or losing my money.

"I know you don't love me."

Jackson's face turns desperate, but there's something hiding underneath, flickering just below the surface. His eyes narrow.

"Why? Because I just spent almost the first year of our marriage away from you? Because I didn't call, or write, or message you enough?" The venom in his voice knocks me back, and I have to reach out my hand to steady myself on the table. I take a step away from him, towards the front door of the cabin. I don't know where the car keys are.

"Yes," is all I say.

"What do you want me to say? I did that for us."

I move in towards him again, my heart pounding violently in my chest. "You abandoned me and ignored me to make our marriage stronger? Is that it? And you show up, just before I inherit two million dollars from my dead father, with no coincidence other than that you want to be my 'loving' husband?"

My shouting seems to make Jackson speak even more quietly.

"What are you talking about?" The words barely come out of his mouth.

"I'm talking about how you conned me," I say, whispering the words to match him, trying to keep my emotions in check.

"*Conned?* I conned you? What is wrong with you?" Jackson reaches out to grab my arm, but I pull myself away from him.

"There's nothing wrong with me. Except that I believed marrying someone I barely know was a good idea. Except that I trusted you!" My words can't come out of my mouth fast enough. They're jamming up, like cars on a highway at rush hour. The sounds collide in my throat, choking down how devastated I feel that this is happening, and that I'm the one who's doing it.

"I didn't marry you for your money."

I catch his words, and throw them back at him.

"So you *did* know that I'd be rich in a few months! You just needed to figure out a way to avoid being near me for long enough so that you could tolerate being married to me until the money came in. But I've got news for you. I'm driving back now, and I'm going to file for an annulment and you won't see a cent."

"I don't want your money. Don't you understand?"

I ignore him. "How did you find out? Did you look me up? Have you been following me for a while, biding your time?"

"It's not important how I found out. What's important is that it had nothing to do with why I married you."

"The hell it didn't!"

We are like two animals in a cage. I'm on my end of the kitchen table, and Jackson is standing on the opposite side. The physical barrier feels good, like I can throw out my worst fears and they won't bounce back to haunt me.

Although I know that's just a fantasy. They're already hurtling back against my bones, battering my body down to its softest, most tender part.

I feel like I'm dying. Because I wanted to be married. Because I want my husband.

Just not like this.

"Listen to me," Jackson pleads, but I'm beyond listening.

"Where are the keys? I'm leaving."

"Dani told me," Jackson says. "She confronted me, before the wedding. She thought you'd told me, and she wanted to make sure that I wasn't marrying you for your money."

None of what Jackson is saying makes any sense.

"I don't believe you," I blurt out. "Dani would never go behind my back."

But even as I say it, I picture my mother and Dani, together in the living room of my childhood home. And another person, with checkmarks and pamphlets and promises that they only want to help me. *Dani lies*, a voice inside me whispers.

Jackson finishes my thought before I can.

"She wanted to protect you. She thought you'd told me

about your past--your inheritance." Jackson stumbles over his words, trying to get them out. "I think she figured out, almost as soon as she'd said 'inheritance,' that I had no clue what she was talking about, but she didn't want to admit it. Either to me or to you."

Unconsciously I nod. I could see Dani coming in like a fury, ready to rip into Jackson if she thought he was trying to use me.

I realize this means that Dani must believe that Jackson married me because he loves me. Otherwise she would never have let me marry him. Not without telling me everything she's suspected, which Dani has never mentioned.

I loosen my grip on the pale wood of the table and think about all these revelations over the last few minutes. The last few days.

Jackson seems puzzled by my sudden quiet, but he doesn't interrupt my line of thought. Instead, he stays on his side of the table, and I watch silently as he moves his hands towards my side by the slightest of nudges.

"I was so lonely," I finally say. I can't look my husband in the face. It's too humiliating. I've put on a brave face since we said goodbye at the airport, nine months ago, and since Jackson's returned I've been the happy, supportive wife.

For the most part, I amend, thinking about our fizzling honeymoon, just two days in.

I go on. "I don't understand why you would leave, and pretend almost like I didn't exist. I know you said it was work, but you had time to post all those photos and comments online. How could you not have had time to send me a message? To let me know that you still wanted me?"

Jackson pulls back a chair from the table on his end and sits down. I wait a moment, and then follow. I stay, staring at my hands, unsure of what he'll say next. In my mind I start to pack my things.

I think about what it will mean to separate our lives from each other. I suddenly feel exhausted.

"All of those posts were because of work."

I start to protest, not believing this same, worn excuse, but Jackson holds up his hand and I stop myself from interrupting, despite how much I want to tell him he needs new material.

"They had me working seventy-, eighty-hour weeks, plus I was expecting to represent the bank brand while out and about in Sydney. All the managers have social media accounts, and if you don't post regularly and keep their interest, it can affect their openness to your ideas and performance in the office. I wanted to succeed so badly, and I threw myself into every hoop I had to jump through. Being separated from you was awful, and having my free time eaten up by more work expectations, I was running on almost no sleep and absolutely no privacy. I was on the bottom of the ladder at the bank. The higher-ups gave me this opportunity to prove myself in Sydney, and I had to take it. Because it wasn't just me anymore."

Just for a second our eyes lock across the table and I look away. Part of me desperately wants what he's saying to be true.

"This was my chance, after fucking up so much of my life before, to show that I was capable of caring about someone else."

I was picturing Jackson in his sterile apartment in Sydney alone and fatigued, and having to pretend to enjoy every second of it, but then what he's just said registers and I jump in. "Doesn't that seem ironic? That you ignore your wife to show how much you care?" I try, but I can't keep the sarcasm out of my voice. I lean back in my chair and cross my arms over my chest.

I scan the room, looking for the car keys.

Jackson shakes his head. "You're right. In the short-term, it seems like I don't care. But in the long-term, Mary, I built a career over those long months. I have job security, a higher paycheck. I proved to my superiors that they can count on me. I worked my ass off so I could come home and be the best husband I could be."

He sits on his side of the table, turned away from me, his hands now folded in his lap, and stares at the swirls of dark and light grain in the surface of the wood. "I did it for us. And I know I put my job before you, and knowing that you were so hurt and lonely tears me up inside. All I can say is that I'm so, so sorry, and that it will never happen again."

He turns towards me, and his eyes are so open and crystal clear as he drinks me in that I feel my heart strain at the corners of my chest.

But my mind is roiling with one question, flashing and ripping through the fabric of my thoughts: *Can a marriage really be built on top of so many secrets?*

Followed by another: *Could we just start again?*

Jackson doesn't have much family. With his parents dead from their respective overdoses, Jackson had been bounced around in foster care for a while until he turned eighteen. Which is where he met Aunt Rachel. *Aunt* isn't an official title for Rachel; it's one earned through love and affection over the years. She was Jackson's social worker, and the two of them stayed close. According to Jackson she's the nearest thing to family that he has left.

We were at Jackson's welcome-home party, and while his college friends were regaling Jackson and Dani about some trip they'd taken back in school along the Appalachian Trail, I'd cornered the one person who could tell me about what Jackson was like when he was a boy.

"Was Jackson lonely when he was a teenager?" I'd asked. "He hasn't told me much about his childhood. . ."

Aunt Rachel's usually bright voice instantly turned serious. The woman is a fortress, and if she weren't pushing sixty, she'd be able to play linebacker for the Eagles and still make a Bundt cake to enjoy at the end of practice. "He doesn't like to talk about it. Most children who've been through foster care don't."

But I couldn't stop myself.

"It's just that Jackson didn't have any siblings, and I keep picturing him at these foster homes he's mentioned." I went on and on. "Even though he said they were fine––that's the word he used, fine––I can't help wondering if some of the things he does now are connected back to being alone when he was younger."

And that's when Aunt Rachel reached out her hand, as though to put her palm on my forearm in a gesture of comfort, and knocked her drink all over me. She never got a chance to answer my question.

And I really don't blame her for spilling her drink on purpose, because she loves Jackson. And I'm learning there's nothing simple when it comes to loving my husband.

I picture my husband, tapping out messages at 3am on his phone while we're on our honeymoon.

I think about Dani trying to protect me and, in so doing, revealing something I may have never told Jackson about, because I wasn't willing to risk being vulnerable in that way.

I think about me and the pieces of my father's death––and what happened afterwards that Jackson still doesn't know. And that I never want to tell him.

And then I think about my mother and father, and how marriages can be built on so many things. If Jackson and I build ours on a set of lies it might not matter all that much––as long as one thing is entirely true.

When I stand up I'm not precisely certain what I'm going to do. I just know that I want to be closer to Jackson, and that I'm sick of having a table separate us.

As I walk over, he jumps up from his chair, and swivels his hips so that he's facing me straight on as I come around towards him.

"I don't want to leave," I tell him.

"Then don't," he tells me. His mouth is set in a grim line, as though he's waiting for the second part of my statement that will seal our fate.

But what I say next must surprise him, because something bright and luminous shifts across his face when I ask him, "Do you love me?"

He doesn't hesitate. "Yes."

I nod. "I love you too," I say, and his mouth cracks into a hint of a smile.

I don't return it, but I do inch myself closer to him.

"Let's start over," I whisper, my mouth just below his.

Jackson doesn't say a word, but his body answers as he wraps his arms around me and pulls me into his chest. We kiss, passionate and long, and I feel myself letting go as my head swims with the memories of every kiss we've shared, and lets them go on the rays of sunshine streaming through the windows.

We stumble back towards the bedroom, pulling at zippers and buttons and anything else that's keeping our skin from touching each other's. Our bodies link together like magnets; each time we pull apart we're drawn back together with currents of electric tension. My body is flooded with light and warmth and every sensation is magnified.

It's like the first time. Like a renewal of where we could be if we'd just kept loving each other.

As our limbs tangle into each other, our breath joining in one fluid motion, I tell myself, over and over, that this is enough.

This has to be enough.

12

I haven't been with a lot of men. There was a boy, Tom, back when I first moved out of my mother's house and was living with Dani while I finished the last few weeks of high school. I was already eighteen by that point, so there were no real services to help me. I needed to finish school, get a job, and get an apartment quickly. With a restraining order following me like a toxic vapor trail, I was lucky to get a job at one of the grocery stores in town in the deli department. Dani's mother said I could stay with them as long as I wanted to, but living there was almost more tense than living with my own mother, if you can believe it.

Dani was planning on bailing out as soon as she graduated. When she ended up getting expelled for smoking pot in the girls' bathroom just a week before graduation, she came home the same day and packed up all her stuff. She and I moved into our own apartment above a Suds and Go Laundromat at the outskirts of town, and the rest is history.

Her mother called me a few times, asking if I wanted to come back, but I never picked up. She just left voicemails. I couldn't face her, especially because I knew she hadn't called Dani to ask her the same thing.

So there was Tom, who was cute and sweet, and worked in the bakery at the grocery store. We fumbled around on my futon in that dingy apartment a few times, but it didn't really go anywhere. I wasn't looking for a relationship, and he didn't know what he was getting into with me. I ended it one night when he asked if I wanted to meet his parents. There was no way I was ready for that.

And, sure, there were a few other men over the years that slipped in after a night out with Dani, dancing in her fake furs and drinking sickly sweet cocktails at some of the bars. But they were all just placeholders, really. The sex was almost pragmatic. I came a few times, but none of the men I was with before Jackson seemed to understand my body the way he did.

Does.

Nothing's ever felt as good as Jackson. He made my skin tingle with his hands. His tongue. His body.

In the bed in our honeymoon cabin, Jackson grips me in his arms and cradles me, the naked skin of his chest smooth and supple on my thighs. He hoists me up a little further, until his hands can reach underneath my hips and he can balance the weight of my body on him, while touching the secret place between my legs that sends shivers up my spine and convulses the muscles in my legs. My breath is hot and rapid in his ear, and I tell him to please, don't stop.

I read that somewhere once. That men like nothing more than to hear those three words when they're with a woman, making her body vibrate on a frequency of thirsty satisfaction.

Please, don't stop.

I tell Jackson this, over and over again, and he obeys with a relish that makes my mind feel close to collapsing in on itself. Just when I'm about to scream out in a mixture of anguish and pleasure, Jackson flips me onto the king-sized bed. The sheets must be some form of luxury, because they feel silky smooth as my skin rubs against the soft fabric.

I spread out, my arms and legs cast wide and my body vulnerable to my husband. Inside, I silently fight the doubts whispering in the corners of my mind. If my marriage is going to work, I can't leave room for fear. Instead, I need to offer myself, voluptuous and whole. Marriage is a give and take, after all, and now it's my turn to be the giver.

Jackson gazes down on my naked body, so full of desire that I sit up suddenly and cup him in the palm of my hand, pressing against the stiff fabric of his jeans. I start to pull at the zipper and buckle, groaning with impatience.

My husband mimics me, and soon we're both ripping at the last shreds of his clothes, desperately trying to marry our bodies together.

As soon as Jackson's pants are off, he leans over, putting one hand between my legs and the other on himself, ready to join us together and let me ride another wave of total, unreal pleasure. But I stop him.

Because it's his turn.

Dani told me once that she likes giving oral sex better than actual sex, because it allows her to be in total control. I always thought she was a little crazy for thinking that—I mean, they don't call it a *job* for nothing. But I've come to realize what she means. Kneeling on the luxurious bed in this isolated cabin in the woods, making my husband moan with pleasure and beg me to keep going, is more of a power trip than anything else I've felt in my life. I feel so incredibly wanted in this moment that I don't want it ever to end.

Eventually, though, Jackson presses his hands on my shoulders, pulls himself down on top of me, and sinks his body into mine in one fluid motion of total synchrony that I almost pass out from the pure, primal gratitude it sends through my body. And just as suddenly as he strokes our bodies together, a wild wave of greediness crashes over me and I grip my legs tight around his body, pulling him as close as he possibly can be physically.

The temperature of the day is rising, and the air in the bedroom is getting thick with the heat of our lovemaking and the smell of sex. Sweat drips down my neck and under my breasts, and Jackson bends to lick the moisture from my body even as he continues to rock his hips into mine. An aching is growing in my body, leaving my mind desperate with the sheer pleasure of my approaching climax. It's overwhelming, and for a feverish moment all self-control leaves my body and I scream out my husband's name, shrill and loud. If anyone were listening to us, they would think Jackson was trying to kill me.

And it's that thought, rising to the tip of my consciousness in the midst of the chaos of sensations rocking my body, that does it. Right after I scream out Jackson's name, I laugh. Not a small, sexy giggle. A broad, deep-throated guffaw that echoes against the log walls of the cabin.

It's a sound of total release, and I shift my eyes to meet Jackson's, hoping he'll know exactly how fantastic he is making me feel. But when our eyes meet, my husband's body still plunged deep into mine and demanding with each movement a reciprocation of my own pleasure, I have to fight the urge to look away.

Because in that moment I'm not looking at my husband. I'm looking at a stranger, pressed into my naked body.

It only lasts for a second, but I swear it's as though Jackson doesn't know who I am. And in return, I feel just as unsure of exactly who we both are.

The pulse of fear that I tried to suffocate a few moments earlier pounds again with a vengeance.

And then it's gone, and Jackson is back with me, pressing his lips onto my mouth and locking his eyes with mine as we both fall off the edge into the sweet, cool hum of release. Jackson rolls onto his side and rests his arm across my stomach.

"That was amazing," he says.

Lying down on my back intensifies the sensation of my heart rate dropping as my body sinks back into equilibrium. Jackson's breathing beside me starts to slow, and then I hear it ratchet up again.

"Wasn't that amazing?" he asks, and I feel his hand grip more firmly on my hipbone.

I don't know what to say, and so I kiss him instead.

13

"Let's go for a hike." Jackson stretches across the bed as I struggle to get out of the sheets. He yawns and falls back onto the mattress. "If we stay here another second, I think you might kill me from dehydration."

"That's why I'm getting up," I explain. "Sustenance."

I start to make my way over to the kitchen, but before I realize it, Jackson is up out of the bed and has his arms swung around me.

"Gotcha," he says. "Not so fast."

He pulls me back to the bed, and I willingly topple over him.

"I shall get up, and bring you refreshment," he says in a way that is more charming than silly. I can't argue. I wouldn't mind lying alone for a few moments, reminding myself to enjoy the sensation my husband has left on my skin.

Husband, I think. I let the word sit firmly in my mind, not willing to let it go again like I had been ready to do just a few hours earlier. We're moving forward, I tell myself. No more looking back.

I push the anxiety down before it can burst in my chest. It's just my post-sex haze, I tell myself. I always feel this way.

"Where did you want to go hiking?" I call out, and to distract myself I grab my phone from the bedside table to start looking through the hiking app I downloaded before our trip.

Jackson returns triumphantly with a large glass of orange juice for us to split and a granola bar partially unwrapped and with one bite missing, and I grasp the glass and drink greedily.

Jackson takes it back from me and jokingly turns it over.

"Sorry," I say sheepishly. "I was dying."

"I have that effect on women," Jackson says over his shoulder as he heads back to the kitchen. "I love them to death."

I know he's joking, but that word—death—still sends a sliver of ice up my spine that I have to shake off.

We can do this.

"I read in the paper insert that the Storm King trail is pretty gorgeous. There's a waterfall at the top, and the hiking isn't too difficult," Jackson calls out from the kitchen. I hear the whoosh of the faucet and a few seconds later he's back with a glass of ice water.

I tap in the trail name into my phone and try to look up pictures posted online, but the reception won't connect. The search bar with the words *Storm King Trail* just sit while the small wheel circles round and round on the screen in the browser. I look up at Jackson.

"Sounds like a perfect fit," I say.

Jackson murmurs his assent and, setting down the glass, turns to kiss me just behind my ear. His fingers are so strong as his right hand moves across my shoulders and clasps the base of my neck, gentle yet firm in their hold on me.

I set my phone down.

"Did you want to go this afternoon?" I ask. I'm a little disoriented with how quickly everything seems to have changed.

Could it really be that easy? Just hitting reset?

I refuse to let my mind track back to that moment, with Jackson's weight bearing down on me, where we seemed to lose each other.

My eyes fall on Jackson's nightstand, and the local paper we'd seen earlier today stares back at me with that headline. *Same Individual Suspected in Hiking Trail Sabotage.*

Jackson's eyes follow mine.

"The Poconos is a huge area with several different parks inside it," he says. "The likelihood that we'll be in the one area where this individual has decided to mess around with the trail-heads or whatever is very, very low."

"You seemed so worried earlier," I remind him.

Jackson gives a shrug, shifting his weight off me and giving a perfunctory pat to my hipbone, but I can tell bringing up our earlier fight bothers him.

"We can't stay in bed all day, can we? And the start of the trail is just a few minutes' drive down the road," he continues.

"Do we have time for me to take a shower, first?" I ask.

Jackson strokes my face. "We have all the time in the world. Although I have to say I kind of love how you look now, all disheveled and spent." My husband leans in and kisses me. He inhales long and deep. "And I love that you smell like I've been all over you."

"Well, you have been," I reply, and start to head towards the bathroom, but Jackson follows his hand along my arm and gives a little tug on my hand as I turn away.

"Mary," he says, almost in a whisper.

I turn back towards him, suddenly aware of how utterly naked I am. Despite the warm day, a chill passes over my body. The sweat from earlier has dried on my skin, and I'm anxious to hop into the shower.

"What is it?"

"Thank you," Jackson says. He won't look at me. "Thank you, for giving us another chance. I promise I won't let you down."

A warm flush rises up my skin, replacing the creeping cold I'd felt a moment ago.

"I love you," I tell him.

"I love you too," he says, and lets go of my hand so I can head into the bathroom, and have a few moments of privacy.

14

The bathroom in the cabin has a gorgeous walk-in with gray slate tiles and a huge rain shower fixture in the ceiling. As soon as I step into the bathroom, I crank the faucet to as hot and heavy as it will go, and wait for the bathroom to fill with steam and soak into my bones. It only takes a minute or so for the water to heat up, but it's enough time for me to spot Jackson's travel case on the long marble sink and pick it up on impulse.

At first, I'm not sure what I'm looking for exactly. Until I find them.

They're not hidden at all, but sitting in the universal orange-brown bottle pharmacies use. Jackson's sleeping pills.

I read the label—it's Ambien that he's taking—and notice something. The dosage seems really weak: 12mg of medicine per tablet. I don't know anything about sleep medication, but I do remember something Dani told me once. She'd been volunteering at the hospital for almost our entire senior year, because Ms. Chiu had suggested Dani would be good at nursing when one of our classmates had a full-blown seizure in her chemistry class and Dani had known exactly what do to. Dani said it seemed like a lot of people were on something when they came in, and one night she'd done some shadowing of a nurse on the psych ward, where antidepressants were passed out like lip gloss. I remember her saying that everyone was on at least 30mg, and that some people were in the triple digits. I know that medicines aren't all the same and that antidepressants are different from Ambien, but still. *Could just 12mg of something make a person forget they'd hidden a gun?*

Steam starts to cloud the mirror above the sink, obscuring my reflection. I look straight in front of me, tracing over the patches of light and dark where my hair and eyes and face all blur together into an abstract kaleidoscope. Jackson's face, back in the bedroom, flits up and fills in the blotches where my face should be. Was it the medication that made him look at me that way? Or was it the fact that we *are* really strangers? And that, even though I've decided to keep trying at our marriage, I'm not planning on sharing certain parts of myself with my husband. Ever.

I wipe my hand over the mirror in one quick movement. Just as a clear space appears in the mirror, I see something move behind me. The door to the bathroom snaps open, as if someone has pulled the doorknob from the inside where I'm standing.

Even over the sound of the shower, I can hear Jackson in the kitchen, opening cabinet doors and running something under water in the sink. He couldn't be trying to open the bathroom door on me. I push the door closed, and turn the lock.

I know the door probably popped open, just because of the change of humidity and temperature in the room from turning the shower on so high. It's something that would happen all the time in my first apartment with Dani, and we'd joke about how we must have a stalker or a peeping Tom.

Looking back on it now, it doesn't seem at all funny.

The sensation that someone might be trying to sneak in on me in the shower, however imaginary, forces my hand over to

Jackson's travel bag, where I slip his pills back where I found them. I shouldn't be snooping on my husband like this. If I want to know about his medication, I should just ask him.

Still, I check the lock on the door again before I slip under the steady stream of the showerhead. The water feels luscious as it runs over my skin, and I try to just sink into a state of relaxation.

I close my eyes and tip my head back, letting the water pour down over my face.

As I stand there, trying to relax on my honeymoon, I think about what it was like a week ago: seeing my husband again after nine months apart. Jackson's flight home from Sydney was delayed, and so I'd found myself anxiously pacing around the airport for hours, trying to pretend that I wasn't half as nervous as I felt. Finally, he'd called me while I waited in the shops at the airport, and after I raced to the gate to meet him, I ducked into a small hallway that led to an employee entrance and reached into my bag to grab my compact and dot a little bit of powder onto my nose. I wanted to make sure I looked presentable, given that I'd just run across Philadelphia International Airport. I needed only a moment, and I didn't want Jackson to catch me before I was ready to see him. My back was to the throngs of people passing by. As I rustled around in my purse, the light from the larger terminal blotted out over my shoulder.

Someone was behind me, I realized. I stood to the side, assuming that an employee was coming for their lunch break and needed to pass by me. But the shadow didn't move. Whoever was behind me was standing there, staring at me from behind. Which was when I suddenly realized how detached the entranceway was from the rest of the airport, and that I didn't want to be there anymore with a stranger closing in around me. My hands went cold and clammy as I strengthened my grip on the compact.

I decided to turn to my right, and rush past whoever was lurking behind me and propel myself towards the open atrium of the airport and everyone moving in it. Towards my husband, newly home, waiting for me at the gate. As I twisted, though, two hands gripped my shoulders and a voice barked, "Not so fast."

I instinctively fought against the man's grip, and was about to scream when I felt lips press against my mouth. I reared back, disgusted and ready to take on my attacker and figure out exactly what I was going to do to save myself.

But in front of me was a mirage. My husband, tanned, a little leaner perhaps, and still gorgeous.

"I found you," he said, a wicked glint in his eye that told me he thought I was in on the joke.

I work a lather of shampoo into my hair and rinse it out, and then rub soap over my body and wash off the thin layer of sweat and sex dried on my skin.

When I get out of the shower, I check the lock on the door again before toweling myself off. The door is held fast, and nothing seems out of place.

I only need a few moments, staring at myself in the mirror. Just a few deep breaths, before I feel ready to go out again and join my husband.

15

After I dry my hair and get dressed, Jackson and I gather some water bottles, granola bars, and sunscreen. I set my phone down on the kitchen table as I try to fit a pair of binoculars into our hiking bag, squeezing them in around our rations.

I finally get them in and zip up the pocket. We're about to leave when my stomach gives a very decisive growl. I blush, but Jackson laughs.

"Maybe we should eat something first," he says, as he pulls open the fridge door. "Let's eat outside. I think I saw a picnic table out back."

I go to help him prep the sandwiches, but Jackson shoos me away. "I've got this. Why don't you take out the drinks, and I'll be there in a second."

So I head outside to put the glasses down on the picnic table around the back corner of the house. There's a buzzing all around us as bees go about their work in the gardens surrounding the cabin, and the sun feels delicious on my skin as I sit and wait.

After a leisurely round of sandwiches eaten—Jackson's done

an excellent job with ham and cheese—we stash our dishes and head out to the car.

I've left the car unlocked, and as I pull the door open I remind myself to lock up when we return. Before I climb in, I watch as Jackson pauses to lock the door to the cabin.

Then I remember that I left my phone on the table in the kitchen.

I open the door to call out to Jackson to grab it for me, but my eyes catch something nestled in the crease of the driver's seat. I reach down to retrieve whatever it is. The screen lights up as my fingers wrap around it.

It's my phone. The screen says it's locked for the next two hours.

Because someone has tried to unlock it without the passcode.

The car door opens, and a wave of damp air floods in.

"Ready to go?" Jackson asks.

I put my phone in my pocket. A red checkered shirt flits across my mind. The headline in the paper. My husband's face, bent over a glowing screen in the middle of the night.

Reset, a voice begs me. *Reset.*

"Ready as I'll ever be," I tell my new husband.

16

The trailhead is visible from the road, despite the dense foliage of the pine and elm trees towering over us as we make our way in the car. A few cars are parked in the gravel turn-off, but we don't see any other hikers as we park and fill our backpacks with the water bottles and granola bars Jackson grabbed from the kitchen on his way out.

Jackson rubs sunscreen on my shoulders and neck with an intensity that would be foreplay, if my mind allowed it.

How did my phone get in the car?

Who was trying to unlock it?

I want to ask Jackson about it. Maybe he tried to map the trailhead, hoping to get a better connection outside the cabin, and didn't want to bother me with the passcode? I use it so rarely since it's linked to my thumbprint to open. He's said previously that his phone service seems to have been garbled since he returned from being abroad. There have been texts and phone calls, from me and from other people that he's entirely missed.

I can rationalize it until I'm running myself in circles. But the fact is I don't want to bring another accusation up to Jackson. Not now, after everything that's happened so far since we've come here, for what is supposed to be our romantic, *reconnecting* anniversary getaway. *The missing shotgun, the sleeping pills, the prowler harassing hikers.*

Of course, I've considered the reality that, if Jackson didn't try to open my phone, someone else must have been inside our cabin.

Suddenly the quiet forest seems terribly loud, like an airplane about to take off. Jackson's asked me to put sunscreen on the back of his neck, but my hands are shaking so much I can't manage to smear the lotion onto his skin.

Jackson whips around.

"What's wrong?" His arms encircle me in a tight embrace. I press my hands against his chest, just needing a little air, but he holds firm for a second longer. The smell of sunshine and sunscreen envelops me in a cloud that should be happy anticipation.

I shake my head. I shake the fears out of my skull.

"I'm fine. I think I just need a sip of water." I grab the bottle from our bag and take a few swigs of water. "Let's go," I say, and venture a tight smile.

As the miles pass, the steady rhythm of our feet on the dirt-packed trail starts to relieve the tension tugging at my shoulders and my chest. It's hard to feel threatened in such a beautiful space. The Storm King trail is ten miles long, half of which climbs at a steep ascent to a waterfall which, as Jackson points out, should be running with a steady stream given the recent rain the area has had.

The tops of the trees tower over us in a protective canopy, although rays of sunshine peek through the boughs and fall on us to illuminate the trail. We've been going for almost four miles and have yet to see any other hikers.

Jackson is holding the pair of binoculars I brought along for our trip, and will sporadically stop at different lookouts to take a view of the forest valley, or a bird he sees flying overhead from tree to tree. Hikers might be few and far between, but with Jackson's eye we've managed to spot two downy woodpeckers, a grosbeak, and one wild turkey, the latter being on the ground, not up in the trees.

Bird-watching is a hobby my father loved, and one he passed on to me. To my surprise, Jackson and I share it. Investment bankers never really struck me as the slightly disheveled, canvas-hat-wearing birders my father spent time with on the weekends when he was feeling well enough—Friday nights were always rough for him—but one of our first dates had involved Jackson suggesting we go over to Millbrook Marsh for a bird-watching picnic. We'd spotted little that day, with the sky being overcast and eventually dripping with rain, but we'd had a great time matching each other's gaze with our binoculars trained on the same tree-hole or grassy copse.

We'd also spent a fair amount of time in the car afterwards, making out like two teenagers.

I instinctively blush as I remember the afternoon, and Jackson must catch me reminiscing because he says, "Do you remember that day we went birding at the Marsh?"

I tell him that of course I remember.

"Did I ever show you the pictures of the kookaburra I saw eating a lizard outside my apartment?" Jackson's eyes are trained on the rocky incline we're about to ascend.

He steps up and turns back to me to take my hand and help me up the large boulder at the base of the hill.

I go silent, because no, he did not share those pictures with me, although I'd seen them on his social media accounts, posted for the world to enjoy.

"I didn't, did I?" He doesn't look at me, but his hand still holds onto mine.

"No," I say simply, and keep climbing up the hill. My voice isn't harsh, or hurt. It's simply a fact.

Jackson seems to accept this, and starts telling me the story as we climb up a steeper part of the hill. The terrain is rough, and eventually both of us fall silent as we focus on placing our feet carefully amongst the rough stones littering the train.

As we climb, higher and higher, I consider my birthday tomorrow, and what it means. I picture telling Jackson that my father didn't just die in a car accident when I was seventeen, almost eighteen. That he was a drunk, and the accident didn't only kill him. My father crashed his car into someone else—a teenage girl who was driving home from work that evening: Abby.

I think about telling him that, up until my father died, I hadn't even known that he had a lawyer. It seemed like something only rich people would have—people who lived over the hill in Houserville Estates, not in our shady little street with Sears' dowdy houses and climbing honeysuckle.

My mother wore large black sunglasses the day his will was read, which had become a fixture for her out in public after my father died. At home, I'd walked in on her sobbing only once, although I could hear her crying sometimes at night, locked behind her bedroom door, when she thought I was asleep. I'd knock, but she'd just pretend she didn't hear me, and so I'd wait outside her door, whispering to her that everything was going to be okay.

There was one time I came in after school and found her, sitting on the edge of her bed and weeping into one of my father's old shirts. I'd sat down next to her and tried to comfort her. But when I wrapped my arms around her shoulders and pressed her into a hug, she shrank away and pretended that she needed to get up and gather more tissues.

That day, the lawyer had announced that my father had made significant changes to his will only a few months prior to his death. His pension from the paper mill was intact, and handled through the labor union for my mother, but apparently my father also had significant investments, along with a million-dollar life insurance policy. And he had signed all of it over to me, to stay in trust until I turned twenty-five. My mother was expressly forbidden to have anything to do with my inheritance.

Part of me wonders if my father had just been playing at loving my mother; if he'd regretted marrying someone so young and vivid. She was so passionate about everything, including him for a period of time.

As soon as we were clear of the door of that slimy lawyer's office, my mother excused herself and rushed off to the bathroom. I knew she didn't want me to follow her, but I couldn't let her be there alone.

When I opened the door, I found her standing in the corner of the dreary corporate bathroom, her dress and new shoes covered in sick.

She hadn't made it in time.

Later that evening, when I heard my mother crying, I tried her door again.

And this time it was open.

I blink. Jackson's voice has gone silent, and his shoulders are turned towards the path.

The slow crunch of our hiking boots in the dirt fills the silence, and I'm glad that I didn't follow my impulse. There's no way Jackson would understand, and if there's one thing I know from all the pain and loss I've been through in the last seven years, it's that people tend to hate what they don't understand. Maybe not at first, and maybe not with awareness.

But with a dark and pulsing malice, all the same.

A metallic smell of running water starts to fill the air around Jackson and me, and the sound tinkles in the background of the quiet forest. Up ahead, I see a steep drop-off and metal safety bars slung along both sides of the trail, which narrows considerably at that point.

My mother couldn't cope with my father's last betrayal. And I'd come to hate my father for it, for what it did to our family, even as I missed him each and every day.

"That's the perfect spot for a picture," Jackson says, as we take another step towards the summit.

17

"Let's stop here for a moment," Jackson calls up from behind me.

We've been hiking in silence for the last ten minutes or so, with the noise of the forest washing over us. The tattoo of a woodpecker breaks through the quiet ambient sounds of wind rustling leaves, and the soft pulse of water rushing over stone grows stronger the higher we climb.

I glance up ahead of us, and suddenly the waterfall looms into view, rushing in white, foamy streaks. When I look back, to acknowledge what Jackson has just said, I see something move in the shadows of the trail below us.

The branches of an ancient rhododendron bush rustle as whatever was just there moves through them.

"Are there hikers behind you?" I call down, but Jackson can't hear me over the din of the water. Sound traveling up the mountain seems to move faster than it does traveling down.

I look again at the spot on the trail, and for a moment I think I spot a silhouette of a person, but then the light moves behind a cloud and the limited streaks passing through the forest canopy make everything outside of them bleary.

Just like yesterday, by the hot tub, I can't be certain of what I saw.

Jackson catches up with me, and the smile he gives me as we physically reunite at the lookout isn't contagious, but I pretend that it is. I smile back, and there's a few moments of what Jackson's Aunt Rachel would undoubtedly call 'heavy petting' before my husband pulls away from me.

"Isn't it beautiful," I say, purposefully turning away from Jackson and towards the waterfall, now only a few hundred yards higher up the trail.

"Picture?" Jackson asks. "I can upload it to my Instagram when we get back to the cabin," he tells me.

My mind rushes over the months of pictures catalogued in my husband's online life. Of beaches and kangaroos and jackfruit cocktails. Of anything other than the two of us: together and happy.

We're going to be just fine. I force the words to float in front of me.

"You take it," I tell him. He has longer arms, and a flare for framing the shot. I know this from all the pictures he posted during his time away from me, cataloguing the life he said he curated for his bosses.

Jackson sidles back against the railing next to me, offshoots of the waterfall running behind us and down the slate gray rocks that litter this part of the forest. I hold onto the railing and smile. I lean my head into his like I'm supposed to. Jackson reaches his arm out, and the two of us show on the screen of his phone, glowing from our hike and squinting just a bit from the sunshine that's streamed through the clouds at that exact moment.

His finger clicks on the dot, and the two of us are frozen in time for a moment before the photo minimizes in the bottom right of his screen.

Jackson glances behind him at the streaming water.

"I want one just of you." He steps away from the edge and crosses to the opposite side of the lookout. There's a metal railing on that end as well, and he leans his tall frame against it, relaxing into the scenery.

I blush, and the surprise I feel at my husband wanting a picture of me cuts deep. I'm not really a selfie kind of person. Especially not after those PG-13 pictures I sent to Jackson during the first months we were apart were apparently tossed around Australian customs.

"You should see how gorgeous you look with the water behind you," Jackson says. "I want to capture this moment forever."

This time I don't blush.

I stand back against the railing, careful not to lean too heavily against it. The lookout we're standing on is positioned above a steep drop-off on both sides, and even as I stand and wait for Jackson to take the picture, pebbles fall from the packed dirt and tumble down the side of the mountain.

It's easily a thirty-foot drop, lined with the same ragged rocks we've been battling with on our entire hike.

I swallow involuntarily as I look down.

Best not to do that again, I tell myself.

"Let's start moving," I call out to Jackson. The rush of the water has picked up for some reason, and I'm having trouble making my voice carry above the noise.

I step forward, but Jackson still has his phone out, a frown tugging the corners of his mouth down.

"I can't get you in the frame," he yells over to me. He steps closer, and his voice is suddenly clear in my ear. "Can you stand there one more time—it really is the prettiest shot."

I push down the nervous tension rising in my stomach and

patiently move back to the place Jackson is pointing to with his left hand, his phone poised in his right.

My mind wanders to those stories that litter social media, of vacationers and hikers who've fallen to their deaths after trying to get the perfect picture for their *influencer* accounts.

"That's enough." I step away from the railing and begin to move towards the safety of sturdier ground, but Jackson reaches out and places his hand gently on my arm.

"I almost have it," he says, his eyes a mixture of expectation and intention. "Seriously, I wouldn't ask if it wasn't such a beautiful picture. I have hardly any photos of you, and this would be a perfect one to print out and frame on my desk at work."

That's stops me. Aside from our wedding photos, which are still waiting to be ordered and printed, Jackson doesn't have a single photo of me in a frame.

It was a noteworthy absence when he unpacked his bags in our apartment, nine months of clothes and tchotchkes, and keepsakes spilling out of his suitcases, but no pictures of me.

I want Jackson to have a piece of me when I'm not with him, so I gingerly step back over to the railing, inwardly sigh, and then smile for the camera.

"Lean back just a little bit," Jackson tells me, and I oblige, resting my hands on the railing. *Almost over*, I tell myself.

But as I lean against the railing, something shifts. I feel the ground below begin to slide beneath me. The railing is coming loose, and my center of gravity pulls me down the side of the cliff face, into the pouring runoff of the waterfall.

I scream my husband's name.

The newspaper headline, the one Dani warned me about, flashes across my mind, and as I fall off the side of this mountain, into the jagged rocks waiting to pummel my body, I think of the stranger who is out there, terrorizing vacationers and hikers. I wonder if I saw him, earlier at the cabin, or on the trail when the shadow of someone seemed to pass through the bushes, and wonder if he's watching me fall to my death. And enjoying it.

Jackson runs over to me, fear making his eyes bulge. His breath is heavy and rapid.

"Jackson!" I yell again, my hands slipping in the wet gravel and mud. My left hand is clamped around the base of the railing, which has slid out of its posthole and is still attached to the lookout by only a few larger pieces of gravel blocking its fall. The weight of my body will pull it down, and myself with it, any second now.

On his knees, Jackson reaches out to grab me, and I let go of my right hand, which had been clawing at the gravel and dirt, and grip onto him. He starts to pull me up, but something happens as I feel my body being hoisted back to safety.

I stop moving.

Jackson isn't pulling me towards him.

I look up to see something sharp play at the corners of Jackson's mouth, turning his familiar lips into an unfamiliar wound. His eyes are far away, trained on something in the distance.

I call out to him again, but he won't look at me. His grip begins to loosen, and suddenly I'm falling down into the ravine.

I can't believe it. My husband isn't going to save me. Jackson has let go of my hand.

He wants me to die.

My mother's warning rings in my ears as I start to fall.

A surge of adrenaline catapults up my chest. I don't want to die. I won't let this happen.

I reach my arms back up the cliff face one more time, my muscles screaming from holding the weight of my body and my hands slick against the broken railing, which is slipping out of my grasp. I scream, the sound primal and urgent as it leaves my lungs.

Jackson turns his eyes to me as I fight for my life, his gaze dreamy.

I can't keep the pain from my face as I struggle to pull my way to safety.

And then something seems to snap inside Jackson. He moves so quickly, like his body was a recording of himself, working at twice the speed that is normally possible. My husband reaches down, and his strong hands wrap around my body and pull at me, hand over fist, gripping at my shoulders, my hips, my legs, until all of me is safely on sturdier ground. Then Jackson picks me up in his arms and runs up the mountain, away from the broken railing and the steep drop-offs. He doesn't stop until we're on a large rock, almost the size of a car, planted firmly in the mountainside.

We're both breathing heavily, and it's several seconds before either one of us can say anything.

My entire body is shaking. I try to raise my hands to my face, but they're trembling so hard that I can't steady them. I eventually put them in my lap.

Finally, Jackson turns to me and says, pain forcing his voice an octave higher than usual. "Oh my God, Mary! You almost died!"

I don't wait to hear more.

I jump up and run down the mountain, and away from my husband.

But just as I'm clearing the distance between us, just as my feet bring me closer to safety, an arm whips out from somewhere, hidden in the shadows of the forest, and wraps around my neck. I'm pulled over and down towards the ground. My hiking boots dig into the trail's loose gravel and mud.

"I've got you," a voice says over my right ear.

My world crashes down around me.

18

I fight against the rough hand that's wrapped around my face. I can't scream, because the dirty palm of whoever has grabbed me is pressed too hard against my mouth. I move my arms from against my sides, where he's pinned them with his other arm, and realize as I'm trying to break away that my legs and feet are free.

It takes a split second to steady myself against my captor, who smells of damp and body odor. I can't see his face, but know that he must have a beard because his chin is so close to mine as he whispers again, "I've got you," that the short hairs scratch my cheek.

With all my strength I pound the heel of my hiking boot into his instep. He howls with pain and lets go of me as instinctively he reaches to grasp at his foot. I don't wait to look at him.

I run.

Too late, though, I realize that I've twisted around in my attempt to escape, and that I'm running back up the mountain, not down towards safety. Jackson is just in front of me, racing down the mountain himself. His skin is red from exertion and the humid air that's invaded the forest since we began our walk.

I have no idea what Jackson is thinking as his eyes meet mine. His face looks pinched and hollow, transformed from the vibrancy he had just a few minutes ago while we hiked up the hill together. While he urged me to take another step closer to the edge. And then his gaze moves past me.

To the man who tried to take me.

The expression 'between a rock and a hard place' has never been more real to me than it is right now. Between a killer and a kidnapper.

Something shatters inside me and reassembles into utter certainty.

There's no coming back from this. Not for me. Not for us.

Our marriage is over.

I just hope my life isn't over as well.

I'm frozen, unsure of where to turn. I watch my husband come towards me and the overwhelming emotion that floods my body is fear.

Fear of what he might do to me. Fear of what he wanted to happen up there, on that cliff side by the waterfall.

Fear, too, that the man behind me will hurt both Jackson and me.

I swing around, now determined to face this outside threat first, even if it means having to trust that Jackson won't try and hurt me as he closes in from behind.

I scan the ground and see a large branch that's fallen from one of the elm trees, thin enough that I can hold it in my hand, but thick enough that it could work as a weapon if I swung it hard.

"He's coming," I whisper to Jackson, who's close enough to hear me now.

My husband reaches out towards me, his hands pressed outward like he's approaching a startled horse, but I shift to the side. "Don't touch me," I hiss.

I don't have time to care about his reaction, and turn back towards the oncoming threat.

The man is coming around the bend in the trail. I hear his hurried footsteps crunching through the fallen leaves and scuffing themselves on the stones. Based on the cadence, he doesn't seem to be limping.

The pain I caused his foot must have only been temporary.

"Stay away from me," I call out. I hoist the branch onto my shoulder like a baseball bat, poised to swing out.

From the bushes at the corner of the path, the man emerges into full view. He does have a beard, and is wearing a khaki button-shirt, a wide-brimmed hat, and green trousers that seem almost old-fashioned in their cut and styling.

There's a gold star affixed to the left side pocket of his shirt.

"Mary," Jackson says under his breath. "What's going on? Why are you threatening a park ranger?"

"I'm sorry I scared you," the ranger says. His hands are raised in appeasement, just like Jackson's were a few moments ago. "I'm Park Ranger Mike Hampton. You seemed terribly distressed as you were coming down the trail. I was worried you might hurt yourself. The terrain can be pretty treacherous in parts on this route."

"I'm fine," I say. I take two steps back, the branch still poised on my shoulder.

"No, you're not," Jackson says to me, but also loud enough for the ranger to hear.

Jackson walks past me and over to the man. "She nearly fell off the trail up ahead. The railing had been tampered with, and when she leaned against it for me to take a picture, the railing gave way."

I don't add to Jackson's explanation that he was the one who encouraged me to lean against the railing, to stay on that crumbling piece of trail for longer than was safe, or that once I fell he stood by and considered letting me plummet to my death.

The ranger's face has a stoic calm to it, but his eyes narrow as Jackson speaks.

"We've had reports of problems throughout the forest," he tells us. "I don't know if you've seen the headlines in the paper––"

"We did," Jackson interjects, his eyes fixed on the ranger's face. "We're here on our honeymoon."

I flinch at the mention of why we came to the Poconos. We've only been at the cabin for two nights, but it feels like a lifetime ago.

I see the ranger notice, but he trains his gaze back on Jackson almost immediately.

Jackson continues. "And we picked up the local newspaper when we bought supplies. We didn't think it was anything too serious, though."

"You can't be too careful," the ranger responds.

Something passes between the two of them as the ranger's words hang in the air, and a hot fear burns in my chest that they are silently agreeing with each other that I'm crazy.

But then the ranger turns his attention back to me, and the intensity of his gaze feels like trust. "Can you show me where this happened?"

I nod, the adrenaline leaching out of my body. I drop the branch and start making my way, once again, up the hill.

I'm safe with the park ranger here, I try to console myself.

Jackson stays below as ranger Mike and I examine the place where the railing gave way. As I explain what happened, he nods reassuringly and listens with an intense focus.

He gingerly leans over the edge to examine where the posts of the railing came loose. After a few minutes, he gets up.

"This all seems very familiar," he says. "There are tool marks in the dirt and against the railing where someone's worked to loosen it from its footing. Like I've said, we've had other incidents this season, which have occurred in different areas each time. Whoever is doing this seems to be randomly choosing places."

Ranger Mike looks directly at me. "I'm sorry this happened to you."

His voice is deep, like you'd picture a stereotypical cowboy's voice to be, and it deepens as he apologizes to me. The sincerity in his words is a balm to my shaken body and mind.

"Can you come back to the cabin?" I blurt out. "I'd like to go over a few things with you, in more detail, if that's possible."

I try not to sound desperate.

The ranger gives me a considered stare, and then says, "Of course. I'll need some more information from you anyway, to write my report."

He pulls out a small notepad, I assume to write down our cabin's address in order to meet us there.

"I'll ride with you," I tell him. "It'll be easier to find the cabin that way, and we're just up the road."

I don't tell him that I'm afraid to be alone with my husband.

Not yet, at least.

19

"Tea? Coffee?" Jackson asks ranger Mike.

We're sitting around the table in our cabin. Jackson wasn't thrilled that I wanted to ride with the park ranger, but he didn't fight it. He's putting on a show of being the good host now that we're back, although he seems wary of the ranger. He kept glancing back at the two of us while he was in the kitchen searching out cups and spoons.

My husband sets a mug of coffee in front of me, and even though I thank him, I know I'm not going to drink any of it.

I didn't say anything about Jackson to Mike on our ride over to the cabin in his jeep. He asked me a few questions about our time in the cabin and how we decided to go on that particular hike, but otherwise we rode in silence. I could barely focus on what he was saying.

I needed time to figure out what I was going to do.

I wish I could call Dani. I need her reassurance that I'm not being paranoid. But the phone reception has been non-existent every time I've checked since we returned from our hike, and the gray clouds looming over the mountains mean that a storm is coming.

My ability to call my friend isn't going to get any better anytime in the near future.

Which leaves me with the park ranger as my only ally.

With a small notepad in hand, the ranger asks us to recount exactly what happened up on the mountain. "I'll need as many details as possible for my report," he says. "Nothing is too small or irrelevant."

It sounds like something directly out of a cop show, and part of me wonders how often park rangers end up needing to write up reports like this. Is this really what they're trained for?

"Did you hear that on a *Law & Order* episode?" Jackson asks.

I want to kick him under the table.

Looking at the ranger's expression, he wants to do more than that.

"Maybe I should talk to your wife alone," he says. "She was the victim, after all. You were just the bystander." Mike's emphasis on that last word brings a flush to Jackson's face. I wonder if the ranger has his own suspicions about what happened to me.

Jackson falls silent.

"I'll also need a photo of each of you for the report," the ranger tells us. "Why don't we do that first?" He gestures to the back wall of the kitchen, which is painted a plain white and clutter free. "Just stand over here. One at a time."

I don't look at Jackson to commiserate about whether or not this is strange. Instead, I go over and stand against the wall and stare straight ahead at the ranger. He pulls out his phone, takes something off his keychain, and types in a code to unlock the phone.

"What is that?" Jackson asks. He's still seated at the table, a steaming mug of coffee in front of him. "Why not store your fingerprint like everybody else?"

Mike raises his phone and snaps a picture of me.

"Should I turn to the side?" I ask.

"No," the ranger replies, completely serious. "It's not a mug shot."

I move away from the wall and, surprisingly, Jackson takes my place without a fight. Standing behind the ranger I watch as he raises his phone again to take Jackson's picture. I notice that he actually takes a series of shots, one strung after the other, and each flipping down into the bottom of his phone's screen like a compressed accordion.

All three of us then move back towards the table. "People don't realize how vulnerable they are, or how much privacy they give up just for the sake of convenience," Mike says as we settle back into our chairs. "It's standard for rangers to have a two-step authentication for our accounts. You'd be surprised how often government databases get corrupted by outside users."

"So you think someone's trying to break into your phone and read your messages?" Jackson sounds like a peevish teenager, trying to get a rise out of the ranger. I'm appalled at how petty he's being.

"Not exactly," the ranger says, and shifts in his chair slightly. He looks over at me, across the table. "Tell me what happened."

I swallow hard, trying to gather my thoughts.

"Start from the beginning," Mike prompts me. I start by telling him about the near-empty parking lot when we began our hike, our ascent to the lookout, Jackson's suggestion that I pose with the edge of the waterfall at my back, and how the railing gave way so suddenly. I decide to skip over the moments where Jackson froze, refusing to help me to safety.

I can cover that with the ranger later, after I leave with him.

Once I've finished recounting the entire incident, up until I ran down the mountain and into Mike, he studies his notes and flips back through his notepad a few pages.

While he's thinking, Jackson leans towards him. "What does

your badge say?" My husband squints, as though he can't read the embossing on the gold star.

The ranger doesn't look up. "It says *Park Ranger*."

"Isn't there a form we need to sign? Some sort of official paperwork you need to complete?"

"That's what we're doing." A note of tension edges into the ranger's voice.

I don't know what Jackson is getting at.

"Honey," I say, trying to keep things moving in the direction I need them to. "Can you go into the bedroom and get the newspaper we were reading? I want to show the ranger the article we mentioned."

Jackson ignores me. "Why does your shirt have a hole in the sleeve? Isn't that against uniform protocol?"

Admittedly, as I study Mike's uniform, it does look a little rough and ragged on the edges. But surely that can happen to park rangers? Their uniforms get worn out, just like any other piece of clothing.

"Our clothing budget keeps getting cut," the ranger says grimly.

"And why was my wife so frightened of you when she first saw you? She was scared to death, grabbing at branches to protect herself." Jackson stands up, his hands balled into fists against the wood grain of the table. "What did you do to my wife?"

Mike stands up, too.

I feel as though I'm surrounded by two gorillas, battling out their territory. A wave of disgust pushes me back from the table.

"Why was she running away from you? She looked scared to death when I found her," the ranger counters.

"Stop it," I say, firm and loud. "This is ridiculous."

"I'm sorry, Mary, it's just..." Jackson begins, but I cut him off.

"I want you to leave, right now." I can barely get the words out through my clenched teeth.

The two men look at each other, and I realize I need to be more specific.

"Jackson, just go," I say.

My husband looks wounded at my words, but silently gets up and walks back to the bedroom. I hear the door of the screened-in porch creak open and shut. A breath of relief leaves my lungs.

Ranger Mike and I settle back down at the table. I let out a deep sigh, and he offers me a conciliatory look.

"It's just not your day, is it?" he says, and despite myself and everything's that's happened today, the corners of my mouth turn up for a split second before the ache in my gut takes over again.

It certainly isn't.

He goes on. "So tell me more about before the hike. You thought your phone was tampered with? Did you see anyone around the cabin, or any other signs that someone was prowling outside?"

What did he just say about my phone?

My heart freezes. I try to not let it show, though, and instead shake my head in response to his question.

The ranger flips a few pages back in his notepad. "We've been tracking this particular individual across the Poconos," he tells me. "But he doesn't leave any physical evidence of who he might be. No fingerprints, no hairs or threads of fabric. No eyewitnesses. And all of his booby traps are rigged with materials that are either natural or found in any hardware store."

I swallow hard, but can't say anything just yet. My mind is whipping itself into a frenzy.

How do I get out of this situation? I ask myself.

"Lately, he's been escalating. We've suspected for a while that he might shift to choosing his victims beforehand."

I think of the shadowy figure I saw on the trail and try to calculate if there was time to pass around Jackson and me, move up the trail along another, steeper shortcut, and dislodge the railing before we arrived.

I just don't know.

But I've also made a decision.

"Just think if he used all that intelligence and effort for something other than harassing hikers?" I'm testing the waters with my comment, playing with fire.

Just like my mother is fond of saying, flattery will get you everything.

And sure enough, something I've said catches the ranger's attention. His shoulders shift back, and he sits up a bit straighter.

"Some people in the park service have even described him as a 'mastermind.'" He stares back at me, and the energy in his gaze makes me uncomfortable.

The air in the cabin shifts, like an electrical charge through a body of water.

A huge thunderclap echoes through the house, and I flinch involuntarily. I watch lightning flash across the sky through the window just above the ranger's right shoulder.

The hairs on the back of my neck stand up.

Because I recognize his expression, his body posture.

"He must be brilliant," I say, continuing to play along.

It's pride. That's what this man sitting across from me is feeling. *Pride about what he's done.*

I instantly regret sending Jackson away from us.

Or maybe I don't. I can't fathom how my life has taken me here, with a husband who wants to hurt me and a man who wants to hurt anyone.

"Do you have everything you need?" I ask, standing up under the pretense of clearing away the dishes. I want to get as far away from this imposter as I possibly can.

I don't dare glance over my shoulder as I put the dishes into the sink, but I hear the man's chair scrape back, and the sound of keys tinkling as he pulls them from his pocket.

"I believe so," he says. "But before I go. . ."

He drops his voice and takes two quick steps over towards me. I instinctively move back, and the look on the man's face collapses into one of regret.

I must look terrified.

"Before I go," he repeats, gently, cautiously, "are you sure you're safe here? If there's anything wrong—if you feel you're in danger—we can leave right now. You don't have to go through this alone."

A small part of me is tempted to run out the door with him, away from my fracturing marriage, but the much larger part knows that he's a fraud.

I never told him about my cell phone being misplaced this morning. In fact, I haven't told anyone about that.

The only person who would know is whoever moved my phone. Whoever's been hurting hikers out here in the honeymoon capital of the Northeast.

But just as I'm certain of what I need to do, something in the corner of my mind won't let go. I think about our car ride over here from the trail, how shaken I was by what had happened, and how distracted I'd been while he asked me questions.

What did I tell him? I can't remember what I said, not exactly.

This man, whoever he is, extends his hand towards me. "I can keep you safe," he says, his voice barely above a whisper.

There's a sound from the back of the cabin. The screen door shrieks, and Jackson's footsteps are audible as they approach from down the short hallway.

When he appears around the corner, a tornado of emotions swirls in my chest. Relief mixed with anger. Fear commingled with love.

"I think that's enough questions for my wife," Jackson says, and moves to the door. "She's had quite a shock, and I think it's time you left."

Our visitor's eyes lock on mine, a question passing between us, but in the split second I have to think I make my decision.

I look away.

He steps back, pulls a sheet of paper from his notepad and scribbles something down, and then walks to the door, past Jackson.

"I have both your phone numbers. I'll be in touch if I have any further questions, or any updates on the case. My number's there" —he turns and looks at me— "if you need anything."

And with a quick nod towards Jackson, he's gone.

As soon as I hear his jeep's tires driving away over the gravel lane, I run out the door of the cabin, past Jackson, and out to the shed.

The shotgun shells are in my pocket, where I pulled them from the kitchen cabinet when I was clearing away the dishes. I put them there, behind the knives, after Jackson had confessed to moving them and not remembering because of his sleep medication.

Just for safekeeping.

I run fast enough so that Jackson can't even call out to stop me, and sprint to the shed.

It's started to rain, and another angry thunderclap crashes above me.

The shotgun is right where we left it yesterday, and I snatch at it and whip open the barrel, just like I saw Jackson do when he handled it in front of me.

Jackson's coming up on me.

The rain is pelting down now, and the sky has turned an eerie green as the storm intensifies. A surge of wind whips around the shed so powerfully that both Jackson and I stagger.

I fumble with the shells in my pocket, and silently curse myself for not thinking ahead enough to pull them out as I made a run for the shed.

Finally, just as Jackson makes it to the shed, I manage to slide the shells into the barrel. They fit inside with a satisfying snap, and I hoist the gun to my shoulder, like I've seen people do in the movies.

My arms tremble as my breath catches at the back of my throat.

I point the barrel of the gun straight at Jackson's chest.

"Step back," I tell him.

Jackson holds his arms up and stops moving towards me.

"You can't get rid of me that easily," I yell above the rain smacking onto the shed's metal roof.

But the words don't have the effect I intended. A wave of déjà vu sends my mind spinning, and I stumble back a few steps.

"Don't do this," Jackson calls out to me, his voice pleading. He is drenched with the rain, his shirt stuck to his chest and his hair matted around his face. "I never meant this to happen."

I freeze.

But I keep the gun aimed at my husband, the feeling familiar and new all at the same time.

It's not the first time I've threatened someone I love.

On the day of her actual birthday, my mother said she didn't want to celebrate, and she'd spent most of the day in her room. At least that's where I found her when I came home from school, the door slightly ajar, the air pungent with the smell of unwashed clothing and unmoved limbs—and something else. Something chemical and harsh.

I wondered if my mother had been sick again. I'd read that antidepressants could make you nauseous, but I hadn't been able to find the pill bottle and determine which specific medication she was on, if any at all. I knew better than to try to talk to my mother about it.

Lately, she hadn't wanted to talk about much of anything.

I went into my mother's room after knocking quietly on the door.

She raised her head from her pillow, and the creases in her cheek made her face look like it had been fractured in a mirror. I asked her to come into the kitchen.

Without a word, my mother propped herself onto the edge of the bed with her hands, and then reached her arm out to me to steady herself as she stood up. She felt so light, like a bird with hollow bones.

The kitchen's lights were bright and gave my mother's skin a sallow color.

"I said I didn't want to celebrate."

Even though my mother whispered her words, her tone was vicious.

It wasn't the reaction I'd hoped for when she saw the cake with the lit candle, the prettily-wrapped box, and the card I'd propped against it.

I had a choice—I could keep trying, proceed as planned, or abort and let my mother slink back to her den of bad breath and misery. One look at my mother's sunken cheeks, one second of looking at her—really looking at her—was all it took.

"Sit down, Mom. You don't have to have any cake. Why don't you just read the card and open your present? I'll make you a cup of tea."

"But I told you, I didn't want anything." A softness had

invaded my mother's voice, and she sat down in the chair I offered.

I filled the kettle under the faucet and set it to boil on the stovetop. All my mother had been drinking for the last three weeks had been mint tea. She said it calmed her nerves.

I'd also read that mint can be a good antidote for nausea, and so I tried to bring a cup to her in the mornings and evenings. Most of the time she ignored what I brought, but sometimes she'd take a sip and chat with me about my day.

"It's not much," I reminded her. "But I hope you'll like it."

My mother ripped off the paper with her nails, which were bitten down to the quick and raw on the edges.

She stared at the picture on the box. I had no idea what she was thinking.

"The woman at the store said that they were the perfect addition to any elegant kitchen." I was embellishing, but it was close enough to the truth, I thought. "She said the right tools are essential, and that everyone is becoming their own personal chef." At least that part I got right.

My mother made some small sound of assent, and reached in to open the box. She pulled out the largest of the knives, the chef's knife, it said on the diagram on the outside, and held it in her hand.

"There's a card, too."

Setting the knife on the table, she unwrapped the envelope and took out the lined paper I'd used. I remember the paper made that delicious sound letters do when they slip against skin.

I watched as her eyes skimmed the lines I'd written, and I recited them to myself from memory.

Happy Birthday, Mom! You're a wonderful mother, and every day I try to be the kind of woman you are. You've made me who I am. Without you, I'd be nothing.

Love,

Mary

When my mother finished with the letter, she folded it up and slid it back into its envelope. Her shoulders were hunched over the table from reading, and when they started to shake, I put my hand out and pressed it over her right hand, which lay flat against the tabletop.

I thought she was crying.

Just then my mother leaned back, whipping her hand from mine and tipping her chin towards the ceiling. She let out a sound that was more awful than the protesters at my father's funeral shouting things about hell and death. It was more terrible than hearing the police say that my father had died in a car accident. And that he wasn't the only victim.

She laughed so hard and so loudly that hiccups erupted in her chest, and she couldn't catch her breath. I just stood there, feeling like someone had cut my stomach open from navel to collarbone.

"I've made you who you are, have I?" My mother flicked her fingers at the letter, like it was a piece of trash. "You expect me to be *happy* about that? You expect me to *want* you!"

I couldn't speak. My mother's voice echoed inside my head, like it was coming from far away. I started to gather up the cake and the letter. When I reached for the box of knives and the chef's blade on the table, my mother touched me.

But it wasn't a gentle touch. No. She reached her fingers around my wrist, and yanked me back down towards her so that our faces were just inches apart.

"My parents kicked me out when they found out I was pregnant. They didn't want anything to do with me, calling me a whore and a slut for slumming it with some college drop-out. The only reason your father and I got married was because I was pregnant with you," she said. "You were an accident—a mistake! And somehow, while my life was collapsing around me, I'd deluded myself that it was really a gift, getting pregnant. I'd seen women walking through the grocery store or sitting in the park admiring their delightful children. Congratulating themselves on being such wonderful mothers that they could give birth to perfect miniatures of themselves. But I never felt that way. I never had any reason to adore you. Because if there's one thing I'm certain of, it's that you are your father's daughter, *not mine*."

I could barely hear the next thing my mother said to me. The roaring in my ears was too loud.

But I did hear it, all the same.

"You're nothing like me. I tried so hard to raise you right, and yet you're still the same stupid, pathetic, grubby little girl you've always been."

A fleck of spit flew from my mother's mouth and landed on my cheek.

"I see the way people look at us, how they look at me when we're together. There's pity in their eyes, because even strangers can see how you suffocate me. How you force me to be someone I never wanted to be. I can't breathe when you're near me, and you are *always* near me. Always there, looking at me with your sad little eyes. You are a constant reminder of the worst decision I ever made. I wish I had died, and your father was stuck here with you."

I don't remember grabbing the knife.

I don't remember the feeling of its cool steel in my hand, or the electrical currents running through my brain that made me raise it and then strike out at the woman whose love I wanted more than anything else in the world.

What I do remember is the blood. So, so much blood, seeping down the smooth white of my mother's forearm.

And that strange alchemy of frustration and anger, and the total and complete wish that everything in my life was different, pumping through my body afterwards.

When my mother passed out, I had to rush to catch her from falling. After I called 911, I pressed a kitchen towel around my mother's arm to try and stop the bleeding. We'd lain there for what seemed like an eternity, my arms wrapped around her unconscious body, waiting for the screech of the sirens to grow louder and louder. Hoping they would replace the torrent inside my head.

20

"What are you doing?" Jackson cries.

A streak of lightning lands in the clearing behind the cabin. Despite the rain, the air feels like a thousand pinpricks on my skin.

One one-thousand. Two one-thousand.

The thunder cracks almost instantaneously, so loud that Jackson reaches up and covers his ears.

"It's dangerous out here," he yells to me above the clamor of the storm. "We need to get inside."

"Don't come any closer to me." The gun slips slightly and I steady it against my shoulder.

"What's going on?" Jackson looks frantic, but there's a steel edge to his voice. He takes a step closer. "Did that ranger do something to you? Did he hurt you?"

"Get back," I shout at him as he tries to move under the roof of the shed. Near enough to grab the gun from me, just like he yanked it from my reach when he'd banged down the front door last night.

Jackson's mouth shifts into a silent howl of fear and desperation and something else. It takes me a moment, between flashes of lightning and my pulse rocketing through my temple, to realize what it is.

Resignation.

Like he knew it would always come to this.

I fight the urge to vomit as my stomach roils, trying to process what my husband's face is telling me. Which is that he never expected us to live happily ever after. He never expected us to be happy. Period.

I want to shout *Why?* like an arrow pointed at the softest spot bellow his collarbone, but I swallow my words.

Jackson clenches his hands in the air before raking both of them over his face. "I don't understand. I'm scared. You almost died today on that stupid lookout because I wanted some goddamn picture, and that fucking ranger was staring at me like I'm some kind of murderer. And now you're pointing a gun at me! None of this makes any sense!"

I don't believe him.

"You wanted me to die." I somehow say this calmly, like I'm explaining arithmetic to a child.

A burst of wind whips itself through the shed, and for a second the rain blots out my vision as it slings across my face.

It's only for a second, but it's long enough.

Jackson lunges at me. Before I can tighten my grip or fight back, he's taken the shotgun from my hands. Standing in the rain, holding the loaded gun, my husband surveys me.

My skin tingles as his eyes travel over my body and I wait for that crooked smile to spread across his face. Because he's won.

He has the gun. He can do whatever he wants to me now.

I shrink back, certain for the second time today that I'm going to die.

But instead of aiming it at me, or commanding me to tie myself up, or turn around so he doesn't have to look into my eyes while he gets rid of me and collects my inheritance, Jackson collapses against the wall of the shed, the shotgun propped along his side like a discarded walking stick.

Now that he's shielded from the storm, and the beating drum of the blood in my body gradually slows from the riot it was a few seconds ago, he looks different. Like a filter's been lifted from in front of my eyes. And the sight of him sends a shiver through my body.

His skin is ashen, his lips trembling and almost blue from the chill of the rain. He looks older somehow, as if these last few hours have marked him permanently. Deep creases crest his forehead, and there's a slump to his shoulders that I've never seen before.

My impulse is to run away from all of this—this chaos surrounding us––but I stop myself. The gun is still nestled close to his body, only a few seconds of quick movements away from being pointed at me, and another hair's breadth from being fired.

I picture Jackson avoiding my pleading eyes as I reached out to him. As I felt my body losing its grip on solid ground, the sharp rocks waiting below.

I don't know what to say, but apparently Jackson does.

"I'm done," he murmurs, so softly that I find myself leaning towards him in order to hear above the whirling force of the storm coming down around us.

My phone is in my pocket, burning a hole. I know I could unlock it with my thumb, and I know the landscape of it probably well enough to navigate unseeingly to my recent calls, and click on Dani's name. But I don't dare take my eyes off my husband to see if there is any reception. With the storm, I'm certain any attempt to call someone for help would be useless. I'll need to wait until the storm clears.

He says it again. "I'm done."

My husband shakes his head, as though baffled by my silence. "I'm so sorry. I'm going to stop. I promise."

I shake my head, like I can knock the words he's just said out of my mind to keep them from sticking. "Your promises don't mean much."

I sound bitter, even to my own ears.

"Till death do us part," he recites, and looks up at me, his eyes sagging under the weight of some emotion I cannot read.

Bile rises in my throat. My vision blurs, and I force every fiber of my self-control to keep myself from crying. My husband doesn't deserve my tears.

"I couldn't live with myself if something happened to you. That's why I'm not going to take them anymore. I never would have started if I'd known they would put you in danger."

"What are you talking about?" But even as I say the words, I realize what he's saying.

The sleeping pills. The ones he started taking while he was in Australia.

The ones that clouded his memory. That made him do things sometimes that he didn't realize he was doing.

Oh. My. God.

He thinks he's found a way out. He wants to blame this on his pills.

Jackson leans up against the shed's metal siding, and I see his body shift as his shoulder blades bump against the metal grooves and he slumps down onto the floor. He brings his knees up to his chest and circles his arms around them like he's a little boy again.

He starts to rock himself, back and forth. That same violent wave rocks through my body, urging me to let my insides collapse on themselves and just give in to whatever he has planned for me, but I fight it back.

"I already told you—I couldn't sleep last night. After you fell asleep, I lay awake, thinking about you, and work, and just. . . just life. My mind was racing. I ended up taking more than I usually do, just to knock myself out and stop my thoughts from suffocating me."

My chest heaves, and I catch myself before asking him about the late-night messages. He doesn't know I watched him without his knowledge, pacing and reaching out to someone in the middle of the night.

A small voice whispers inside me that all this might be in my head. That maybe Jackson is telling the truth. But I push it down, far down, because there's nothing wrong with me. Except for my husband.

"Why didn't you wake me up? We could have talked about whatever was bothering you." I don't correct him, to say that he told me earlier today—when he accused me of hiding a fucking gun from him—that he only took one pill. I have to play along. My mind is working through the contingencies, trying to calculate how I can still get out of this alive.

The shotgun slips from Jackson's shoulder, its sleek body creeping down the wall of the shed just a fraction.

"I was embarrassed. I didn't want you to think there was something wrong with me."

He tries to give a short, dry laugh, but something catches in his throat and it turns into a cough.

"I did a great job, didn't I?" he finally manages to choke out.

I pause, my body looming over my husband's.

"That's what happened up there, on the lookout." It's a statement from me, not a question, because that's what he wants to hear. I picture my husband in the middle of the night, staring out the window in our living room with unseeing eyes.

Jackson nods his head. "It's a side effect of the medication sometimes. When I take too much, it doesn't just mess with my memory. It can leave my brain all warped and cloudy the next day. I'll just space out, and when I come to again I have no idea what happened."

He leans forward and reaches out for my hands. I let him.

"I should have told you. I should have never put you in danger like that."

My skin burns.

Thunder rolls outside as another streak of lightning scars the sky.

"So you weren't trying to kill me for my money?" The last word leaves a bitter taste in my mouth, and I cringe. I'm getting twitchy, and I remind myself that he still has the upper hand.

Jackson looks confused.

"Why would you think that? I'd never hurt you."

My husband's face twists into a grimace. "Your birthday isn't even until tomorrow. I wouldn't inherit anything anyway. Besides, I just spent the last nine months away from the person I love most in the world to make myself as financially independent as possible. So that I can *contribute* to our family."

I pause. Either Dani didn't tell him everything, or Jackson is pretending he doesn't know. My father was very specific in his will. He left it that if I died before I turned twenty-five, the money would be donated to a local women's shelter. If I was married, however, the money would go to my spouse. Not to my mother. It was just one more hurt that my mother would have had to endure.

I decide to crouch down beside Jackson. His hand reaches out for mine, his fingers icy against my own.

"It's not your fault," I say. I stare out into the yard outside the shed, willing myself to be strong.

My mind moves back to the ranger that was here, and his odd behavior. It's something I can use, I realize.

"You thought there was something suspicious about that park ranger?" I begin.

The storm outside seems to be moving away. The lightning and thunder have grown more distant, and the rain has shifted to just a gentle pelting on the roof of the shed. A few beams of light scatter over the forest.

"He's no park ranger," Jackson says. "I'm certain of it."

He leans back absentmindedly, and his shoulder jostles the shotgun. I reach out to steady it from falling over, and lie it on the packed dirt floor of the shed. Jackson doesn't react when I touch it.

I remind myself that the shells are still in the barrel, where I loaded them.

"Why do you think that?" I ask.

Jackson shakes his head, as if he's trying to get his thoughts straight. "There's just something about him. His uniform seemed generic. He didn't have any official forms. And he drove a jeep."

My husband turns to look at me. "I nearly lost it when you insisted on riding over with him. I don't think I took a breath until we were all back at the cabin and I saw you were safe and sound."

"He said something strange while he was here, interviewing me while you were in the back room." I don't need to add that Jackson's banishment was my doing. "That ranger––" I pause, leaning into this role I'm playing. "That *man* kept mentioning how brilliant the person is who's setting these traps for hikers. He seemed to be almost proud of the work this guy is doing."

Jackson makes an indiscernible noise.

"And that's not everything," I go on. In the back corner of my mind I've been weighing options, trying to determine which pieces of information will help me survive, and which will force Jackson's hand. I decide that what I'm about to say will probably help me more than it will put me in danger. Even if Jackson did it, he can play it off as another sign that we are being stalked by someone else. It's worth the risk.

"Today, before the hike, I found my phone in the car, even though I'm certain I left it in the kitchen here. I didn't mention anything to you, because I didn't think it was all that important." I start to speed up my words, but force myself to slow down. Liars tend to talk fast.

I correct myself. Bad liars talk fast.

Jackson always speaks with purpose, measuring his words out before letting them loose.

"When the ranger was interviewing me," I go on, "he asked if anything else had happened to make me think the person harassing the hikers might have selected us specifically. Anything else besides my phone being misplaced."

I wait expectantly. Jackson doesn't know that I may have mentioned something to the ranger while we were driving back to the cabin from the trail—the ranger had asked a lot of questions, and my mind is buzzing with everything it needs to do to help me survive. I can't remember exactly what we said in the car ride over.

But that doesn't matter, because I don't really believe that this ranger is a greater threat than the one sitting next to me. I just need my husband to believe that's what I think.

"He already knew my phone had been moved, but *I didn't tell him that*," I add.

Recognition lights up Jackson's face, but it's soon replaced with another emotion.

"You think he was lurking around here, trying to scare you? Scare us?" Jackson's voice trembles. He's made himself look furious. "Do you think he was the person you saw outside the other night, by the hot tub?"

"I don't know for certain," I backpedal, Jackson's intensity playing at my uncertainty. "I don't know what I saw that night." I shake my head.

Jackson's quiet for a moment, and then his grip tightens on my hand. "How would he have known where we were going?"

My mind and body are starting to weaken under the strain of these mental somersaults: pretending to be frightened and conjuring up a bogeyman to stave off the one I'm married to.

I force my mouth to move. "I tried to search up the trail on my phone. The connection was bad and I couldn't get to any information, but the trail name stayed in my browser. It was the last thing I did on my phone." I don't tell Jackson that my phone was locked, and that whoever messed with it wouldn't have been able to get in to see what I was searching for. "That's how he would have known where we were going, and been able to damage the railing in time for us to reach that spot on the trail."

I'm hoping I sound believable to Jackson. Because if it wasn't someone coming in from the outside, stalking us, the only other person who could have tried to get into my phone is my husband. I need him to believe that I think it was someone else.

"But you have a passcode on your phone," Jackson reminds me. "I don't even know it."

Sweat pricks the back of my neck.

And then another very real possibility occurs to me.

"Or maybe he didn't even need to see anything on my phone. Maybe he overheard us talking about it. Maybe he was outside, listening to us."

I watch the words register on my husband's face. A moment passes, and then Jackson scrambles up, yanking me up with him, and starts to run to the car.

"Jackson, wait," I call out. My hands reach for the shotgun, but my husband's grip is too firm.

I don't want to go anywhere with him, but he's already pulling me away from the shed.

"You almost died today, Mary. And then, afterwards, that sicko stayed around to watch. He drove you in his car and came back here and pretended to help us while you told him how terrified you were. He probably enjoyed every goddamn moment."

Jackson's words blend together. His bottom lip trembles as he pulls me to the cabin and inside the door.

"Grab your things. We're going." Jackson heads towards the bedroom, under the guise of grabbing our suitcases, and as soon as he disappears around the corner I lunge for the car keys he put on the kitchen table when we arrived home with the park ranger, and sprint out the door.

I climb into the driver seat of the car. My hands shake slightly as I try to put the key into the ignition, and I fumble with it for a few moments that stretch into an eternity. Jackson left the windows down, and the sounds of slamming cupboards and Jackson's voice calling out to me float over the rain-drenched air.

Finally, I slip the key in and turn.

There's a horrible grinding noise, followed by a loud clunk.

A fresh sheen of sweat breaks out across my forehead, despite the coolness brought in by the storm.

I turn it again. And another time.

Something is wrong. Very, very wrong.

Just as I'm realizing that I can't leave this nightmare, Jackson appears outside the car window.

"The car won't start," he says, his voice and face inscrutable to me.

"No," I tell him.

Together, miming what responsible, safe adults do, we pop the hood and I check the fluids and the battery.

"I don't know how to fix this," I tell my husband, and he doesn't seem at all surprised.

The day is waning away, the forest slowly turning pink, red, and orange as the sun sets.

As I stand outside the car, waiting for a sign of what the hell I'm supposed to do now, Jackson walks around the grounds, his phone in the air trying to get service. I don't really pay attention to what he's doing. I'm just trying to get the car started.

Yet another mistake I make. I should have watched his every move.

"I can't get anything," Jackson tells me. He leans over my shoulder, pressing his strong body into my side. Panic rips through me, but I manage to reach my arms up and wrap them around his shoulders, like he wants me to.

"We need to stay here for the night," he says. "It's getting dark. We can't just go roaming around in the wilderness, hoping to get a signal."

"You're right," I say. "We'll stay just for the night, and then we'll go first thing in the morning."

I start to unwrap my arms from him, hoping to break away towards the shed.

"I'll go get the shotgun," I tell him.

His eyes lock on mine.

"No, we'll go get it together," he replies.

We trudge to the shed, his hand coiled on my waist. The little light that is left casts a dim glow around the cabin, and Jackson turns on the flashlight on his phone to guide us.

When we get to the shed, he moves the light around the small space. He traces the shed again with the glow from his phone.

We fall down on our hands and knees, looking in the now darkened corners.

He must have done it when he was in the cabin, I think, slinking through the door of the screened-in porch. Or when he was roaming around, supposedly to get a cell phone signal as I tried to fix our mysteriously broken car.

Even though I already know what my husband's done, I continue our pantomime.

Time stretches as we search. The shed grows dark as the battery in Jackson's phone dies. After a few breaths together, in the small space of the shed, we silently turn, Jackson grabbing the axe resting on top of the stack of firewood, and race back to the cabin, throwing the lock behind us.

The shotgun is missing.

And we are alone.

Just my husband, and me.

21

Jackson has us huddle in the cabin, our two bodies intertwined in a knot of limbs and hot breath and my rapidly beating heart. I go with him around the cabin as he draws the shades on the windows, checks the locks on the doors, and then pushes pieces of furniture in front of the doors for good measure.

Sure enough, the door to the porch through our bedroom was unlocked when we checked.

"We're safe," Jackson keeps saying, over and over again, as if somehow he can make himself believe that this is what's happening between us.

I'm trying to pretend there is someone outside, trying to hurt us—the two of us together—because I know that's what my husband wants me to believe. I'm trying to pretend, all the while waiting, looking, counting, watching for the chance that I will make it out of here alive.

The night is close around us in the cabin, and the air inside stifling, even in the cooling temperatures of the evening. Sweat drips off both of us, and I take a chance and unwrap my arms from Jackson's and pull myself off the couch, my legs sticking to the leather of the cushions. I wince as I move so abruptly. The bruises from my fall earlier today are starting to show on my legs and arms, and my muscles are tender.

If Jackson noticed the ring of black and blue forming around my right arm where the ranger grabbed me, he doesn't say so.

For some inexplicable reason Jackson hasn't turned on any lights. Our car is still in the drive. The house is bolted shut. It's like Jackson is playing at being held captive, trying to act out some scene from a movie he's watched a long time ago, where he only remembers shades and edges of the plot.

I can't help thinking this is all a game to him. I figure he's decided to wait until my actual birthday—tomorrow—before he tries to hurt me again. I remember reading in a novel once, some whodunnit with a Scottish detective who wrote excellent poetry and cared too much, that the best lies are based in truths. You lie about what you ate for dinner and what you did and said the night your wife disappeared, but only so much as telling the detectives what happened the previous night. It's true, and not true at the same time. More believable, because you actually know it happened, and it helps trick your mind into leaving out the important details. Such as that you killed someone.

That's what it feels like Jackson is doing, with all his precautions and clammy palms and hand-wringing. He's playing at being scared of someone outside, because he wants the police to believe him when he has to explain what happened to me.

What's going to happen to me.

Sometime, in the night, I need to get away from him.

"But what are we going to do?" Jackson almost whimpers into the empty, still air.

A surge of anger floods my body, and I fight the urge to slap my husband. Part of me wants to goad him into just doing it already. My head is spinning, trying to think five steps ahead, and my body has turned cold and tense from the adrenaline that's now leaking out of me the longer he forces me to sit here and just wait.

"We need to contact someone," he says. "We need to figure out how to get a signal and get in touch with someone who can help us."

I tell him that's a good idea, and a seeming calmness settles into his shoulders for the first time since we came back inside after finding the shotgun missing.

Part of me wonders if it's here, inside the cabin. If that's what he's planning on doing.

He clears his throat. "What are you thinking?"

I tell him nothing. I'm thinking about nothing.

I already checked the back porch when we went around, pulling the shades down, but the reception I had when I was able to talk to Dani seems to have dissipated with the storm. There's no connection available within or around the cabin at all.

The scent of the flowers from my mother fills the room the longer we have the windows closed, and the fragrance starts to prick at my nostrils, sickly sweet and slightly rotting. I already thought about what she must have done to get them delivered and waiting for me, how she must have contacted the owners of the cabin and the florist, and coordinated everything to be in place when we arrived. She's already done her duty, I realized. Counting on her to reach out tomorrow, on my actual birthday, or to have another delivery stop by would be too much of a risk for me.

And too late, by my best guess. If I haven't made it out by daylight tomorrow, I might as well give up, because I'm already dead. Jackson won't have to wait much into the day to have a reasonable story to feed everyone about what happened.

I force my mind away from that inevitability, and instead think about my mother, thankful that Dani is there to help her if she needs it. A small part of me wonders if my mother's trying to get a hold of me, even now, and an even smaller portion of my mind wonders if she would believe me if I told her what was happening. If she'd actually get help.

I can't read her card on the flowers from where Jackson and I are huddled, but I can picture it in my mind. Would she send something like that without meaning it?

Was it a sign that she'd forgiven me? Or that she hadn't forgotten?

I shake my head, because it doesn't matter. If I don't figure a way out of this, none of it will matter, and my mother will just be another woman grieving the loss of her daughter. Just like the woman at my father's funeral.

I can still picture their signs, vivid in bright red lettering against the white background of the poster boards. *Justice for Abby*, they said. *Murderer. Drunk. Burn in Hell.*

The protesters were already there, shouting angry volleys at my mother and me when we arrived at the church.

My mother's face was stoic, her body numb. The shouts from the crowd seemed to absorb into her, and lie like dead weight on her shoulders. There must have been twenty of them, teenagers who were probably there for the rush of it, middle-aged PTA mothers all pious in twinset sweaters, and older, boozy cranks looking for some excuse to hate someone besides themselves. They were all of them scarlet-faced and loud, except for two: an older man and a woman, standing separately from each other, but in the same corner of the group, quietly watching as we filed inside.

Over the years the man's face has blurred into soft edges in my memory, but the woman's face is burnt into my mind like an overexposed photograph. Her straight white hair, hanging in limp strands around her face. Her clothes, saggy and worn-looking, but dark in color and nicer than what most of the protesters were wearing. She didn't hold a sign, she just watched us move into the church with eyes that sank into her face, as though they were tired of looking out. As if they'd seen enough. I wouldn't be certain of her name until I saw it online, tagged below a picture taken of the throng outside my father's funeral in a local news article. Becker. Her name was Cheryl Becker, and my father had killed her daughter.

When the service had ended, the shouting throng of people was still there, but the man and woman had left. As we made it through the crowd of people, I saw my mother glance at the spot where they'd stood, and something inside of her seemed to release as she walked by the hollow left by the two quiet observers.

"I think we're going to need to cover some distance—to hike out further and see if we can call someone. Maybe a higher elevation will help us connect to the network." Jackson's nervous babbling invades my thoughts.

He goes on as I silently listen. "I only brought the one flashlight, but I think there might be a few others under the kitchen sink." He turns towards me, and because we are now sitting next to each other on the small sofa, I can feel his breath on my cheek as he asks, "What do you think? Is it too dangerous to go out tonight?"

I shift back, and turn myself to face him. His mouth is set in a firm line, like an em-dash across the blank page of his face. Although his eyes aren't blank. Narrowed in the corners, they're encouraging me to do something.

I take a gamble that he's testing me, to see if I'm really going along with this charade.

"Going out in the dark would be too dangerous," I tell him. "We need to stay here for the night and go out as soon as it's light outside."

My husband doesn't say anything for a moment. His eyes are

stormy, and his mouth gutters like an extinguished candle. In the darkness, Jackson suddenly looks so young. The axe he brought in from the shed lies like a dead body on the floor beside the couch. When I'm not looking at Jackson, I'm looking at it.

A moment later he seems to decide something, and gets up so quickly from the couch that he almost knocks the heavy piece of furniture over. "I'll take first watch," he says.

I shake my head, because Jackson wanted me to believe earlier that his thinking is blurred by the medication he's on, but then stop myself. I begin to smile, only to shift and hold my mouth mid-rise in some hideous grimace, because I'm not sure what I should do. I'm running out of options playing the scared, clueless wife. "I'm not going to sleep, anyway. Let's stay up together."

We wordlessly move over to the fridge, neither of us hungry, even though we haven't eaten much of anything since breakfast. Anxious for a distraction from my waning acting skills, I start pulling food from the refrigerator and Jackson begins to heat a pan with some oil.

I find the bread and cheese we bought at the supply store and make up some cheese sandwiches, which Jackson grills on the pan until they are golden brown. I'm careful, and watch him as he cooks, under the pretense of being together for safety. The smell of the food forces a growl from my stomach, the physical systems of my body betraying me with their everyday needs.

We take our sandwiches into the living room and huddle together as we eat. I reach over and turn a light on, not wanting to sit in the dark any longer and thinking some small resistance might be helpful, to keep Jackson off my scent.

"What are you doing?" Jackson asks. I notice he takes one requisite bite of his sandwich, and then puts the remainder on his plate, untouched.

"They know that we're here. There's no point in making things scarier than they already are."

I take a small bite of my sandwich, and the salt and warmth of the food hits my tongue like a celebration. My mind is weary but my body is starving. The tension that I've been storing in my jaw for hours releases just the smallest bit.

"You should eat something." I point my chin towards Jackson's plate. "It'll help."

Jackson silently reaches out and takes another bite of sandwich, chewing it like it's ash in his mouth. He swallows and takes another bite.

"You know what this reminds me of," he says.

Something flutters up my throat and chokes me. "No. I don't."

Jackson looks across at me, eyes wide and unyielding for a moment.

"It reminds me of when I was a kid, and we would get shipped off to this run-down camp for three weeks in the summer. The cabins were just concrete slabs with beams and tarps thrown over the roofs, and the lake was full of leeches. Most of the other kids were there through some government program—such as Fresh Air, but with parole officers—and the equipment was all broken and rusted. At least two kids ended up at the hospital each year just from impaling their hand or their leg on a janky kayak or volleyball net."

I blink, because this is more than Jackson has ever told me about his childhood. I put down my sandwich.

Why is he telling me this?

"Every night I'd dread 'lights out' because it was the time that all the bigger kids—and these kids were the tough, nasty kinds of kids—would make our lives a living hell. They were really creative about it sometimes." He pauses, and reaches his hand out to wrap his arm around my shoulder and pull me in towards him. "And sometimes it was exactly like you'd expect."

I say what I think I should. But also, I'll admit, what I feel, in that one contained moment.

"I'm so sorry."

He shakes his head. "It was a long time ago. But some memories, you know, they stick with you. Just the feeling of them. And that's what this feels like. The anticipation can be the worst part."

I involuntarily turn to look at Jackson, expecting some sign that he's taunting me. I try to draw my mind to the hours ahead, waiting with him until he decides it's over. But instead there's an air of earnestness around him as he tips his chin down towards me and kisses my forehead gently.

We sit quietly for a while, and I find my mind constructing a picture of Jackson as a boy, crouched in the night against some unseen threat.

Just like we are now.

Something pulses at the back of my mind. I think about his Aunt Rachel, spilling her margarita all over me at his welcome-home party.

I decide to risk it. I don't have much else to lose, and it's still a long way until morning.

"We?" I ask.

"What?" Jackson moves away from me, shifting his shoulders back from the center of the couch, but keeping his arm on me. With his left hand, he takes a long drink of water.

"Earlier, you said 'we.' '*We* would get shipped off.'"

Jacksons rubs his hand along his jawline, leaving a string of crumbs from his sandwich over his cheeks and chin.

I hold my breath, hoping that I can tip him towards spilling something from his past, and force his attention away from me. A plan is starting to form in my mind.

"I had a sister," he begins.

I couldn't have anticipated this.

Had.

"What was her name?" I manage to choke out.

My husband bites his bottom lip and turns his gaze towards our curtained window. The corner of the kitchen. The now-empty plate in front of him. "Gail," he says, finally. "Her name was Gail."

His grip on my shoulder tightens, and I fight the urge to give a little yelp as the pressure on my body intensifies.

I don't know what he wants me to say, so I wait.

Jackson's breath comes long and shallow. He won't look at me, and for a moment I think I see the end flicker across his face.

I get ready to bolt. But just then a rustling outside breaks into the quiet air of our cabin.

Jackson turns towards the noise, which is coming from the larger window by the front door, and in a split second he's shifted back to being my protector, rather than my captor.

"It's okay," he tells me, and with his hand over mine he coaxes us towards the window like some amalgam of tragic heroes in a children's ghost story, clutching at each other as though that will somehow protect us from whatever is outside.

The scraping sounds continue, followed by a series of louder crashes, and an alarm goes off inside my head that maybe, just maybe, I've gotten this all terribly wrong.

Jackson grabs the axe in his right hand as we move towards the window.

The rustling turns to a harder noise, like a tapping hammer against the windowpane.

My stomach churns with hot acid and the sandwich sits in there like a solid weight. I don't know what's happening.

I want to scream. I want to be anywhere but here, decoding the clues for where to direct my fear and my cunning.

Jackson raises the axe, ready to swing out, and he gestures for me to move and unlock the front door.

I lock eyes on Jackson, who gives a small nod, a hint of determination in the set of his mouth, and whip the door open. The two of us burst out onto the front porch with a cacophony of noise, shouting expletives into the dark. Jackson holds the axe, poised above his head like a talisman, but doesn't swing down.

In the darkness, two eyes stare back at us, low to the ground and iridescent as the dim light from the cabin streams out onto the porch. The flowerpots near the front steps are turned over, their contents spilled out over the wooden boards. I move closer, just enough to see the rest of our visitor.

Jackson lowers the axe and lets out a sound from deep inside his chest that is part sigh and part howl. He leans against the frame of the door and lets his body trail down until he's sitting on the ground.

I watch as those two eyes, framed in the familiar black rings of a night bandit, rest on me before scurrying off into the darkness again, a ringed tail trailing behind it into the shadows.

"A fucking raccoon," Jackson says. "It was a fucking raccoon."

I let out a deep breath, not one of relief but one that is a sucker punch to my stomach. Because I have my answer.

Before we turn to go back inside, I look out into the black night wrapped around our cabin, like an ocean. The wind whispers softly in the tips of the trees, all its energy spent from the storm earlier.

I wonder if anyone can see me, looking out into the forest.

And as my husband urges me back into the cabin, I wonder if anyone is watching me walk back into his trap.

22

The incident with the raccoon seems to have loosened something in Jackson. Once we're back inside the cabin, he makes a beeline for the bedroom.

"We need wine," he says to me, and for the first time since the storm we are separated from each other.

I measure the distance to the front door. I get up, make my way over from the kitchen where Jackson left my side, but he returns too quickly, with a bottle of wine we'd set on the back porch for safekeeping when we first arrived. It's a screw-top, so Jackson doesn't need a corkscrew to open it.

The axe is propped up next to the front door, and I act as though I was moving to a different seat, choosing a chair by the fireplace, away from where my eye can keep drawing itself to the slick edge of the blade.

"I was saving this for your birthday," he says. "But I don't see any harm opening it early."

He glances at his watch. "Besides, technically, it *is* your birthday now, isn't it?"

I look down at my phone. It's 12.30am.

I can't drink the wine.

"Happy Birthday, Mary," Jackson intones, and passes over a large juice-glass of wine, which I set on the coffee table in front of me.

He takes a sip from his own glass, which is not nearly as full. He spots me eyeing it, and explains, "I figured one of us should stay as alert as possible. Since I've been having trouble sleeping anyway, I thought I'd be the designated. . ." He searches for a word, but doesn't find it. "I'd look out for you."

I don't move, and Jackson misinterprets my hesitance.

"Any effects of those stupid pills will have worn off by now," he assures me. "I won't blank out again."

I reach out and wrap my fingers around the glass obediently.

"Take a sip," Jackson directs me.

I lift the glass to my mouth, hoping to just mimic drinking it. As I go to set the glass down again, though, Jackson raises his arm and tips it back into my mouth, the wine splashing down onto my tongue. I involuntarily swallow some of it. It leaves a harsh taste in my mouth, strong and sour, as though the wine has already turned to vinegar.

"You need to get some sleep," he intones, as if this explains what he's just done. I suppress a shudder and work to keep my face neutral.

"You're right," I say.

I try to remember when dawn will come. The sun rises earlier now.

I do the math. Only four and a half hours left to go.

I need to fill this time. I need him to think that I'm on board.

"Are we going to be okay?" I ask my husband, because it's the best distraction I can think of.

Jackson doesn't respond right away. He takes a deep breath, and when he starts again it's as though he's continuing a different conversation.

"My sister was two years younger than me," he says, his voice soft yet firm. "She died when she was sixteen."

I'm still, knowing that I need to do something to respond. I wrap my arms around him, but he remains stiff against my embrace. Eventually, I let go.

A growing piece of my heart turns dark, as I realize that the only reason he's telling me about his life is because he thinks I'll never have the chance to betray his trust.

"I don't like to talk about her. Her death ripped me apart inside. We'd always relied on each other, for everything. After our parents died, it was just the two of us. Really, though, it was just the two of us well before that. I wouldn't have survived my childhood without my sister." Jackson pauses. "I wasn't always the best brother," he says. "I could always rely on Gail, but for a while there, she couldn't rely on me. I—I don't know. I needed space, I guess. I regret it so much, now that she's gone."

He gives me a look both empty and so full I can barely look at him.

"I couldn't tell you about her." He stops, shifts his shoulders. "That's not true. I *didn't want* to tell you about her, because I've spent my entire adult life trying to move forward."

I don't dare breath. I don't make a sound.

"My sister was murdered." His voice turns bitter, pinched on the word. "The man who killed her was never convicted. A technicality helped to ensure he was never even tried. And I've been living with this. . . this bitterness, ever since."

Jackson reaches out to take hold of my hand, his skin suddenly soft again and his body molding into mine. "I've worked so hard to put that rage away. I never wanted you to worry about it being a part of me. That's why I didn't want to tell you. I even asked Aunt Rachel to not hide it from you––she's too good a person to do that––but to keep it private for me until I felt ready to tell you." He dips his head, and his eyes stare out into the dusky corners of our cabin. "I'm sorry I didn't share that part of me with you. I didn't want you to see the side of me that's so broken."

"You're not broken," I tell him as gently as I possibly can, because I'm certain that's what he wants to hear.

I'm trying to focus, but my vision is getting fuzzy around the edges. I blink and push through the wave of fatigue that tries to suck me under.

What is wrong with me?

Even with Jackson pushing the wine on me, I barely take more than a few mouthfuls.

"Maybe I am," my husband says, and it's the last thing I hear before I fall into a dark and fitful sleep. I dream of wolves, and rivers.

And then I dream of nothing.

23

DAY 3

When I wake up, light streams through the closed curtains.

I'm lying on the couch in my clothes from yesterday, a blanket covering me.

For a few heartbeats I'm so disoriented that I swivel around, trying to get my bearings. I have a ferocious headache, and my mouth feels like it's full of a mixture of cotton and asbestos.

I hear the tinkling of water, the rush of the shower from the bathroom. The sound brings my thoughts back to my body. I desperately need a drink of water.

My mind screeches to a halt as I realize what's happened, sunlight warming my skin.

I've slept through dawn.

I stand up, and as I do so, my body bumps against the coffee table and my glass from last night tumbles over, spilling a few drops of wine across the pale wood. Just then the water from the bathroom turns off, and I hear Jackson's footsteps in the bedroom and then, a few seconds later, down the hallway.

I try to run out of the cabin, willing to trek across the miles of forest barefoot, but my legs wobble underneath me and I crumple to the floor when I try to take a step.

My husband appears, naked and dripping except for a towel wrapped around his waist.

His face crumples when he looks at me.

"Oh my god, Mary."

And that's when I do it.

I start sobbing. For the first time since all this terrifying awfulness started, I let the fear and the pain and the overwhelming sadness come out.

Because my husband is looking at me like he's seen a ghost.

"It's my fault," he says, rushing over to me and pawing at me with hands that I don't want on my skin. "I shouldn't have poured so much wine in your glass. Not with everything else going on. I just wanted you to be able to get some sleep. I only put half a pill in your wine."

I don't dare turn my head towards Jackson. He's testing me— baiting me to lash out at him for admitting to drugging me last night. I'm sure of it. And I don't want him to see my face as the truth registers with me.

He was going to do it last night. He just couldn't get enough wine in me, paired with what I'm sure was far more than half of one of his sleeping pills. And now I've missed my chance.

My brain feels cracked and murky after whatever Jackson gave me last night. My mind won't focus, but I have to get it to work somehow. I need to find a way out.

My sobs slow down and eventually stop. My head is pounding, and suddenly my balance gives way. The room spins as I slip out of Jackson's arms, still slick from the shower, and hoist myself up on the kitchen counter.

"Here, drink this." Jackson passes me a glass of water, which I gulp greedily. Like an idiot.

"Everything was quiet the rest of the night, so I thought I

could slip away and take a shower and then be ready when you woke up."

"Ready?" My mind swirls, and I'm desperately trying to grip onto something solid and sure. I run through everything I can remember, ending with Jackson's revelation about his sister. The memory shoots through me like a bolt of electricity.

Thoughts churn in my head like quicksand, turgid and warped. I need to say something, to keep him believing that I don't suspect him.

"Jackson, I'm sorry about last night." I say the words as though I'm learning to form them for the first time. "I'm glad you told me. You don't have to carry the burden of what happened to your sister on your own."

I think I may have crossed a line just now, because Jackson clenches his jaw, just briefly, at my words. But then he relaxes again. "You're right. I need to let go."

"That's not what I'm say––" I begin, but Jackson cuts me off.

"Are you still okay to try and hike to higher ground? The sun rose about twenty minutes ago. If you can't go, though, I can try and get a signal myself."

I shake my head. My vision warps for a second, but I ignore it.

"I'm fine. Just give me a minute."

I carefully make my way to the bathroom, brush my teeth, splash water on my face, chug down two Ibuprofen, and change my clothes as quickly as possible.

When I come out, Jackson is dressed and lacing up his shoes.

"I'm ready," I say, and for whatever reason, Jackson gestures for me to take the axe as we head out the door.

24

Outside the cabin feels surreal. It's promising to be a beautiful day, the sun rising over the small hills to the east of the cabin and covering the forest floor in a deep orange glow.

My phone is tucked inside the backpack I'm carrying.

The forest is coming alive with noise as birds wake up and call to each other. The harsh pitch of the chickadee breaks through the wall of sound, followed by the metallic caw of a crow. I look up and see a turkey vulture already circling overhead.

The woods seem empty, save for the birds above us and the scuttle of small creatures that disturb the leaves below us as we step.

I need to wait for the right moment. I stare at the horizon in front of us, trying to gauge how quickly I can run.

"Should we follow a trail?" I ask Jackson.

"I think we should head in the opposite direction of where we were yesterday. I couldn't get any reception up there, and I remember seeing signs to a lookout when we drove into the cabin the first day. It was just past the bridge over the waterway."

I nod, take a timid swig of water from the bottle I filled, and we start walking in the direction Jackson pointed out.

Just like our hike yesterday, our steps make a pulsing rhythm as we walk, and eventually the percussive beat of our feet joins together as we walk step in step.

I risk a look over at my husband—I'm being careful not to walk ahead of him, where I can't see what he's doing—and as I take in his intent focus, the flush in his cheeks and the steady tracking of his eyes over the area surrounding us, I realize something.

My husband is frightened. Truly frightened.

And for a moment, it makes me wonder if I have everything entirely twisted into something unrecognizable. If it's possible that I'm misreading the clues scattered around me.

It wouldn't be the first time, a caustic voice inside my head reminds me.

My mother waited a few days after her birthday, and our trip to the hospital where a very young and attentive doctor gave her fifty stitches in her arm, before she made it clear that I was not going to be forgiven.

I came home from the grocery store to find Dani's beat-up Chevy in our driveway, along with a car I didn't recognize. The front door was hanging open.

Dani, my mother, and an unfamiliar man sat in our living room with strained looks on their faces, several pamphlets spread over the glass coffee table.

"Mary?" The man said my name as though it were a question, and I instantly decided to dislike him. He wore baggy khakis and a button-down shirt in cornflower blue. He was slim, with a high and tight haircut and shiny brogue shoes. "I'm Ian."

I didn't see the clipboard he was holding until he moved up from his chair.

I remember my mother wouldn't meet my gaze. Dani caught

my eye for a second before looking away.

"Your mother and Dani are very worried about you," he said calmly. He still had that clipboard in his hand. "And I'm here to help them talk to you about their worries."

I felt nauseous. I'd been trying so hard to make my mother happy. To love her out of her grief. And to make up for what I'd done to her.

In the days since our trip to the hospital, I'd apologized and apologized to my mother. I'd made her favorite kind of cookies —oatmeal chocolate chip, which she hadn't eaten. I'd cleaned the house, and brought her cups of tea. In my hands were ingredients to make a special dinner for her tonight: pasta puttanesca. She'd ordered it at an Italian restaurant we'd gone to as a family one night, back when I was still in middle school. She'd talked about that meal for weeks afterwards.

Things were getting better. I was paying my penance. I just needed to do everything right. I was certain that if I kept trying she'd remember we were a family.

And that she loved me.

"I don't understand," I said, not to Ian, but to my mother and Dani. "What am I doing wrong?"

"Nothing," Dani started to say.

"Everything," my mother said at the same time.

"Let's start over," Ian cut in. He explained he was a social worker from The Meadows, the inpatient psychiatric clinic on the edge of town. "We have a lot of options available to help you. There's mobile therapy—that's where the therapist works with you in your own home. There's outpatient group work." He picked up a pamphlet from the coffee table. "And if that doesn't work, there's also inpatient treatment. But we reserve those for the most severe cases."

I felt like I couldn't move.

"Would you be open to seeking treatment?" Ian asked me.

When I tried to talk, my mouth wouldn't form the words. I looked at my mother, but she just stared back at me.

"I think inpatient is the only option." My mother's articulation was crisp.

Something clamped itself around my chest, and suddenly I couldn't breathe.

Dani and Ian both rushed to my side, but my mother stayed where she was.

"You see how she's struggling," she added. "She needs more than a one-hour counseling appointment every week."

"Mrs. Smith, you realize that inpatient treatment is reserved for the most severe cases. Your daughter isn't exhibiting violence, against herself or others. I don't see why inpatient would be necessary."

"Who said she hasn't been violent?" My mother sat down on the couch and began to sob.

In the end, though, there still wasn't enough to justify taking me against my will to the psychiatric clinic. Pennsylvania laws about involuntary commitment are very strict, Ian said. A single incident wasn't adequate. My mother needed to prove a history of violence, which she couldn't.

After he left, my mother, Dani, and I sat in a circle and stared at the glossy brochures left on the coffee table. I felt as though I had no skin.

Finally, my mother stood up. "I don't want to hurt you, but we can't go on like this. We need to figure something else out."

I raised my eyes, hoping to find some understanding—some forgiveness—in her face. But when I looked up, she wasn't looking at me. She was looking at Dani.

Two weeks later, I found out the solution to our problem.

I stood in the driveway, staring at the papers in my mother's hand that said I couldn't go near her. That I had to leave the only home I'd ever known.

25

The footing is difficult to navigate in places away from the trail, and I have to keep shifting my attention from the open expanse surrounding us to my feet in order to avoid tripping over rocks and roots hidden by the underbrush and leaf litter. I'm already unsteady on my feet, but I don't want Jackson to know that.

We continue on in silence. When Jackson reaches out to touch me I instinctively flinch.

"There's a stream up ahead," he says. "We'll have to cross it."

I know what he's referring to after spotting it on our initial drive to the cabin, and I was avoiding thinking about it until we were right up on it. What my husband called a stream is more like a small river. With the rain from last night, the water level is higher than normal and small rapids have formed in pockets where I'm certain slippery rocks are waiting underneath the surface.

Jackson steers us towards a fallen tree trunk that's leveled itself across the riverbanks, making a lopsided bridge from one side to the other. Debris from the storm is covering portions of the trunk, and it's hard to see whether the tree is solid, or if parts of it are rotted through. A number of smaller, but still sturdy limbs have fallen around the base of the trunk, making a nest of strange angles at the bottom of the rotting tree.

I glance up and down the riverway, but there's no other option visible. Just a long, wide stretch of rippling water.

Jackson starts to climb up on the trunk, but I call out to him to stop.

I have an idea.

"Wait, let's check to see if we have any signal," I say, trying to sound reasonable. I keep the axe in my hand, and my husband in front of me. I pull out my phone from my backpack and turn it on. We'd turned both our phones off when we left in order to save the batteries as much as possible.

I wave the phone around in the air, and Jackson does the same with his. There's nothing coming through. The top of my phone reads *out of service* in impassive lettering.

I shrug my phone back into my bag, careful to power it off again, and step up onto the trunk.

"What are you doing?" Jackson is right on me. "Let me go first, to see if it's safe."

"I'm smaller than you are," I argue. "It's safer for me to go over initially. I can spot the rotted-out places and let you know where to step."

I don't wait to hear what he has to say. I start clambering over the trunk, hands and feet in a bear crawl. The axe in my hand leaves me unsteady.

But before I can make it far, Jackson follows right behind me.

I feel his hands grasping at me, and I think that this is it. The water hurtles underneath me, flowing fast after the rain last night. I try to estimate if I could survive the rapids if Jackson pushed me in.

I struggle against his touch, but my hands slip and I have to focus on gripping onto the slick wood. The axe falls from my hands and teeters on a knot in the decaying trunk, just below my feet. Before I can manage to grab at it, Jackson reaches around me and catches the long wooden handle before it falls into the river below. In the clamor of the moment, I realize that his feet are still on the riverbank. He hasn't climbed onto the trunk.

I don't hesitate. I move ahead, climbing further out onto the trunk. It's easier now that my hands are free.

My foggy brain is too late to focus on what's just happened.

I glance over my shoulder, willing my body to keep moving forward.

Jackson raises the axe in the air, as if to show me that I have nowhere to go. His mouth is set grimly in a fierce line as he watches me.

He doesn't say a word.

The wood is soggy under the ribbed sole of my hiking boot. As I step, I feel it sink down in a way that makes my pulse amp up its steady beat. I look across and estimate that it'll take at least fifty steps before I'm across. My fingers grip into the bark of the fallen tree, which is covered with moss and slick from the rain. I can hardly keep my grasp as I pull myself to the next foothold.

I move quickly, not daring to look back over my shoulder. Fear pulses through my limbs, waiting for the crack of the blade hurled at me. Even with everything that's happened, until we started today's hike, I still didn't fully believe that Jackson wanted to hurt me. Not entirely. There was still a small portion of my heart that believed he really loved me. But now I know how wrong I was.

I'm certain, after watching my husband hoist the blade of the axe in the air, its metal tip glinting in the sunshine filtering through the trees, that he's capable of hurling a weapon at me, making it look like an accident. Or that he could claim that someone else stole the axe, only to terrorize us in our escape.

I take another step, and another. The trunk seems to be more solid as I get further away from the upturned roots at the riverbank, and I start to move faster.

I gulp down a surge of panic.

Keep moving, I tell myself. *Don't look back. Just keep moving.*

I'm about halfway across when it happens. I take a step into a spot covered by leaves and brush, and instantly know I've made a mistake.

I hear it before I feel it. The crackle of the tree's integrity falling away as the weight of my body pushes against it.

It sounds like a gunshot, the way the wood severs itself from being one piece into many separate shards. The trunk wobbles slightly, and then more profoundly. I hear Jackson call out my name, but I can't look back. I'm seconds from being plunged into the river, which rushes up at me like a frenzy of animals waiting to swallow me whole.

My hands are still balancing the weight of my body, and I sink them into the soft wood, piercing through the layers of moss and fungi that have sprung up on the decaying tree. There is another crack, but this one sounds from far away somehow. I take a chance and glance over my shoulder to see Jackson. He's not upright anymore. He's crouched near the ground, his legs tangled amidst the other smaller branches. As I watch he stumbles and tries to stand. His hands wave in the air, frenzied and disjointed, like he's not sure what his body is doing. A tree limb teeters on the edge of the riverbank by his feet. The axe is gone from his hands.

There's another, final snap that echoes over the sound of the water, and I feel the trunk of the tree rend itself in half. I just have time to see Jackson stumble over, his hands at first wrapped around his stomach and then roaming around on the ground below him as if looking for something, before I need to turn back and grip my fingers as hard as I can into the wood, Jackson's face burned like a negative into the film of my vision.

Pain. He was in pain.

My body is in motion, swinging down in a parabola from the middle of the makeshift bridge and falling into the water waiting below. The river is too deep from the rain, and where I am on the trunk will be submerged in icy rapids if I stay where I am.

I scramble up the trunk, my hands frantically grasping at anything hard on the surface that can brace the weight of my body. I'm above the water level, but the trunk is sinking further down from the edge of the river. If I want to make it up over the bank and to the other side, I need to move. Now.

Even as my mind registers this, I also desperately want to turn around so I can see Jackson.

The sounds I heard—were they really the rupturing of the tree bridge? Or were they something else? They sounded like gunshots, the hard snaps reverberating across the forest, so loud that they rounded towards me over the water's angry murmur.

I need to get to the other side.

Focus. You can do this.

I fix my fingers in the wood, putting as much strength as I can into my hands and forearms, and brace my feet as best I can on the knots that have grown into the tree over the last hundred years. I move up the trunk, until I'm moving inches, and then feet. The adrenaline that my body is pumping through me has kicked in, finally, and a new force field of strength wraps itself around my body, propelling me up.

Finally, after what feels like a day, but must have been only thirty, maybe forty, seconds, I feel my forearms sink into the soft, yet stable, mud-packed ground at the top of the river. I give one final push, a primal growl escaping my lungs, and hoist myself up and over.

I'm on the other side. A gasp escapes my mouth as I shoot up to see down towards the lower bank where I left Jackson.

Jackson, who I thought was trying to kill me.

My husband, who I've assumed for the last twenty-four hours has been playing a game of cat and mouse, wanting me to die to take my money. I've ignored his fears that someone else was out here, wanting to hurt us. The certainty that I felt only a few minutes ago has evaporated with the collapse of the tree, and the image of Jackson looking back at me from the other side of the riverbank, his face wracked with a fresh agony somewhere in his body.

Jackson was never trying to hurt me. The threat is coming from the outside.

Someone else is here, trying to terrorize us.

I stop myself, the correction ringing in my ears. Not trying.

They *are* terrorizing us.

The realization of my mistake threatens to overtake me, but I can't let it. I force down the shame and regret flooding my body, and focus on the other side of the water.

I'm prepared to see so many things—Jackson, bloody from a bullet wound, collapsed against a tree. Jackson, held at gunpoint by ranger Mike. Jackson, still standing but bleeding through his shirt from some unknown wound.

But what I see doesn't match any of those.

The riverbank is empty. Jackson is gone. Somebody has attacked Jackson, and now my husband is gone.

All that's left is a flat patch of leaves, and what looks like a dark pool of oil or thick, black mud, but which I know with a frigid shiver at the base of my skull is neither. Of course it's neither. Because it's blood. My husband's blood.

I force my mind to expand on the picture inside my head— Have I seen anyone else in my memory of those last few moments? Is someone rushing up to my husband out of my periphery? Was there a person waiting in the shadows for the right moment to ambush us? But the edges of my field of vision are blurry inside my head. All I can conjure in those seconds just before the tree came crashing down is Jackson's face, his mouth twisted in a fresh pain, but his eyes willing something else. Pleading. Telling me to go, just go. . .

"Jackson," I cry out, hysteria pulling at the edges of my voice. "Jackson!"

I pray that Jackson has gone in search of shelter somewhere, to hide from whoever is doing this to us. Because the alternative —that this person has him, and is hurting him—is too much to bear.

There's a sound of rustling from behind me, down the river-bank in the direction where the sound of what I thought were shots came from. It can't be Jackson—there was no other way to cross the river for miles, except for the path I took, which is now sunken into the whitewater.

I don't wait to find out what or who it is. My husband is somewhere, bleeding, and in need of help.

I need to get to the top of the lookout. I need to call the police.

My feet start to move before my mind can catch up, the frenzy of my desperation pushing my legs forward, despite the fatigue and dehydration from the night before, from the days preceding this one.

I keep running while I reach into my backpack and grab my phone, powering it on and cursing the little insignia that pops up, taunting me for several precious seconds as it promises my phone will come alive soon. When the home screen finally lights up, I instantly look to the top left corner.

No Service still, in those infuriatingly clear white letters.

I keep running, not daring to look back. Or around me.

Because, if I do, I might know I'm being chased.

26

I feel as though I've been running for hours up this mountain, over jagged rocks and fallen branches, although I know that it can't have been that long. The sun is still rising in the east over the mountainside.

I check my phone again—still no reception—and the clock reads 7.30am.

When I look up ahead, I see a path opening up on the right-hand bank of the hill. It must be the access point to the lookout.

I'm getting close.

I turn, and hurtle my body towards the clearing, but the bushes in front of me shake violently, and I hear the scratching of fingers against bark. Or claws against stone.

I freeze. I have no weapon, no protection. Under what I thought was Jackson's suspicious gaze, I didn't even grab a kitchen knife and tuck it away in my pack.

All I have are my hands, my phone, and a half-full orange Nalgene water bottle nestled in my backpack.

I scan the woods around me, looking for a potential weapon, and see a rock that could fit into the palm of my hand with a sharp edge on one side.

It'll have to do. I bend down quickly, grab it, and hoist it over my shoulder ready to strike out.

There's no point in hiding. Whoever is behind that bush has been tracking me. They shot my husband. Hiding won't do any good.

It's time to fight.

"Come out and face me, you fucking bastard," I yell, my bravado lost as my voice cracks on the hard syllables of *fuck*.

The bushes stop moving, and there's a pause like the eye of a tornado, all calm before hell breaks loose again.

I tense my grip, ready to let the stone swing in an arc where I'm estimating Mike's head will be when he steps out.

But it's not the fake ranger who appears. Or any human being, for that matter.

Out of the bushes steps a fox, all spindly legs and bushy tail, eyeing me with an intense curiosity that tells me she's used to hikers, and not amused by them.

Even in the state I'm in, a portion of my brain can't help but admire what a gorgeous creature she is. A beam of sunlight breaks through a covering of cloud and lights up her crimson fur like a holy flame. She blinks at me, squinting in the sunlight, yawns calmly, and takes a few steps towards me. I try to think back to the little I know about wild animals—whether or not I should make eye contact, whether she might feel cornered, and whether I should turn and run in the opposite direction.

Before I can decide, she reaches out with her narrow mouth like a blade, and, without thinking, I raise my hand, fingers curled in. She slinks back at first, and I instantly regret not having paid more attention when Dani would tell me about her hiking group meet-ups she'd rotate through when on her health kicks, and the wild animals they'd see on the trails.

The vixen sniffs cautiously, the wet of her nose touching my skin, and then, with a swish of her tail, she wanders off into the cover of the forest floor again without a look back at me.

I pause for a second, stunned at this close encounter with the wild.

And then I start to run.

It can't be far, I tell myself.

27

I'm right in my estimate. I reach the lookout via the path cut into the forest in just a few more minutes. When I get there, I don't even have to pull my phone out of my backpack to know that there's finally a signal. The buzzes and beeps of incoming voicemails and texts from the last several days vibrate through my spine.

The lookout is empty save for a green sedan, and any excitement I feel that I may have stumbled upon another hiker or someone else who can help seeps out of me when I see the state the car is in. It's clearly been parked in this spot for a while. Leaf debris litters the windshield and the roof of the car, and there are bird droppings peppered across the hood and side windows. I cautiously peer inside, thinking perhaps I might still find someone in there, taking a nap, and hoping under my breath that I don't recognize a checkered shirt, or a shiny badge.

But as I look inside, the car's seats are covered in a healthy dose of empty Trail Mix bags and discarded granola bar wrappers. There's nothing personal inside the car, though—no key chains or rearview mirror ornaments. Except for the food disarray, the rest of the car is immaculate, and something inside tells me this car is a rental. It's either a hiker who's traveled in and gone for a longer hike.

Or something else.

I don't have time to worry about it too much, though. After surveying the car and making sure I'm alone, I reach back and pull my phone out to see I have four voicemails, and seven new text messages.

I don't stop to read any of them. I click to the keyboard and dial 911.

The phone is silent for a few seconds, and then—my heart drops as I hear it—there's a busy signal. I cut the call and dial again.

Busy.

I can't believe it.

I click into my contacts, and dial Dani.

She picks up on the second ring.

"Mary?" Her voice sounds all wrong, like she's saying my name backwards.

"Dani, you need to call the police. Someone is here. Someone has hurt Jackson." Now that I finally have another human being on the line who can help, my lips can't keep up with the words as they spill out of me.

"I don't understand," Dani says, and her voice has its familiar cadence back again. "Slow down. Start from the beginning."

"I need you to call the police," I repeat.

"I will, I will. But they're going to need to know why, and where."

I hear something scraping in the background, and picture Dani at the store, pulling out a pen and pad of paper to scribble everything down.

"There was an incident, on our hike yesterday. Someone set a trap and I almost died."

"Oh my God," Dani interjects. "It's that person from the paper—the one attacking the hikers. Oh my God!"

The background noise hums in my ear, and a long whistle floats over the line. Dani's breathing picks up.

"I think so," I tell her. "We lost all our reception, and Jackson and I hiked up the mountain so that we could call somebody. But we got separated, and I think whoever is out there has him. And he's bleeding."

"I'm calling the police right now. It'll be okay. Do you want to stay on the line with me while I call? Do you want me to call you back?"

I tell her no. I can't risk wasting the precious battery in my phone.

I repeat the address for the cabin that I gave her when we last spoke, and she says it back to me.

She starts to say something else, but her voice is interrupted with a beeping.

An unknown number is calling me.

I ignore it.

"Help's on its way. I'm on my way," Dani says, and she sounds so calm and capable that a small hinge that's been coiled in my chest releases itself. I take a deep, deep breath.

We're coming, Jackson.

I hang up the phone.

The caller from earlier must have gone to voicemail, because my phone buzzes again with another message.

I start to move away from the lookout, ignoring the view of the valley stretching in front of me, but when I reach to put my phone in my backpack, I see the text messages that loaded into my phone once I had reception again. They're all from my bank —our bank, I should say.

It's the one Dani and I used for our small business loan, along with our money market account. I have the account set to give me alerts when there are changes to be made: deposits and withdrawals—I set it up a while ago, one slow day at the store when I was missing Jackson and needed something to do on my lunch break besides stare at my lack of messages on my phone.

I'm used to seeing the information coming through as Dani manages the balance with our daily receipts and expenses. But, even in my frenzied state of needing to get back to Jackson, one text stands out and I have to look at it again. I blink, and focus my eyes, thinking that I've misread a comma or a decimal.

No, I read it right the first time.

There was a withdrawal.

For $50,000. The majority of our savings for the business.

Why would Dani take out $50,000 from our bank account?

I start running again, down the mountain this time, but I don't put my phone away. There's a hum inside my head, and my gut is telling me that something isn't right.

I click to look at the details of the withdrawal. It was done electronically at 10.30am yesterday. A few hours before Jackson and I left for our hike, and just a little while after I spoke to Dani on the phone. My mind reels. Why wouldn't Dani tell me she was draining our account?

I check my footing, which is precarious at best, and click over to the voicemails waiting for me, thinking that maybe some explanation is sitting there. Two are unknowns. One is from Dani. And one is from our bank manager.

I notice there's nothing from my mother.

I click on Dani's first, listening only for a few seconds before I stop. In the message, she says she's just checking in. She asks if I'm okay, and whether everything is safe at the cabin. Asks if I'm still nervous about being all alone there with Jackson.

I listen to the bank manager's message next. Chip Duncan, who we've worked with since starting Kitchen Kabinet, has a nasal twitch to his voice only outmatched by his business acumen. He starts his message without any preamble, just launching into why he's calling.

"Mary, I just saw the withdrawal from your money market. I made sure your overdraft protections kicked in, but I have to advise that with such a large reduction in your assets here at PNC Bank that you're not likely to get your request for another loan approved. Things aren't looking good. Call me as soon as you get this."

Another loan? But we were still paying off the first. Why would Dani need more money, after the $50,000 she'd just taken out, draining our account?

Something smooth and razor-sharp crawls up my spine.

The call I overheard her take at the store that she'd brushed off as a telemarketer. The way she'd tensed at the number coming up, again and again. The way she always looked so perfect and put-together, with Prada handbags and Miu Miu mules. I think about my best friend's insistence at the store that we should sell more expensive products, increase the revenue for the business. Overextend our financial foundation because it would pay off tenfold in the end. And I'd agreed. I'd let her manage the money. While I'd worked with our customers and had taken care of the face of our business, Dani had been in the back, slowly bleeding our store dry. Hiding it from me.

And then other things occur to me.

Dani, the more avid hiker of the two of us, warning me about the dangerous person out prowling the Poconos trails. How she went behind my back and told Jackson about my inheritance, pretending the entire time that she was on my side. Even our most recent call, back at the cabin, takes on an entirely different meaning. When she told me not to tell Jackson everything, she wasn't talking about the guy I kissed at the club. She was talking about the money. She couldn't risk me telling Jackson the truth, and having him confess that he already knew. Because Dani had told him.

In the delirium of the last few days, everything suddenly makes sense.

Dani, my best friend since we were just kids, the person who saw me through my father's death, and my mother's abandonment, and my husband's trek across the world without me. She wants my money, and to get it she needs both my husband and me dead.

I let out a scream, fear and grief and rage all mingling into one fierce sound that echoes through the trees, but then silence it almost immediately. My brain is on fire, and a deep wound opens inside the back of my throat as I try to regulate my breathing, and not be annihilated by the betrayal of a woman I've loved like a sister since I was sixteen. A woman who I would have given my money to, if she'd only asked.

She must have planned it the entire time. Killing me on the trail—or killing one of us, at least. And then picking the other one off, afterwards. Blaming everything on the rogue sociopath attacking hikers in the woods. And then being free of me, and my cautious lifestyle and my scrutiny of her life. Dani would then be able to do whatever she wanted, live as recklessly as she cared to do so, with two million dollars.

And now she's coming to our secluded refuge in the woods. Because of me.

A bird sings out above me, bright and clear, and I look up to see a chickadee cracking a seed on the branch of the elm looming beside the lookout clearing. He sings again, the call like the taste of summer melon, and another notch in my mind that I didn't know was there catches and holds. The sound I heard behind Dani's voice, just now. That whistle. It matches exactly.

Because Dani's here, in the woods.

I need to get back. I need to save Jackson.

Before my best friend kills him. If she hasn't already.

28

My mind is working at lightning speed, trying to think ahead to the river and how I'm going to cross it. I start to run down the hill towards the water, adrenaline surging through my body, and then I stop and make a ten-point turn to the east, towards the road. It's going to take me longer to get to Jackson than if I crossed the river, but it's also the closest crossing left, and I don't want to waste precious time stumbling around, looking for logs and stones to get me across.

I also don't want to be tempted to swim across, and then end up sucked under.

I don't want to leave Jackson alone. I need to save him.

It's not lost on me what a difference time and a few text messages can make, and my cheeks burn from exertion, but also from shame at having thought my husband was capable of the terrible things I imagined.

I pump my arms against my sides, my breath straining at each inhale and exhale. My heart is going to burst out of my chest and my legs are on fire, but I keep going. The words that my gym teacher—*our* gym teacher, Dani's and mine—from high school used to say, as we'd limp along during the mile-long race at the end of each semester, cycle through my mind: *Pain is for the living.*

I keep moving. My head is a symphony of words and memories and fuzzy recollections: last night with Jackson and hearing for the first time about his sister; Dani and I going dancing; the man who cornered me in the alleyway, and the other man who came to help; kissing someone who wasn't my husband, and having Dani see this.

Falling from that cliffside; grasping out for dear life, the jagged rocks almost snapping at my heels below.

My mother and I, sitting across from each other in the lawyer's office, and hearing my father's will being read. The yelp of pain and surprise escaping my mother's mouth as she and I learned that my father had decided to betray her, not just by dying so stupidly on the road in a car accident, but also by stockpiling his money, hiding it from her in secret accounts, and then leaving every cent of the stockpile to me, with enough conditions and contingencies to let him exert control over both of us from beyond the grave.

The small crowd of onlookers who came to my father's funeral, not to mourn him but to attack him. The shouts and biting words making the air vibrate around us.

Dr. Bradbury, lean and masculine across from us at his gleaming desk. Explaining to me how he was going to save my mother.

The thought of my mother getting weaker and weaker with the chemotherapy brings a swift convulsion to my chest, like I've just been trampled on. I stumble over my feet, and trip face first into a hedge of green moss and wet leaves.

My mother! How could I have left her with Dani? How could I have been so stupid?

I spin around, my hands held out as if I were holding a weapon, although I don't have anything to protect myself with

except the forest's offerings. *Sticks and stones may break my bones.
. .*

The sick song trills in my head.

I debate going back to the lookout so I can call and warn my mother. *Why didn't I call her first? Why didn't I think, after I realized what Dani was doing, to use the reception and call my mother?*

A metallic taste vibrates in my mouth.

The pills. Those fucking pills Jackson gave me to help me sleep last night, mixed in with my wine. He gave them to me, even though he knew they would mess with my thinking.

Or because he knew, a small voice chimes in from somewhere inside of me, but I push it down. I need to focus on Dani. I can't keep chasing shadows and straw men when there are very real, very dangerous threats surrounding my husband and I.

I whip out my phone, but, as expected, there's no reception where I am. I stand, indecision gripping at me like a vise, until I finally force myself to move. There's no time to go back to the lookout.

I have to accept the fact that, if Dani is already here with Jackson, whatever she's done to my mother is already finished. Bile rises in my throat, and I have to reach out and grip at the trunk of a nearby tree, but it passes quickly and I start moving again.

Sounds from the forest flood my senses, and every rustle of the canopy of trees or the snap of a twig by some small creature sends a jolt up my spine. I scan my surroundings as I make my way over the ground, but I can't see anyone lurking nearby. What I can see is the road, off in the distance, which means that I'm now only a mile or so away from the cabin. I have to go onto the road in order to cross the river with the bridge that spans the water.

A flare bursts out from the blood pounding in my ears. I have to cross at the bridge, but I can't stay on the road. I know what I heard, and however certain I am that Dani has Jackson with her right now, there's also still the small possibility that she's still on her way from somewhere else in the forest, and driving down to the cabin.

I can't risk her seeing me.

I pick up my pace again and sprint to the road's edge where I crouch in the drainage ditch along the side. I hold my breath, willing my pulse to slow down so I can listen for the sound of a car in the distance.

Even after my breath calms down, I can't hear much over the roaring of the river below the bridge. It spans about fifty feet across, which means that I'll have to be exposed on the road for at least forty-five seconds as I run across it, before I can disappear in the undergrowth of the woods again.

I don't have time to be cautious.

I walk up onto the bridge, and not hearing any immediate sounds of traffic over the rush of the water, I tense the muscles in my legs and spring into action. My backpack pounds against my shoulders as I race across the bridge. My feet feel as though they're flying, and I pray under my breath over and over that I won't stumble. I won't trip.

That I'll just make it to the other side.

Time never moves as slowly as when you are trying to race against it.

The Ibuprofen I took this morning is wearing off, and the pain in my head comes back like a bolt of lightning, just as I cross the midpoint of the bridge. My field of vision goes blank, and I blink my eyes, remembering from some dark recess of my brain my mother once telling me about hysterical blindness. Where stress can make a person believe that they've lost their sight.

I will the medication Jackson gave me—I won't let the word *drugged* rush into my thoughts like it's begging to—to leave my body. I'm sweating so much from exertion and fear that it must be almost out of my system.

Stop fucking with my brain, I want to scream.

I blink again, and the colors and textures of the Poconos are back in front of me.

But so is the slithering black body of a town car, moving almost soundlessly down the road. I can't see inside the blacked-out windows.

I return to the crossing of the bridge and hurl myself to the edge. I'm only a few feet from the other side, and the safe recess of the embankment. My body collides with the ground and I start to roll down and over the edge, but something stops me.

My backpack's strap has caught on the smooth metal pole bracing the bridge.

The car is closing in. I can see it in the corner of my eye. I yank at my arm, which is caught in the loop of the strap, but my shoulder is kinked in such a way that I can't loosen it. I tug as hard as I can on the strap itself to try and slip the backpack from where it's holding firm, trying to pull it free and screaming inside my head at the sheer idiocy of it all.

It feels the same as it did when I was on the trunk across the river, waiting for it to collapse and feeling exposed to the primal violence that was surrounding us. That is circling closer and closer, suffocating Jackson and me. The car is just below the peak of the bridge, and I'll be in full view of the driver in just a few more seconds.

I give one more tug, my shoulder blade jabbing in a strange way against my ribs, and there's a satisfying rip that loosens the noose of my backpack and my body that had been holding me there. My arm comes free, and I roll off to the side. The main pocket of my backpack has also come loose, and it spills out its meager contents onto the side of the bridge, where they roll down into the ditch, trailing my body as I roll under for cover.

I've just hit the small pebbles and muddy bottom of the ditch when I hear the whoosh of the car go by. I glance up and see my backpack sagging like an empty skin against the railing, my water bottle wobbling along the side in the grassy verge beneath the concrete of the bridge. A few granola bars are spilled out below it. And sitting on the ground, next to me, is my phone.

Someone is calling me.

29

I snatch my phone, amazed at the call coming through, and see a few bars of reception have appeared out of the ether. I recognize the number as the same one that was on the two other voicemails earlier. The ones I didn't have time to listen to.

Because I was running to save my husband.

A million options swirl through my head of who it could be, and why they're calling. I swing my thumb over the bottom to answer the call, but it drops immediately. I click to dial back, ignoring the shards of pain shooting through my skull, but my screen sits immobile for a few seconds before the call times out. *I don't have time for this*, I think to myself, and start running again.

I'm almost there.

I see the chimney poking through the trees. I can get there quicker than that black beetle of a car, if that's where it's headed, because of the straight line I can cut through the forest instead of following the winding road.

I come up on another fallen tree whose trunk is splayed across the ground, creating a shelter of sorts. I brace myself against it and peer down into the valley. I now have a clear view of the cabin.

And what I see brings an avalanche down onto my chest.

Panic. Relief. Anger. Resignation.

Jackson is there, his face bloody and his clothes torn in places. His hands are behind his back, as if they're tied together.

And so is Dani, buzzing around him like a cloud of flies.

A scream claws at my throat, but I force myself to shove it down.

I scan the area around the cabin, trying to put together a plan. There's no other car but ours parked in the drive. Which means that the black car wasn't Dani's, but just some random driver's.

My mind flashes to the car parked at the lookout: the one that seemed to have been parked there for a while. *How long has Dani been here, watching us?*

I don't see the axe Jackson had, or any other weapons lying around. I think about the back door to the cabin, and wonder if I can somehow pry it open and sneak into the kitchen where the knives are.

As I'm weighing my options of attack, Dani leans down so her face is next to Jackson's. She shoves her hand deep into the pocket of her fashionably high-waisted jeans.

I suck in a breath, picturing my best friend about to pull out a gun or a blade—something to end my husband's life or taunt me into coming out of my cover.

I start to stand up, ready to rush down the hill and tackle her body to the ground.

But that's not what happens. Instead, Dani pulls out a wad of white bandages, and starts dabbing at Jackson's face. Even from this distance, I can see Jackson's body relax. He leans towards Dani.

And then, my breath held like I'm waiting to watch the world burn, he puts his forehead against hers, and they stay together like that for one second, two seconds.

For an eternity.

He pulls his hand from around his back, not tied up at all, and puts it on Dani's shoulder.

Dani jerks back, suddenly moving over to our car, and pulls out her phone, calling something over her shoulder to Jackson. She's waving her phone in the air, staring up at the screen.

I glance up at the sky, assuming the signal won't go through, but the clouds and turbulence of last night's storm seem to have finally cleared, and a pale blue sky peeks through the tops of the trees. The air is still, without even a hint of a breeze.

My phone is still in my hand, on silent, and it vibrates as I watch my best friend trying to call someone. I don't even look at the screen as I swipe to the right, expecting to hear emptiness as the call drops, or for my best friend's voice to stab the air as the call connects.

"Mary Smith? Hello? Is this Mary Smith?"

But the voice I hear isn't my best friend's. It's a man's voice, one I don't recognize.

Until I do.

"This is Ranger Mike Hampton. I've been trying to reach you. Hello?"

I still don't say anything, but he must hear my breathing across the line.

"It's about your husband," he says. "It's about your husband and his sister."

30

"What are you talking about?" I whisper into the phone. I'm still watching Dani, who is pacing back and forth on the gravel drive. Jackson moves to sit up, catching Dani's attention, and she swings her long, lean body back over to the porch, where she says something to Jackson that makes him sit still.

"After we met, I called up one of my friends in the sheriff's department. You were acting so frightened, and you seemed almost scared of your husband." Mike pauses. "I didn't want to leave you alone with him, but I couldn't force myself to stay or force you to come with me."

I instinctively cringe as he says the word, 'force.' Twice.

"I don't understand. What does any of this have to do with my husband?"

"Seven years ago your father died in a car accident?" He says it like a question, and I find myself nodding in response, watching Dani move closer to Jackson on the porch steps, before remembering to murmur a "yes" into the phone.

"And I also discovered that Jackson's younger sister was killed seven years ago."

"Yes, he told me. She was murdered," I tell him, a flare of irritation setting my voice on fire. "What is your point? I don't have much time."

I could tell him that I'm watching my husband and best friend circle each other at the cabin. That I need help, and that he needs to call the police.

But I don't trust him. I don't know what he's playing at.

"That's just it. She was living with a foster family at the time she died. Your husband had already turned eighteen and was living on his own. The family's name was Becker. Does that sound familiar?"

A dark coil starts to unwind inside the base of my throat.

I turn my face to the ground, trying to steady my breathing and silence the pounding in my ears.

I do know that name. Mrs. Becker's grief-stricken form, drawn and hollow, materializes as a ghost from another life. I see her standing like a wraith outside my father's funeral, the throng of angry mouths shouting around her. I didn't know her name—my mother had refused to talk about the girl who died when my father crashed his car, or her family—but I saw a picture in the paper the day after we buried my father.

Cheryl Becker. She was listed as Cheryl Becker. She was protesting the death of her daughter, Abby, and the lack of charges against the perpetrator on account of his own death.

Nothing had been mentioned about Abby being in care. Or about her having a different last name.

Jackson's words float to the surface. *He was never convicted. He got off on a technicality.*

"Mary? Mary, are you there?"

"The girl who died in the crash with my father. She was Jackson's sister?"

That coil of black filth starts to wrap tight again around my neck. I can't breathe.

"Yes, she was."

There's a pause on the line. I turn my gaze back to the cabin, but the gravel lot and the porch are now empty. In the few moments I looked away, both Dani and Jackson have disappeared.

"Call the police," I whisper into the phone to the ranger. "I'm at the cabin. I need help. Call the police."

I hear him start to ask me something, a question in his voice, but I don't wait to hear it. I end the call, and huddle down behind the rotting trunk of the tree. A green beetle, iridescent in the sunshine, scuttles across the fleshy bark next to my nose.

The urgency and purpose I'd felt as I raced against time to save my husband drains out of me like a bloodletting. There's no hope for Jackson and me. Because there never was a Jackson and me.

It was all a set-up, but not for the reason I originally thought.

It was revenge, not money. Or, I correct myself—thinking of Dani—it was both.

Maybe Jackson proposed the idea to Dani, one night over drinks at one of her favorite dive bars. Sidling up to her stool, ordering her a drink, and then taking her home. The thought of the two of them together makes my stomach lurch, waves of pain and betrayal wracking my body. I wonder how he would have proposed the idea to her—maybe he did it while they were drunk, because he knew he could back out of it if she didn't respond the way he was hoping.

Except she did. Except Dani agreed that I deserved to die. And that they deserved what was left.

Jackson coming into our shop, out of all the places to buy a wedding gift. Asking for my number, falling in love so suddenly, insisting that we get married and then running away across the world.

He hadn't suggested it until he knew my mother was ill. Had

he planned to pretend to love me for those nine months, and then get rid of me unceremoniously on our supposed anniversary?

Or maybe he'd planned to go all along, and would have invented some other excuse for me not to be able to go. Maybe Dani couldn't stand seeing him pretend to love me for nine long months, while she waited for my birthday to roll around.

I think about Jackson's distance from me while he was away, his unresponsiveness to my attempts to stay close and connected, despite being across the world from each other. He wasn't overworked. He wasn't dazed from his sleep medication. He was just a bad husband. A cheater and a liar.

And a would-be murderer.

My head pulses with the headache from this morning, partnered with the adrenaline still surging through my bloodstream from one too many revelations about the house of cards that is my life.

The trail. The wine.

Is that why Dani was here, now, and she and Jackson seemed to be arguing? He couldn't manage to do it right—to kill me and make it look like an accident—so Dani is here to finish the job?

There's still no activity outside the cabin, but a light shines from inside the front window, despite the brightness of the day.

I need to move, I tell myself. *I can't stay here.*

I think of the shotgun, gone missing last night, and of Jackson wandering around when the car wouldn't start, trying to get a signal. Out of my sight for long enough to hide a weapon somewhere in the woods, or somewhere inside the cabin.

I have to assume that they are armed.

My mind clicks like a record player at the end of a groove. I can't think straight.

I force my legs to stand up, the muscles now aching from my sprint across the woods and stiffening slightly while I crouched in the dirt and leaves to avoid being seen by my philandering husband and my best friend. One thing I'm certain of is that I need to get closer. I need proof of what they've been doing, so that when the police arrive they can't spin this into a story that lands on me being paranoid and delusional.

That restraining order on my record will nip at my heels for the rest of my life.

Sorrow threatens to overwhelm me.

I dial my mother, holding the phone to my ear as I start to make my way toward the cabin, silently willing the net of cell service to extend long enough for her to pick up. Just pick up.

My legs seem steadier the longer I am standing, and I begin to creep down the hill, wincing at every rustle of leaf and snap of a twig that follows me down the deep cover of the forest. I'm not worried about the car I saw on the road anymore, now that I've seen Dani and Jackson together.

Now that I finally understand what's happening.

The phone to my ear keeps ringing. And ringing. Until I hear my mother's recorded voice requesting me to leave a message after the tone.

Not beep. "Tone," she says in her voicemail greeting.

I don't leave a message. Instead, I tell myself that she's fine. That Dani wouldn't hurt her. But I don't believe it for a second, because, up until an hour ago, I would have sworn that Dani would never do anything to hurt me either.

At least not yet, I add, trying to calm the terror clutching at my heart. *She wouldn't hurt her yet. Not until I'm already out of the way.*

I know the words are empty. That, just as I feared when I was considering running back to the lookout, Dani might have already taken advantage of my absence and lashed out at my mother.

In my mind, I see Jackson resting his forehead against Dani's.

I should have gone back, and called my mother when I had the chance to warn her, instead of pushing on to rescue my husband from his fucking mistress. I shouldn't have put my husband—my vile, cheating, fraud of a husband—before my mother's safety.

I try to estimate how long it will take for the police to arrive. On our drive down to the cabin, I can't recall passing any police cars, let alone police departments or deputy stations. It was just miles of winding country roads.

It could be a long time before help arrives, which means I'll have to stay quiet, but I also have to try and get the evidence I need to prove that I'm not making all this up.

I'm thinking clearly enough to know that everything Mike has said to me on the phone could be seen as just coincidence. There's no crime in anything Dani or Jackson have done that can be confirmed with evidence. Using money from the business to pay off debts; marrying someone without telling them about a past connection. And the accident on the cliffside has the perfect cover of being just another incident attached to the stalker in the woods harassing hikers.

Even being drugged with an overdose of sleeping pills can be explained away by Jackson. He can tell the police about how agitated I was, pulling a gun on him, and how I took the pills to help me sleep through the night. That he didn't know I would take so many.

Part of me wonders if Jackson ever really had a sleep problem. If the pills were just there as a back-up for me.

As I think it, I know it's true. The memory issues he pretended to have; the freezing up on the trail as I lost my grip. It was all just an act.

But even with all this certainty I have now, I can't stop picturing the bloody wounds I saw on Jackson as I crossed the river. I'm scrambling over the damp earth down the hill and towards the cabin, and also scrambling in my own head, trying to make sense of all this. Dani was tending to them, so they can't be fake. What about those?

Clearly, part of me still doesn't want to believe this is happening.

I push away the doubt, though, because I can't let it linger and distract me. I've already come close to losing myself one too many times in the last seventy-two hours, in the last nine months, in the last seven years. I need to focus, because I don't want to lose anything else.

I'm approaching the cabin, clawing at the ground in a crouching position, and coming up below the window in the kitchen.

It's open—something Jackson or Dani must have done. Snippets of their conversation float over the air, which is quickly rising with the heat of the day.

I pull out my phone and hit *record* on the voice memo app, and hold it up just below the opening.

"We need to go," Jackson says, frantically.

There's the scraping of furniture. And then a soft whoosh.

"Not with you barely able to stand up," Dani replies, and the sound of her voice hits me like an arrow to my chest. I taste candy apple SweeTARTS, and our first cigarettes, and the thousands of mornings I've woken up sure that there was at least one person in my life who loved me unconditionally.

"What about Mary? Where is she?" My husband's voice is vague as it works its way through the window. He sounds worried, but whether it's about me or the fact that he doesn't know where I am is unclear. Maybe it's both, I let myself think for a brief second.

And then Dani speaks again, and my blood turns to steel inside my veins.

"Shut up," she snaps. "Just be quiet. I need to think."

A whimper floats down from the cabin.

"You said you gave her sleeping pills last night?"

I push my hand further up the side of the cabin, it's shaking as I hold my phone closer to record what they're saying. This confession is what I need.

I hold my breath. I think I hear a car in the distance, but no sirens. Maybe the police are coming in quietly, because they know they'll need the element of surprise.

"Yes, but I don't understand––"

Dani cuts Jackson off.

"Good, that's good." Footsteps start to move across the boards of the cabin.

Come on, I think. *Come on.*

"And you said you lost her when you were hiking out to the lookout, to call for help?"

"Yes. She should be back by now, though. We need to go find her." There's a pleading in Jackson's voice that's unfamiliar.

I hear someone—I'm assuming Dani—walk over to the front door and peer out.

There's the crunch of gravel under tires, and I dare to turn silently, the phone still poised in my hand, and look at the cavalry that's arrived.

It's the black car I saw on the road. It's so shiny that the reflections of the trees overhead almost make it look like it's been camouflaged. The car comes to a halt in front of the cabin, next to our car.

The blacked-out windows reveal nothing, but I'm certain that whoever is inside has not come here to rescue me.

"They're here," Dani says.

"Who? What are you talking about?" Jackson's voice sounds weaker.

I didn't consider that I'd be totally exposed with my position under the window. As I look around the yard of the cabin, hoping to find a place to hide my presence, I know it's already too late. I keep the voice recording going on my phone, but tuck it away into the pocket of my jeans.

The car door opens, and a sleek black shoe hits the white stones, grinding them into the dirt. It takes me a moment to recognize the man that steps out of the car. He's out of place away from his office, but still pristine and polished like a sports car. Like the car he's just driven here, today.

It's Dr. Bradbury, my mother's oncologist.

And then the passenger side door opens, and out slips my mother.

She looks full of life.

She looks like she did seven years ago.

She looks like a stranger.

My mind riots with memories, swirling around in my head like a whirligig.

I remember stepping into my mother's home, under the pretense of checking on her after her first chemotherapy appointment, and finding the air in the front hall thick with the smell of vomit, although I couldn't see her anywhere. I checked through the house from room to room, calling out to my mother, and finding her collapsed, clammy and pale, on the bathroom floor. At first, she lay there as though she was unconscious, but when I put my hand on her face she startled reflexively, and sat up abruptly.

"What happened?" she'd asked, and the coarseness of her voice rattled something deep inside of me. Even after my father's death, my mother refused to show weakness. Seeing her so frail was a shock, I think, to both our systems.

I explained to her that I had to let myself into the house, and that I'd found her on the bathroom floor.

"I don't understand," she'd said. "I wasn't feeling well. I thought I might be sick."

She shook her head.

"I don't remember anything after that."

I paused for a second, thinking through what I was about to do, and then I leaned over and wrapped my arms around my mother.

She was so thin, her shoulder blades like a bird's wings against my embrace. I held my breath, holding my mother. Waiting to see what she'd do.

And then I felt her body relax into mine, almost the way Jackson and I would lean into each other, but different too. My mother let her shoulders drop, and her arms encircled my back and gripped with surprising strength despite her small size.

"I'm so glad you're here, with me," she'd whispered in my ear.

Now, as I crouch outside my honeymoon cabin trying to gather evidence that my husband and best friend want me dead, my mother says almost the exact same words to me again.

"I'm so glad you're here," she tells me.

I know, just from seeing the cruel look on her face, that she means it this time.

31

"Get up," my mother tells me.

White sunbursts cloud my vision, and I can't seem to blink them away. I stay where I am, until my mother walks over to me, teetering on bright pink stilettos, and grips me by the arm. Her fingers wrap hard around my skin. She pulls me to my feet, her strength surprising me.

I turn to look at her, my eyes finally clearing, and take in her solid frame, her firm shoulders, her clear and rosy skin. My mother catches me staring, and a flash of bright steel glistens behind her eyes.

She hauls me to the front porch. Dani and Jackson are still inside, and the good doctor is holding something that looks like a radio up to his ear. I'm still stunned, my mind churning like hot acid.

"We can't go in there," I try to say, but my lips catch on themselves, and I stumble over the words. I say it again, pulling back from my mother's grasp, but it doesn't matter. My mother isn't listening to me.

"They're about twenty minutes away," Dr. Bradbury calls out to my mother. I realize he must be listening to a police scanner.

"What do you want to do?" His voice is a crisp linen shirt. He smooths a wrinkle in his light wool pants and glances down at his nails.

"We'll go inside," my mother tells him. "Come on," she says to me.

I gather all my strength, plant my feet on the ground, and lean my weight away from the steps to the cabin. I'm not willing to accept what I'm seeing in front of me. "We need to leave. Now. They're inside. They tried to kill me. We can't wait for the police. We need to go."

I don't know what to do with Dr. Bradbury, so I ignore him.

Instead, I reach out and put my hand over hers, not to pry her fingers off me, but to hold onto her like I used to when I was a little girl. My hand and hers, one protecting the other.

My mother stands perfectly still as my fingers press into her skin.

"Mother, please. Listen to me."

There's a dark flick to her jaw, and a vein tenses in her creamy-smooth temple.

"Oh, I forgot, sweetheart."

Her mouth is a bruise of deep red lipstick. She lets go of my arm, reaches into her purse, and pulls out something hard and sharp.

It's a knife. *The* knife. The one I bought her all those years ago for her birthday. The one that, when she opened it, opened up a different future for both of us.

"Happy Birthday," she says, eyes like two gleaming diamonds in the sunlight.

32

I obediently listen to my mother when she tells me to open the door and step inside the cabin. As we enter, I spot Dani in the corner, holding something to Jackson's side, and as she looks up a small yelp escapes her throat.

The cabin is crowded with the four of us. Dr. Bradbury has opted to remain outside.

The air hangs around us with the heat of the day, close and tepid, despite the open window.

Jackson looks pale and feverish. Dark circles have risen underneath his eyes. His T-shirt is soaked in blood. It's clear that, from the distance I was at earlier, I couldn't see how badly he'd been wounded.

His eyes meet mine, but he doesn't seem to recognize me. They shift from me, to my mother, to the fireplace and other corners of the room. He's murmuring something, quietly, but I can't hear what he's saying.

I don't have to look at my mother's face. I can feel disgust radiating through her body. Through her breath.

"What. The. Hell. Happened." My mother isn't asking a

question. She's making a demand. And she's looking at Dani as she does it.

The burden of reality that I've tried to deflect from the moment my mother stepped out of the car and into this nightmare slams down on my shoulders and threatens to knock me over.

I have had everything so terribly, terribly wrong.

My mother, knife still held close to my waist, gives Dani a look of laser intensity.

Dani's hands flutter on the side of her hips, then she wrings her fingers like a toddler who's been caught out of bed after lights out.

"I found him like this," she says.

She won't look at me. My best friend hasn't looked at me since I came into the cabin.

"I'm not asking about him." My mother jabs the knife into my side as she gestures with it. Icy pinpricks slide through my veins as the edge of the blade touches my skin where my shirt has ridden up.

"I want to know why I had to come here in the first place."

Dani's mouth opens and closes, no words escaping her lips, and I feel that disgust settling back on my mother's shoulders.

"We don't have time for this," my mother adds, annoyed, like she's at the quick checkout line and someone's bought more than the designated eight items. Like what's happening right now in this cabin is some everyday irritation. Something to check off her to-do list.

The tears well in my eyes before I can stop them, and I force every fiber of my body to keep them where they are.

Jackson looks up at me, and his eyes fix on mine for a moment, no longer clouded by pain but intensely clear. He moves his eyes to the fireplace, behind me, and then back to mine.

A moment later he's lost again, his head drooped into his chest. The blotch of blood on his shirt is growing. The bright arms of the stain are reaching up towards the collar of his shirt. He's losing so much blood.

"None of this was supposed to happen," Dani says. When I look at her there's no emotion in her face, just calculation.

"Why are they both still here? It was supposed to be a fool-proof plan," my mother hisses at Dani's display of weakness.

"Somehow lover boy was able to save her from that cliff face, even though you assured me he'd be too out of it with those sleeping pills he'd been taking to be able to react quickly in a crisis."

"That's what James told me, assuming you read the label on the bottle right when you found them in the cabin. He said Jackson's prescription was the highest dosage already," my mother counters. My mind whirs. James? James Bradbury? Dr. Bradbury?

Dani stands up a bit straighter. She's challenging my mother.

I eye Jackson, who's started to murmur again. Beads of sweat have begun to pool on his forehead. While my mother and best friend bicker about whose fault it is that Jackson and I are both still alive, I try to estimate how many steps it would be for me to get to Jackson.

I blink, pushing a cauldron of grief back down into my gut, and force myself to guess how many steps it would take to get to the fireplace.

I think about Jackson, wandering around in the dark, just after I'd pointed a gun at him and he'd talked me down and held me close to him. About my falling asleep that night, and Jackson assuring me that we'd be safe.

I don't dare to look at the fireplace again, because I can't be certain that someone else didn't take the shotgun after the storm, when we went back to the shed. I can't be certain that

Jackson isn't in some fever dream, and that I'm just grasping for messages in his delirium.

Jackson whimpers. The bloom of red in his shirt is turning darker where the wound must be, in his left side. The clot of blood looks almost purple. My husband's face is so white that I can see the veins underneath his skin.

"Well, he was wrong." Dani spits the words back at my mother. "Because even the dose I put in their wine wasn't enough either. And that was on top of what Jackson put in there last night to calm her down!"

Dani had been in our cabin. She'd tampered with our wine. My mind races over the last three days. I think of the red and black checkered shirt, and the shadow of a figure I saw by the hot tub our first night. I think of finding my phone in the car, the screen locked down as if someone had tried to break into it. Had Dani been here watching us the entire time?

"What did I get wrong?" Dr. Bradbury has silently slunk into the cabin, and his expensive-smelling cologne invades the air.

"Did you check his phone? Has he contacted anyone? Does anyone know we're here already?" My mother's voice remains cool, but I can almost feel her fear pulling at the edges.

Dani shakes her head. "He just had a string of messages he managed to send a few nights ago. The number was international. Something about an account he set up for a client. That was it."

A current ricochets through my skull. I picture Jackson, bent over his phone in the middle of the night on the cabin's porch. How I'd thought he was in love with someone else. How that image of him kept repeating through my mind in the days that followed, convincing me that he was my enemy.

"What about hers?" My mother tightens her grip on me, and I hear her breath, hot and rioting outside my ear.

"Why are you doing this?" I ask my mother. Part of me is still clinging to the delusion that this is all a mistake. Some kind of joke gone terribly wrong.

"As though you don't already know," my mother tells me. "As though you don't know what you put me through." I wish I could see her face, but I can't. Not with the way she's holding me. I can only watch Dani, who looks back at my mother and me with a cautious intensity.

And Jackson, bleeding out and growing paler by the second.

"I don't understand," I whimper. "None of this makes sense."

"Did you like your birthday card? And the flowers?" I feel my mother's head turn slightly, and assume she's surveying the bouquet on the hall table. Our bodies are so close to each other. Closer than we've ever been before, it feels like. But fury and disgust vibrate through my mother's shoulders, and through her hands as she grips me, the knife still slung into the dip of my waist.

"Did it remind you of your gift to me, the year your father died? Right before you slashed my wrist open?"

I wince at her words.

"You'd follow me around like a little shadow, even before your father's accident. As though you wanted to make sure I didn't forget that this life, with you, was my own doing. That I could have had a life that meant something—I could have been someone worthwhile. Glamorous, adored, rich. But instead, I chose you. I chose to keep you, and marry your father, and to be your mother.

"It was just supposed to be a bit of fun," she goes on. "Your father was handsome, and he could be charming when he wanted to be. But after I found out I was pregnant, everything changed. I don't think he ever forgave me for that. For forcing him to be a husband and a father. But, you see, I had nowhere else to go. My parents didn't want me. I was homeless. I needed him.

"I know there are women who love being mothers. Who raise children that are gorgeous, and talented, and so very special. Watching children like that grow up has its own reward, its own elite status, I think. It gives you a satisfaction like nothing else can. But that wasn't what happened to me. Instead, we had you."

The words spill out of her, and I don't know if it's better or worse that I can't look at my mother while she explains to me how I failed her.

"I chose wrong. And then, just when I finally decided to take back control and change my life, just when I thought everything was finally going to be different and better all at once, your father had to go and leave all his money to you. Even after he died, he found a way to keep me in my place. Shackled to you."

"We need to check her phone," Dani reminds my mother.

I try to fight the protest rising in my throat, but I can't stop it.

"We were a family. We cared about each other. Dad loved me, but he loved you, too."

"That's where you're wrong," my mother cuts in.

She loosens one of her hands on me. "Where is it, Mary? Who did you call?"

And that's when I do it, as my mother loosens her grip to search my pockets for my phone. I break loose of my mother's grip, take three steps to the fireplace, reach inside, and pull out the shotgun from the ledge of the flue inside the cavity of the opening.

It takes another second to level it against my shoulder, barrels cocked back with my thumb, but not much longer than that. At this point in my honeymoon, I've had some practice with pointing a loaded shotgun at the people I love.

33

"Drop it," I tell my mother. "Put it down, now!"

My mother cocks her head to the side. She gives me a curious look.

"What do you think you're doing?" she asks me.

I move to the corner of the cabin, keeping my back to the wall. In my head, I try to guess at the time that's passed. Whether the police will be streaming into the driveway soon, or if they are still making their way down the meandering road through the forest.

"I didn't sign up for this, Vivian. She needs me." This from Dr. Bradbury.

My mind catches on that word––*She*. I keep my aim steady and cast my eyes over the awful scene in front of me, but Dr. Bradbury doesn't look at my mother or Dani. Or me. I don't know who he's talking about.

And then, Dr. Bradbury is through the door before I can do anything about it. All of us hear the purr of the engine on the town car, and then the squealing crunch of the tires as he backs out of the driveway, and away from us three women and one bleeding man.

Away from this insanity.

My mother looks shaken for a moment, but recovers quickly. She still has the knife in her hand.

"I'm not bluffing. Put it down."

My mother gives me another unfathomable look, shrugs her shoulders, and drops the knife with a clatter onto the kitchen table. The four of us are positioned like the points on a diamond; my mother and I diagonal from each other, with the front door between us, Jackson slumped into the cushions of the sofa, and Dani hovering at the tip, her body as far away from my mother as possible.

"So what are you going to do now?" My mother sits down at the table without a second thought about the gun I have pointed at her. My hands tremble on the trigger and surreptitiously I try to shift my finger away from the loop of metal. She's assuming that I was lying a moment ago, and in all honesty, I can't say that I wasn't.

After months and months of watching my mother diminish from her treatments, I'm overwhelmed by the healthy aura surrounding her. Even with a man dying beside her—her son-in-law—and her daughter pointing a gun in her face, she looks beautiful. Vivacious.

Something about all of this has made my mother come alive.

"You were never sick, were you?" My voice is shrill, defeated.

My mother shakes her head slowly.

"No, I wasn't. That was something James helped me come up with. We thought you'd get suspicious, what with me arriving back into your life so close to you coming into your inheritance. And then, when you had an accident suddenly after inheriting all that money—Dani and I were going to do the same thing we did to your father—no one would suspect your brave mother, battling cancer. You'd be just another cliché—another kid who grows up and buries their childhood pain in pills and bottles.

Dani would vouch for your history of drug and alcohol abuse, and how it worsened after my diagnosis. But before we could do anything, Jackson was there, sweeping you off your feet, only to leave you alone again. What better way to distract you than to care for your sick mother, who was having such a sudden and difficult reaction to the treatment?"

I think of all the time spent with her over the last nine months. The conversations over tea, the blankets I've brought for her, the chemotherapy appointments where I sat beside her and read her favorite pieces from *The New Yorker* or Dostoyevsky. All the stories of dark Russian realism, where women were always dying.

A metal vise twists in my stomach. The pounding in my ears swells, but I force myself to steady my arms as blood surges through my body.

My mother watches me. Dani watches my mother.

"Saline. That's what Dr. Bradbury used. Saline solution. Instead of chemotherapy. And he also gave me some anti-nausea medicine that, apparently taken in certain dosages, can make you appear as though you have the flu."

The butt of the gun slips against my shoulder, where sweat is slicking my skin. I pull the gun back up.

"How long have you been planning this? An entire year?"

Dani laughs. A grotesque chortle bubbles up out of her throat.

"A year? Are you fucking kidding me?"

"Shut up, Danielle," My mother's voice is ice.

"No, I won't. She should know." Dani turns to me. "We've planned this together since your father died. *Before* your father died, if you count drugging him and basically strapping your father into the driver's seat in order to get his insurance money in the first place. I got the drugs from the hospital—that was another reason I started volunteering there, back when I was still trying to compete with you for the good-girl trophy. Your mother slipped them into his coffee. We didn't know your father had changed the will. That he'd left all of his money to you."

I shift my eyes between my mother and Dani. My mother's look could turn anyone to stone.

But it only seems to make Dani want to talk more.

"So when the will was read, and we found out that we'd have to wait until you were twenty-five to get any of it, well, we tried other options. We had to be creative, because of some of the stipulations your father put in his will. Any sort of physical harm to you would nullify it. But if you were incapacitated mentally, well, then legal authority would revert back to your mother."

A spark catches flame inside my head. I can't think straight, because all my thoughts are burning.

"The psychiatric clinic? The restraining order? That was all a way to get your hands on my inheritance?"

Dani purses her lips. "Not the restraining order."

"I told you to stop talking," my mother roars.

Dani gives my mother an appraising look.

"Vivian, we need to go." Dani takes a step towards my mother. "We can't stay here."

My mother turns her head towards Dani. Her fingertips are just a hair's breadth away from the hilt of the knife, splayed out on the table as though she's examining her nails. But there's something else there, between the two of them as I watch my mother and best friend decide how I'm going to die. A hesitation in my mother's mouth. A thoughtfulness.

I'm not convinced my mother is set on seeing all of this through.

"I love you." I look directly at my mother as I say it. Then I turn my head, the shotgun still pointed at my mother, and say the same thing to Dani. "I love you, both. I don't care about what you've done. I'll share the money with you. I always planned to, anyway. I still love you."

The worst part of what I've just said is that it's true. All of it.

My mother's nails are a gorgeous shade of red, each like a drop of blood as they tap on the pale wood of the table. Each tap bringing them closer to the shiny blade of the knife.

Dani looks like she might be sick.

"And I know Dad loved you," I tell my mother. "He didn't love me more than you. He loved us both, just in different ways."

A small laugh, mean and hard, escapes from my mother's mouth. "You know none of this was really about your father, don't you? I mean, thank you for saying that." She shrugs her shoulders, playing at nonchalance, but it doesn't hide the tension rising up in the veins of her neck. "But this was always about you and me. I couldn't be the person I needed to be with *you* as my daughter."

She purses her lips, and I notice the sheen of sweat breaking out on her face. I watch my mother's eyes as they move across the room, taking in my husband's ragged and bleeding form, and then coming back to me, my arms taut and flexed from adrenaline as I work to steady the barrel of the gun against my shoulder.

"You're different now, though, aren't you? You're more like me than I realized." She gives me a considered look. "We could almost be sisters."

Jackson murmurs again, his voice lost in the soft movement of his lips, which are as pale as his skin now.

Something needs to happen. I need to get Jackson out of here.

My mother casts a sideways glance at Dani, and then moves her gaze back to me so that I see the exact moment she makes her decision. She pushes the knife across the table, towards me.

"We can still be a team, Mary. You and me. We *are* a team. We can have everything we ever wanted."

I can't strip my eyes from my mother. Something rustles in Dani's corner.

The air is suddenly ten degrees cooler in the cabin.

My mother flicks her eyes towards Dani. "She doesn't understand us. She's not part of our family. I see that now."

The top of my lip is damp and I reflexively lick the salt away. My sweat tastes acrid and sweet, and I think again of Jackson's sleeping pills—the ones he slipped to me so that I would be able to sleep and the ones Dani tried to use to poison us—working their way through my bloodstream.

"We should be together," my mother continues. "We should enjoy what your father left for us, *together*."

As my mother finishes her last word, Jackson breaks from his delirium and shouts my name. His voice moves through my body like an earthquake, and my grip on the gun loosens with the pressure of hearing my husband dying.

The inside of the cabin is thick with the vibrations of our four bodies, our breath shaking the air like a spider's tap at a web string. So dense that I can feel what Dani does before she even begins to move, as though her thoughts are shifting the density of the atmosphere around us.

She leaps from her corner, grasping the barrel of the gun in her left hand as she shoves my mother from the chair with her right. She lands with her stomach flat on the table, the knife buried beneath her torso.

I rush forward to grab the shotgun back, but Dani is too quick for me. She's already rolled from the table, the knife slim and shimmering in her hand, the gun swung into the crease of her hip, and I watch as she shoves the blade into my mother's stomach.

My mother makes a sound with her mouth that is more

animal than human. A sound I match with my own, our two voices intertwined stronger than they ever were in life. And then her head slumps forward, the fight gone from her body.

"Move," Dani shouts at me, the gun now poised at her shoulder. "Get onto the porch." She gestures with the gun, and I flow past the bodies of my husband and my mother, unable to get a bearing on whether they're still breathing as I move outside.

The sun dazzles my eyes for a moment after the dark of the cabin. In the distance, Dani and I both can hear the sirens through the trees. Getting closer with each second that passes.

My heart lurches.

"Run," Dani shouts, jabbing the barrel of the gun into the soft small of my back.

I tense my legs, and sprint into the forest, my best friend keeping pace behind me.

I run towards the river.

34

I'm no tracker, but I can see the drops and smears of blood where Jackson managed to bring himself back to the cabin after I was able to cross the river.

By the time Dani and I reach the edge of the riverbed, we're both panting. The trunk is still in the water, its rotting body further covered by the white water.

As I turn, putting my back to the river, Dani levels the gun at me. "It wasn't supposed to end like this, with you and I here, together. I shouldn't have to do this."

"What were you supposed to do?" I ask, checking my fear and trying to stand tall. My knees wobble, but I steady myself.

Dani studies me for a moment.

"Make it look like an accident. And before that, scare you enough so that you and Jackson both thought someone was stalking you. It'd make it more believable if you were already paranoid that some psycho terrorizing the Poconos was out to get you. We couldn't believe our luck when we saw the news reports about someone tampering with the trails—it gave us the perfectr cover."

"So you just lurked around our cabin for the last three days, spying on us and waiting for your chance?"

"I slept in my car at night. It wasn't hard. It turns out you can put up with a lot of things when there's two million dollars at the end of the tunnel." She shrugs. "And it couldn't come soon enough. There are lots of hiding places around here. I put Heather in charge of the store, and I drove out pretty much right after you and Jackson did. When I wasn't at the cabin, I was up near the lookout, where the cell phone signal was better. I still had business to attend to, after all."

I think about the bank transfer. The one Dani made yesterday morning.

"So was it you I saw by the hot tub our first night?" I blush automatically, remembering what Jackson and I did and imagining my best friend watching us during such an intimate moment, thrilling at the idea of hurting one or both of us so soon afterwards.

Dani ignores my question. "After I moved your phone out to the car yesterday, I still had plenty of time while you ate lunch to drive over to the trailhead and mess with a bunch of different railings. I'd already done some prep work the day before. It's the most popular trail in the area—it was a safe bet. One of you should have fallen. It was just dumb luck that Jackson ended up saving you, and that I had two people to fake an overdose for instead of just one."

Dani still has the gun pointed at me. "I didn't want this to happen. You know that, right?"

"What did you want to happen?" I strain to keep my voice as level as possible.

"All I wanted was a chance. Some of us don't have them handed to us. Some of us have to take what's ours. What we deserve to have."

I think of all the times Dani and I slept, just inches away

from each other. All the times she's listened to my fears about my mother not loving me, about how unworthy I was to have this inheritance waiting for me.

A stab of recognition pricks at my chest. "You thought I was ungrateful, didn't you?"

She brings her cool green eyes to mine, and I have to look away.

Not just because I can't manage to see the hatred in my best friend's face. I'm also searching for something.

I picture Jackson's wounds and the pool of blood I saw from across the river. I think about how he raised the axe, and how I turned away because I couldn't stand to think about what he was going to do to me.

But he wasn't aiming for me. He was aiming for something else.

I cast my eyes along the ground, as secretly as I can, and trail the matted grass from where we'd stood just a little over an hour ago until I spot it, the jagged branch jutting up from the scrim of rocks around the river's edge. The place where Jackson must have struck out with the axe, trying to move the branch to brace the trunk I was on and keep it from crashing into the river. He must have fallen when he tried to jam the branch out underneath the trunk, and save me as I started to collapse into the water. The point of the broken limb is mottled and rust-colored.

The sounds I heard weren't gunshots. It was the crack of the wood as Jackson worked to brace the branch against the trunk, and the sound of him snapping it in half as he slipped on the slick surface of the wet wood and fell onto it. Just looking at it, I want to cry out. Jackson must have been in so much pain as he struggled to get himself back up. As he tried to rescue me, after the tip of the branch stabbed him in the side.

I take a step closer to the spear of the limb. A cord of steel ratchets itself up my spine. Next to it, buried slightly in the leaf litter, is the axe.

Dani clicks the two hammers on the barrel back.

"I didn't *think*. I *knew* you were an ungrateful bitch." Dani's words crackle in the air.

"Was it always about the money?" I take another step closer.

"Yes. And no. I don't know."

The sirens are still distant, not moving anymore.

Dani curses under her breath.

They must have gotten to the cabin by now. I tell myself Jackson is being taken care of. That they would have brought an ambulance. That my mother will survive.

Acid rises in my throat, and I force myself to push it back down. I cough at the chemical trickle that threatens to choke me.

"They're going to find you. If you kill me, they'll know that you did all of this. There's no turning back if you do this, Dani."

"They won't even know I was here. Nothing links back to me."

I think about my phone call to her, but stop myself. Instead, I focus on something else, more obvious.

"What about the knife? Your fingerprints are on it."

Which is the exact moment I notice one detail I shouldn't have missed.

Gloves. Dani is wearing gloves. Little leather gloves the color of butter. I bought her those gloves for Christmas last year.

Something dies inside of me.

A bird calls out overhead, something large and predatory that's circling above us. An animal brushes through the bushes at the edge of the river's ravine. My mind flits to the fox which sniffed at my hand, and I wish her away from all this death.

"Then why do any of this? Just walk away. You're not going to get the money now, anyway. If I die, it goes to Jackson. And if Jackson dies, it goes to. . ."

I already know the answer. I knew it the second I heard that voicemail from the bank at the lookout.

"It goes to your mother, and me. And you're twenty-five now, aren't you?"

When our business started to thrive, both Dani and I had drawn up wills. We'd included each other as our second beneficiaries, right after our family. After Jackson and I got married, he became my main heir, and then Dani and my mother would split everything fifty-fifty if anything happened to him. My lawyer had recommended it that way, and it'd seemed so simple. Such a normal thing to do.

If Jackson is dead, and if my mother doesn't survive, Dani will get all of the two million dollars I inherited this morning, on my twenty-fifth birthday.

A sob bursts from my lungs.

There are sounds humming in the forest. It's not clear which are animals, which are people, and which are the rotting of leaves—of life—around us.

"Stop distracting me," Dani lashes out. "I can't hear myself think."

She glances around us frantically. The hum intensifies.

"Turn around. Get on your knees," she orders.

"No," I tell her. I just need her to take one step closer. "If you're going to kill me"––I swallow hard again–– "then you're going to need to do it while you look at me. I deserve that much."

"You don't deserve anything," Dani says as she takes the step towards me that I need.

I plunge forward, and she snaps her finger against the trigger. A click echoes against the soft bodies of the trees surrounding us.

I have my hands around her waist. The click comes again. But no shots.

I was right.

I understand why Jackson moved the shotgun from the shed, and later hid the gun away inside the fireplace while I passed out last night. He wanted us to have protection, but he'd also just faced his wife threatening to shoot him because she was convinced he was trying to kill her.

And that's also why nothing happens when Dani clicks the trigger of the gun. Because, even with the shotgun hidden in the fireplace, Jackson decided to take out the shells. Just like he'd done before, with our first night in the cabin. *Just in case.*

With as much pressure as I can manage, I force my weight onto Dani and pull her towards the ground. The sharp point of the branch is poking from the bed of rock like a spear. I aim for her leg as I reach for the axe.

The weight of both of us topples us down to the ground by the trunk of the tree, but I instantly know I've miscalculated. There's a searing pain in my thigh, and as I look down, I see that in our descent Dani has managed to writhe away from my grasp, and it's my leg rather than hers that's been pierced by the sharp point, my blood mixing with my husband's.

In some recess of my mind, as blood drains from my body, I think about the poetic justice in Jackson and I both dying from pieces of this fucking forest lodged inside our bodies.

Dani rolls off me, and instantly sits up. The axe is buried further underneath the blanket of the forest. I can't reach it.

She scans my body, taking in the throbbing wound in my leg. Her eyes are manic.

A sluice of fear shoves itself down my throat. I start to shout out a name, to call for help, but my words are cut off as fingers wrap around my neck. I put my hands around both wrists, gripping at the arms that surround me and flailing my feet to try and get traction against the soft ground.

The gash in my leg keeps pumping blood, and my heartbeat pounds in my ears.

I can't breathe.

I can't move.

Starbursts flood my eyes. All I can think about, as darkness begins to saturate the color around me, is how the last image I'll ever see is of someone I love wanting me to die just a little faster.

But then something topples over us from the edge of the river, and I hear the soft snap of bones breaking against each other.

35

I can breathe again.

I cough and grasp at my throat. I can't focus my eyes yet. All I see is a dark green slab, edges blurred, holding down Dani, whose right arm is bent up and over like a corkscrew set too far to the edge of a bottle. As my vision clears, I see a face and a scruffy beard. Dark boots, heavy jeans, mud caked up the sides.

I blink, but he's not wearing a badge this time.

Using the handle of the axe for leverage, ranger Mike pulls on Dani's arm, the one plucked up and clearly broken, and she gives out a yelp of pain. "Mary," he barks at me. "Mary, can you stand up?"

I can't say anything. My mouth just moves in empty circles, but I do manage to roll to my side, my leg throbbing. As I work to stand up, I give a sharp cry. The pain in my leg shoots through my body like an electrical current. I grit my teeth, force my fingers into the bark of the tree, and bring myself up to stand.

"Do you see how I'm holding her?" he asks. Dani gives a quick twist to her body, but Mike pulls harder and she instantly goes limp, a whimper escaping her mouth.

I nod silently.

"Come here, now." Mike reaches out with his free hand and pulls me down to the ground as gently as possible and positions my hands on top of Dani's arms with my left hand wrapped around the wooden handle and my right pressing on the flat metal of the axe's blade. "Straddle her like this, so she can't move free."

I do as he tells me, my thoughts still coming in jerks and starts through the fogginess that descended when Dani cut off my breath and that's growing stronger as the wound in my leg threatens to overtake me.

There are footsteps in the woods, clattering across the forest floor. A sharp report of a dog's bark comes from the direction of the cabin. Another follows, closer to where we are now.

"I can't stay here." Mike gives me a look. "You'll be all right." It's a statement, not a question. And then he starts running along the riverside.

As soon as he's gone, Dani gives one more twist to her shoulders, but I do as Mike has told me and hold fast on her arm, ignoring the burning in my leg. She settles herself into the ground, putting her face on the side and burying it into the wet leaves below us.

That's how the police and the emergency medical technicians find us, just a few minutes later. My body, slung across my best friend's, tangled like two lovers and with the wounds to prove that whatever it was we had between was, it was real enough to leave its mark.

36

Dear Mary,

By the time you read this, I'll have turned myself in.

I've always had trouble dealing with people. Back when I was little, I didn't make many friends, partly because I kept having to move from foster home to foster home. And partly because I just wasn't interested. People couldn't be trusted—that much I knew. That's why I was shifting from home to home to begin with, because my parents had broken the one promise they made when they had me, which was to take care of me.

I guess that's something your husband and I have in common, except that he was almost an adult. He had ways of protecting himself. I was still just a child.

And he also had his sister. Abigail.

It's amazing the things you can learn when you don't have to waste your time hanging out with friends, going on dates, being the captain of the glee club or the soccer team or whatever else other kids do. I had lots of time for myself growing up.

Computers always made more sense to me than people.

It's hard to explain why I started setting traps for hikers in the woods. I know it was wrong, but I also can promise you that I never *did anything that would have really hurt anyone. I made sure of it. I just needed to leave my mark somewhere, I guess. Or maybe I wanted people to know that I had control, even if they never met me. If I'm honest with you (and myself), I can't really make sense of it all quite yet. Maybe they'll give me a doctor in prison who can help me.*

My point is that I never would have taken out the railing on that lookout by the waterfall, because the drop-off was so steep. I was there that day, if you can believe it, just to go for a hike.

The woods soothe me. Being in them, away from as many people as possible, helps keep my thoughts from racing around my head like a mouse caught in a cage. I wanted to hear the water and feel its spray on my skin. I usually prefer the trails that have as few hikers as possible—I'm not good at sharing the woods with other people—but that day I needed the waterfall. I needed its beauty.

And then I saw you running down the mountain. You looked so scared, that it overrode all of my instincts to avoid other people. I didn't want to leave you alone. It was like your pain was a magnet for my own pain—like I saw something in you. Leaving you there in that cabin, on your own with a man you seemed so scared of, was one of the hardest things I've ever had to do.

You've probably guessed by now that I don't have a friend in the sheriff's office. I'm also not a real park ranger. You were right—or maybe it was your husband who was. I bought the uniform in an online auction, and the badge came from a children's dress-up costume set. Surprisingly, wearing the uniform and badge kept people away from me when I was out in the woods, rather than drawing them to me.

After I left your cabin, I went back home. I have a small cabin, hidden near the lookout on the way into the valley, just a few miles away from where you were staying. When the storm rolled in, I was worried that I wouldn't be able to get a connection, but I bought a generator and cell phone booster a long time ago. I may not like to live around other people, but being able to hack into other people's lives is almost like a compulsion for me. I have to do it, sometimes just to prove that I can. It's gotten quieter over the years—that need to try and have control over others from a distance. I realize I might have just replaced it with what I've been doing here in the woods, leaving little signals that I exist. Or maybe I'm just broken.

Sometimes people don't know why they do something.

But I do know that night, after I left you with your husband, I used the information you gave me about yourself to do some investigating online. There are a lot of Mary Smiths, but I was able to use the phone number and email you gave me at the cabin to narrow it down until I figured out which Mary Smith you were—and that's when I discovered who your father was. I kept thinking about your face in the car on the drive home, how frightened you were when you told me someone had been messing with your phone, and how you seemed to shrink away from your husband whenever he was near you.

And then I read the news reports about the accident, and what came afterwards. I saw the photograph, the one taken outside your father's funeral. There was Abigail's foster mother, looking like a ghost surrounded by all those angry faces. I'd read later on in the social worker's report I dug up that Jackson's sister had purposefully started calling herself Abby after she moved to that last foster home. She was trying to start over, it seemed, in some small way.

The next day, while I was reading over the headlines about what happened at the cabin, I'd realized that your mother's fake doctor was there too, standing behind Abigail's foster mother. The one who pretended to be your mother's cancer doctor. But that night, I didn't recognize him.

There was another face that stood out to me, though. Another person screaming into the camera, at you and your mother. He was younger than the man I saw on the mountain trail. But it was definitely your husband. I had pictures of both of you on my phone, and I was able to compare the two images of Jackson, the one from the *newspaper article seven years ago and the set of photos I'd taken in your cabin.*

That's how I knew I had to dig further into what happened with your father and Abigail. That's how I found out that your husband, Jackson Morell, was Abigail's brother. He was already eighteen when Abigail moved in with the Beckers, and from everything I read in Abigail's file from her social worker, it seemed like he'd tried to distance himself from his sister after he left foster care. He even went so far as to petition to change his last name, from Davidson to Morell. I found the court documents online. He didn't even want to share that with his sister. It was mentioned, over and over again, that Abigail was lonely.

That she missed her brother.

I kept trying to call you to tell you about the connection between you and your husband. I was certain that Jackson wanted to hurt you, as a way of trying to get some sort of revenge for his own sister's death. It went to voicemail a few times, but I didn't leave an actual message. If you listen back, you'll only hear silence, while I tried to decide whether I could explain all of this in a recording. When I finally got through to you, I'd already decided that I needed to go back to your cabin. That I needed to protect you.

So, in a way, you also saved me. You changed me.

You brought out a part of me that I thought was dead, but now I know isn't. People can care for each other. Even strangers can care about each other.

Because that's how I feel. I care about you.

I ran all the way to the cabin.

When I got there, all hell had broken loose. Jackson and another woman were both slouched over and covered in blood. I'll admit it—I didn't even stop to check for their pulses. I was focused on finding you.

Sirens were blaring in the background, and you were gone. I knew the emergency services would be at the cabin soon, but I needed to find you and make sure you were safe. I traced the perimeter of the cabin, and when I found the trail of blood, I followed it, thinking that you were hurt. I headed in the direction of the river, careful not to be spotted just in case you weren't alone, or that I was wrong about you. I know those woods better than almost anyone, and I covered the ground quickly.

When I found the two of you, I knew I wasn't wrong about you, Mary. I saw how that woman—Dani, I know now—looked at you. I could tell she wanted you dead. And I couldn't let that happen.

I wish I'd watched you and Jackson more carefully, when you first arrived at the cabin. Maybe I could have stopped all of this from happening to you.

I'm sorry that your mother died.

I'm sorry, too, about that woman—your friend.

I'm sorry.

I read in the papers that Jackson will recover. I hope he realizes what an amazing woman you are, and that he works to earn your trust.

Like I did.

Mike Hampton

37

I watch Jackson as he reads the letter. He doesn't betray any emotion. It's like he's reading a grocery list or a shopping receipt.

The doctor said this might be one of the side effects of the pain medication he's on. Blunted emotions. Which is exactly why I'm bringing Jackson the letter now. I want to hear his explanation, free from any emotional camouflage. I want the truth, as neatly packaged as possible.

Jackson should be discharged from the hospital in the next couple of days. The wound was caught early enough to stop sepsis from setting in and, although he'd lost a lot of blood, he should make a full recovery, with maybe a little permanent stiffness in his side.

The injury to my leg proved to be less severe than the medics had originally thought. After a good clean-up and what felt like 300 stitches, I was pronounced almost good as new. On the outside, at least.

Jackson's mouth twitches slightly. He folds the letter and lays it in his lap on the hospital bed.

"It's true," he says. "All of it."

He fidgets with the paper in his lap. "I was a terrible brother. I'm the reason my sister is dead." He turns his chin up and our eyes meet. "She was on the road that night because she was coming to see me. I couldn't be bothered to go and visit her at her foster home. I kept avoiding her, and so that night she insisted on coming over to see me. After I turned eighteen, it was like a switch flipped in me. I wanted to believe that I didn't have anyone who cared about me—I just wanted to wallow in how terrible my life was. But Gail wouldn't let me do that. She kept reminding me how much she loved me, and back then I hated her for it. I just wanted to be a victim. And then I lost her. She was really the victim."

A single tear trickles down his cheek.

I don't reach out to wipe it away.

"I understand if you don't want to be with me anymore. All I can say is that I've spent the last seven years of my life trying to change. To be a better person."

I want to tell him about what happened when I was in high school, after my father died. How grief set off a chain reaction in my life, when I became more and more desperate to know that my mother loved me. And that the more I needed her, the less she wanted me. I want him to know that I *did* hurt my mother. One time. That she used it to take out a restraining order against me. I need him to know everything, finally. Not just the parts that will come out at Dani's trial. If we're going to move forward, he needs to understand what I've been through and what I've done.

All of it.

But not right now.

Right now, there's a question I have to ask. There are a million questions I have to ask, in fact, but I'm starting with just one.

"Did you know who I was when you came into the store that

day?"

Jackson freezes, just for a split second, and then lets out a long breath. Decision made, it seems.

"Yes, I did. I knew who your family was. I wanted to find out more about you, that was all. I wanted to know what kind of person you were." He hangs his head. "I wanted to compare you to Gail—Abigail. It was wrong, I know. But I just needed to see you."

He leans forward in his hospital bed, all the tubes and monitors connected to him tensing at the strain of his movement. "But you need to know that as soon as I laid eyes on you everything else became background noise. You were so lovely, and warm, and kind. All that was real. Every last bit of it."

I want to believe him. Jackson is the only family I have left.

He reaches out to hold me. My husband's hand is cool to the touch.

I picture him, bleeding through his shirt, surrounded by the cruel people I brought into his life. I see him fighting as unconsciousness took hold of him, just so he could give me the signal and tell me where he'd put the shotgun. So he could keep me safe.

Mike Hampton's words from the letter come back to me. Maybe people really can change.

I believe now that it's true for Jackson.

And I want to hope that it's true for me.

Because, if I don't have Jackson, I don't have anyone.

I wince as I stand up from the hospital chair, and very carefully sit down next to him on the bed, careful of the wreckage in both of our bodies from our honeymoon. I don't let go of his hand, but I do lean forward, pressing as much of my body into his that is safe and sound.

For the first time since we left the cabin, I feel our hearts relax into each other.

38

Dani's request to see me comes two days after my mother's funeral. We'd postponed the service, Jackson and I, supposedly because of his recovery at the hospital, which was true. But I'd also wanted to delay burying my mother until I had come to terms with what she'd done to me.

Which was ridiculous thinking on my part. That I could somehow reconcile everything my mother had done—drugging my father and contributing to an innocent girl's death, planning to institutionalize me and, when that failed, waiting years for the perfect chance to kill me, all for the sake of money and pride—if only given another week or two to sit with it. The majority of the time now I feel like I'm living some sort of half-life. At once shallow and murky.

So eventually I told Jackson we just needed to do it. We needed to bury my mother.

"Healing takes time," he reminded me. He reminds me every day, and when he says it I know that it's not just for me. It's a reminder to himself and a touchstone for us, as we try to see if we can salvage our marriage from this wreckage.

Right now, I'm grasping onto the moments, few and far between, when I feel somewhat human again.

At least waiting a few weeks meant that the press interest had died down considerably. My mother's burial came right after a huge raid on a slew of restaurants in town, supposedly serving as fronts for the mafia. Most of the small-town reporters were covering that case, and the national news had moved on from our family's story a long time ago.

That's one good thing to be said for a twenty-four-hour news cycle. Tragedies last only as long as it takes for the next one to come along.

If only that were true for the people the vans and cameras leave behind.

Checking into the prison is surreal. A terse prison guard with tight blond braids checks through my purse and my pockets before scanning my driver's license and then asks me to wait in an airless box of a room. Eventually, another guard comes to escort me down a series of hallways all the same mint-green color, until we come to a room with a broad window facing into the hallway. There's a metal table and two metal chairs in the room.

I can also see Dani, waiting in the corner of the room with her hands cuffed in front.

She won't stand trial for my mother's murder for another six months, they think. Along with charges of attempted murder, battery, and fraud. Of all of them, it's the fraud charge that carries the most weight. Her sketchy investment practices with our company's finances seem to have some hints at money laundering. She started getting personal visits at the store from investors a few months ago, sometimes when I was there and sometimes when she was alone, after hours or before the start of the day. Her last face-to-face reminder came the day Jackson and I left for our cabin in the woods.

Which is why she took so much money out of our account when she did. Apparently, if she hadn't paid up, she might have been dead instead of my mother.

Or they'd both be dead by now. I don't know.

Dani isn't talking about that part of her story. Everything I know so far I've learned from the detectives working on the case.

The guard sits Dani down at the table and motions for me to sit as well. When I do, I try to adjust the chair's position, only to realize it's bolted to the ground.

"You have fifteen minutes," the guard informs us.

Dani looks thinner than before. Her cheekbones protrude from her face like slashes, and there are matching smudges underneath her eyes.

"You look terrible," I say.

Dani runs a hand through her hair, careful not to catch the links of the handcuffs as she does so. She gives me a grim smile. "Thanks."

"Why did you want to meet with me?" It's a question I've asked myself a thousand times since Detective Wright passed along the request to visit her.

She shifts in her seat, and I imagine the bones of her disappearing hips jabbing against the hard metal of the chair. "I wanted to explain to you why we did it. Your mother and me."

I tense. "I already know why." I start to stand up from the table, but Dani talks over me.

"It wasn't just the money. It was more than that."

"You were my best friend. *We* were best friends. I thought. And then I find out that you were just pretending for the last seven years, and however many years before that. You and my mother drugged my father to get the insurance money when he died. And when that didn't work, you decided to get rid of me. Because my mother wanted a fancier life where she could forget I ever existed, and you wanted designer shoes."

Twin flames ignite in Dani's cheeks, making her look feverish.

"It was more than that. You have to understand. I was never like you. I was never *special*."

A pit sinks deep into my stomach as Dani's word conjures my mother, and her insistence inside that airless cabin that I was the exact opposite of what Dani's claiming. That my ordinariness somehow gave my mother permission to resent me; even hate me. It's a realization I've had to interrogate myself with again and again—especially when I relive those last few minutes of my mother's life, when, for just a moment, she seemed to change her mind.

But I don't say any of this to Dani. I can't fathom trying to ask her to reconcile what she saw my mother say and do to me with her own skewed belief that I was still the chosen one out of the two of us. And that somehow this justified what Dani did to me.

Dani goes on. "No one ever wanted me, not the way your father wanted you. Not until your mother did. When she asked me to help her, she made me feel so important. So desired, almost. Like I was the only one in the entire world who could do this for her. That we were a team."

I can tolerate only so much. "*We* were a team. You and me. We took care of each other. We did everything together."

Dani twists her mouth.

"Yeah, and you were always the bright light. The best girl. And I was your sidekick. The one who would get tossed away when they were finished with me. My parents were constantly asking me, 'Why can't you be more like Mary?' You have no idea what it was like being your best friend."

"So, money and jealousy? Is that why you spent the last seven years planning to ruin my life?"

"It was like a game. It wasn't real."

"What? Even after my father died? And Jackson's sister? God, Dani. What's wrong with you?"

Dani starts to cry. "I don't know."

And, in spite of everything, I find myself wanting to comfort her. But I remind myself of what she's done. That she's the reason I'm an orphan. She's the reason I'll never get to confront my mother about what she did to me, and to our family. I let the anger slide like a steel rod up my spine.

"Well, I hope you find out."

For a second time, I stand up to leave. This time, I make it to the door before Dani gets control of her sobs and is able to speak up.

"You have a sister."

I turn. I must have misheard her.

"You have a sister," she repeats.

A spike jabs behind my left eye, overpowering the flare of hope in my chest.

"What *is* this? What are you trying to do? Is this just another part of your little *game*?" I throw her own word back in her face.

I don't hate easily, and I don't hate well, but listening to her try to provoke me by promising a family where none exists makes me think I can learn to be good at it.

"I'm not making it up," Dani pleads, and her tears are back.

"You're a liar. That's all you do. You're just trying to hurt me, one last time. And I won't let you."

I'm at the door now, my fist pounding on the rough metal.

"Her name's Charlotte. Charlotte Bradbury. She's seven years old."

I pause, my fist held in the air. *Seven years old! Seven years ago!*

"Your mother was pregnant when your father died. That's why he went out that night. To get a pregnancy testing kit, because he didn't believe her."

"How would you know that?" I snap. "Stop lying!"

"I'm not lying. I promise you. I just want you to know the truth. Now that it's over. She deserves to have someone in her life besides that weasel."

Dr. Bradbury? My mind finally locks onto that last name.

I sit back down in the chair. I don't look at Dani, but I can feel her eyes boring into me.

"Tell me everything."

39

The days have turned cold again, and I'm waiting for Jackson outside his bank's office. I've left the shop early today, but Heather is there to help out with customers and ring out the cash register at the end of the day.

I still don't do the bookkeeping for Kitchen Kabinet, because numbers were never really my strength and, as it turns out, you can hire professionals to help manage your business affairs. Professionals who don't have any interest in stealing from you, or in laundering money and skimming off the top for themselves.

I'm wearing a new woolen coat—bright red with little toggles at the waist. When I went shopping for it, to replace my old coat which had been worn through at the elbows, it was on a rack beside a display of fake fur jackets in bottle pinks and blues. They reminded me of Dani. Of that night we went out dancing while Jackson was gone, and of how lonely I'd felt even with Dani there beside me.

Maybe back then my heart knew something my mind wouldn't let me realize.

Heather gave me a stack of mail from the store before I left.

There were three more envelopes today, all with the same spidery handwriting. All addressed to me.

The return address is for Rockview Penitentiary.

Mike Hampton writes me almost daily. Sometimes more than once a day.

He doesn't know my new home address, though, which means the letters are sent to the store.

I took them out of the stack of bills and flyers for Kitchen Kabinet and shoved them into my purse before I left the store. I take the letters out now, as I wait for Jackson, and consider opening one.

But I don't.

I haven't told Jackson about them yet. I'm not sure if I will.

Jackson comes out of the front door of his office, coat primly in place and buttoned up, and flashes me a bright smile. I shove the envelopes into the deep pockets of my new coat so he can't see them. My husband walks over, wraps his arm around my waist, and pulls me close to him.

"You look gorgeous," he says.

"Long day?" I ask.

"Not anymore." He presses my hand with his, kisses me deeply, and takes a long breath in. For a moment, we both just stand there, feeling the solid presence of the other person. I take the time to try and organize my feelings for what's about to happen.

We start walking, both of us knowing where we're heading without having to say a word.

I remind myself to put the letters back into my purse when Jackson isn't looking. I don't want to worry him. Not tonight.

When we get to the restaurant—a family-style Italian place with paper placemats and all-you-can-eat spaghetti—the social worker, Judy, is already waiting for us at a table. This is our first overnight visit, and I can sense that both Jackson and I are a little nervous.

My husband grips my hand in his after we sit down, and gives it a long squeeze. I squeeze back.

Judy has dark hair plaited down her back and a practical quality about her. One look at this woman and her focused brown eyes and perfectly-squared shoulders, and you know that this is someone who knows how to get things done. When we first contacted her about fostering three months ago, she didn't waste time equivocating about whether it was too soon, whether we were too young, whether we hadn't been married long enough. She simply started listing off all the things we'd need to do.

If there's one thing I've learned about this type of parenthood, it's that bureaucracy is a well-fed partner of the child welfare system. Jackson and I have joked that our fingerprints will get worn off by the time we'd done all the background checks.

At first, Jackson and I had been worried that one of us would be flagged. Even with the district attorney's office (and, as a result, the small amount of press coverage the case received) placing my restraining order firmly under the umbrella of the emotional abuse my mother had inflicted on me for years, both Jackson and I were still worried the records attached to the restraining order would be damning for me. With everything that had happened between Dani and my mother, and my father's death before that, we'd worried that social services wouldn't even consider letting us bring a child into our family.

On the contrary, though, we discovered that Pennsylvania has a strong push towards kinship care, where children can remain with relatives if their parents are unable to care for them. And, as it turns out, Dani was right.

I have a sister.

A half-sister, in fact.

According to Dani's testimony during the trial, my mother and Dr. James Bradbury had been having an affair for almost a year when my mother discovered she was pregnant. Dr. Bradbury, divorced and paying through the nose with alimony to his first and second wives, wanted my mother to terminate the pregnancy. When she refused, he told her she needed to find some way to support the child. He claimed he didn't have the money.

Which is where Dani came in.

Dani testified that Dr. Bradbury didn't know about the plot to kill my father—his death was just a happy coincidence to him, it seemed—and later he'd assumed my mother was only planning on coercing me out of my inheritance, not killing anybody. Once he arrived in the cabin, however, and saw what was happening, he left. Which makes him both complicit *and* a coward.

Of course, if the fact that he was willing to fake my mother's cancer treatment isn't proof enough, his ability to leave my husband bleeding to death without a second thought tells you about the kind of doctor he is. Well, was. He's not Dr. Bradbury anymore. Although it's possible he makes his fellow inmates call him *Doctor* while he serves five to ten years for medical malfeasance and accessory to murder.

Dani did some searching online and figured out which drug to take from the hospital that would serve as a tranquilizer for my father without being traceable in his system. It's amazing what you can find online. Potassium chloride was locked up, but she was able to take the keys off a nurse administrator who she'd started an affair with a few weeks prior. He never even knew the keys were missing, apparently.

My mother hadn't known that my father had changed his will or his life insurance policy, and so when it came out that I was to inherit the majority of it after I turned twenty-five, she informed Dr. Bradbury that he'd just have to be patient.

And so Dani and my mother worked to find another way to get at the money. Only after their first attempt to get me sent to The Meadows fizzled out, a restraining order against a grief-stricken daughter also proved to be not enough to institutionalize someone. Even Dr. Bradbury's friend, the married judge with the gonorrhea outbreak he'd treated pro bono, couldn't exert his influence beyond the restraining order itself. And my mother's clock was ticking towards the time that she'd start to show her pregnancy.

That was maybe the hardest realization of everything. That my mother didn't want me to know about my half-sister. She wanted to keep her all to herself.

And then she wanted me to die, so that she could buy my sister pretty dresses and horses and a prep school education. She could reinvent herself as the best of mothers.

There's a rustling behind us, and a mop of dark curls and sticky fingers rushes into the chair opposite me. Judy's assistant, some young undergraduate intern with a sad face and black nails, has brought Charlotte back from the bathroom.

"Hi Mary. Hi Jackson." My husband gets the bigger smile. Charlotte likes me, but she adores Jackson. "Judy said I wouldn't need a sleeping bag for tonight. She says you have a bed already. She said it has a bright green blanket."

"That's right. We have it all ready for your sleepover tonight. And your room's right next to ours, so we'll be right there if you need us," Jackson tells her. We spent the previous weekend fixing up the second bedroom in our new house. We used my inheritance to buy an airy split-level on a quiet dead-end street, just a few blocks from our downtown and Charlotte's elementary school.

Jackson and I decided the rest of the money should go into

savings for a rainy day. We have plenty to live on with both of our incomes. After all that pain my father's inheritance had caused, neither of us was interested in letting it transform our lives any further than it already had.

I want to believe that my father left the money to me as an act of love, and that what Dani saw between us—and resented so intensely—was real. That he loved me, and wanted me to be safe and protected. But then I think about him secretly changing his will, and the restrictions he placed on the money so that my mother couldn't touch it. Deep inside myself, I think part of me knows that my father understood what he was doing, and who my mother was. He knew he'd be putting me in danger by taunting my mother from beyond the grave, and yet he did it anyway. He wouldn't be there to protect me, and he was okay with that.

When I picture the smile that spread across his face that night, after my mother told him she was pregnant, and how he rushed out to get a testing kit and confirm that it was true, I have to push down the dark thought that rises up.

That maybe he wanted this new baby more than he ever wanted me.

Charlotte picked out the paint colors for her bedroom in our newly-purchased house, and even came over to help us paint on her last visit, although in a best estimate she probably got more paint on herself than on the walls.

"After dinner, we're going to go walk down to the park, and then have hot cocoa at home before bedtime," I add.

She eyes both of us cautiously. "I need a nightlight when I sleep."

Judy watches us intently, a smile pulling at the corners of her lips.

"Well, we have two for you, Charlotte. One with a frog and one that's just a plain nightlight. Which one would you like?"

Jackson pulls the two lights out of my purse. Judy had suggested we bring them. Since everything that's happened, Charlotte's had some difficulty around bedtime. Her mind starts to hum like a lawnmower—or at least that's how she explained it to Jackson and me while we were painting her bedroom. So far, though, these worries don't seem to follow her to school, which is a blessing. In fact, Judy says that Charlotte's advanced for her grade, and that her teacher recommended her for a special accelerated math and reading program. Charlotte's in second grade at Westerly Prep Elementary School, the same school my mother volunteered at. It was the main way my mother managed to see Charlotte after she and Dr. Bradbury decided it would be best if he raised her alone. Better for Charlotte, perhaps, but also better for their plan to get my inheritance. Apparently, probate can get sticky when another sibling is involved.

Charlotte pauses for a moment, considering. "The frog one, please."

"That's my favorite too." I lean in conspiratorially. "But Jackson liked the boring one."

Charlotte looks between the two of us. "Oh, the other one's nice too," she says, and Jackson laughs.

"No, no, you're right. The frog one is clearly better." My husband looks at the frog nightlight, which is mainly a large green frog head with the light bulb shining out of the center of his mouth, and nods a couple of times. "Yup, definitely better. And, you know what? I wonder if he ribbits in his sleep?"

Jackson reaches over the table and pretends to have the little frog nibble at Charlotte's fingers.

This gets a delicious squeal of laughter out of my little sister.

I'm not as natural with children as Jackson is, and I'm fully aware it's going to take time for me to learn how to connect with Charlotte as easily as my husband does. Right now, I'm grateful that we get to have her in our lives at all, whatever might happen when her father gets out of prison. I'm just so happy to have a family again.

Sometimes, when I'm falling asleep at night, I see my mother in the cabin in the woods. I watch her mouth forming those words, over and over, just moments before Dani plunged the knife into her side: *You're more like me than I realized.*

Unlike the letters that keep arriving, this is something I'm certain I'll never tell Jackson.

The intern, who'd been sitting next to Judy, fades away somewhere, probably to tap at her phone, and Judy gets down to business after we order plates of spaghetti all around.

There are papers to sign, forms to complete, and another round of identification checks that Judy has to notarize. But, thanks to Judy's efficiency, we're done with the paperwork by the time the food gets here. Charlotte sits quietly, doodling on the paper placemat while we dot our i's and cross our t's.

When the spaghetti comes, Charlotte immediately tries to dig in with her fork, and ends up with a wad of pasta clumped around the prongs and nowhere near the size that will actually fit into her mouth.

"Here, let me cut it up for you," I offer, and reach over with my fork and knife. It's something I remember my father doing for me when I was little.

Jackson reaches across the table and wipes at Charlotte's cheeks, where spaghetti sauce has smeared almost from ear to ear.

Charlotte gives him another winning smile. She turns to me, as I cut up her pasta, and says solemnly, "Daddy never cut up my food for me."

Charlotte's nanny took her into her house after Dr. Bradbury went to prison, but she's almost seventy now and was Dr. Bradbury's nanny when he was a boy. She can't take care of her for much longer. Apparently, windfall of money or not, once Dr. Bradbury laid eyes on his daughter, he was enchanted, racking up a hefty sum of credit card debt to give my half-sister the best of everything, while my mother stood patiently on the sidelines, waiting for her time to shine as Charlotte's mother.

From a distance, anyone can be the perfect mother. Or the perfect child.

It's only up close that we start to show weakness.

That's been one of the hardest things about all of this—realizing that my mother was able to love Charlotte precisely because my half-sister never truly needed her. Not like I did.

I look at Charlotte across the table, and take in her long, dark lashes framing her brilliant blue eyes, the flowing curls that frame her porcelain face, so sweet and poised like a little doll.

If she and Dani had succeeded with their plan, I don't know if my mother would have become more of a real caregiver to Charlotte. Maybe she would have moved in with Dr. Bradbury, and gotten to take Charlotte to parent-teacher conferences and bask in the glow of knowing people admired her for having such a beautiful, gifted daughter. Or maybe she would have realized that parenthood is never like that, no matter who the parents or the children are. Maybe everything would have unraveled, and eventually she would have tried to hurt Charlotte just like she'd tried to hurt me.

Sometimes I ask myself which version of this alternate future would have hurt less. The one where Charlotte and I became the same to my mother, or the one where she was forever my mother's favorite.

Mostly, I try not to think about it. Mostly.

"Give it a go." I move my knife and fork back from the plate and let her attempt it on her own.

Charlotte pulls the scrunched-up expression Jackson and I

have come to learn is her 'concentration face' as she grips her fork, shoving its prongs into the pasta and pulling up what appears to be a perfectly-sized bite. She pops it into her mouth and chews, considering.

"Well?" I ask. "What do you think?"

Charlotte dips her fork into her food again and looks up at me.

"It works for now," she says. Before she takes another bite, she gives me a shy smile.

I gaze back at my sister.

Because she's right. And for now, it has to be enough.

The end

ACKNOWLEDGEMENTS

Thank you to everyone at Bloodhound Books for helping me take *The Anniversary* from the spark of an idea to the novel that it is today. Also, big thanks once again for the killer cover—yellow is our color!

Thank you to my writing friends, both in person and online, for brightening my day and making this writing life less lonely. Big hugs to Julia Whicker for her kindness, support, and wise insights on earlier drafts of this novel. The next coffee's on me!

Life is a journey of learning, and thank you to all my teachers for their time, expertise, and guidance. Special thanks to John Hoopes, my AP Calculus teacher, who taught me to never give up.

So much love to my first teacher, my mother. Thank you for putting everything aside whenever I have a finished draft and reading it. Also, thank you for continuing to be my unofficial publicist.

Thank you to my late father, Stephen, for being the best dad and human being I've ever known. You are missed and so loved.

Thank you to my children, Ethan, Katherine, and Elisa, for not being too terribly embarrassed when my answer to a timeline issue is to cover the living room table with post-it notes that detail all the scenes in the novel, including the salacious ones. I love you.

Finally, thank you to my husband, Joshua, who is and continues to be my favorite person. You make everything better.

ABOUT THE AUTHOR

Sarah K. Stephens is the author of three novels and a developmental psychologist at Penn State University. Her writing has appeared in *LitHub*, *The Writer's Chronicle*, *Hazlitt*, and *The Millions*. Aside from *The Anniversary*, her books include the psychological thrillers *A Flash of Red* and *It Was Always You*. Sarah lives with her husband and children in Central Pennsylvania.

Follow Sarah on Twitter (@skstephenswrite) or Facebook (@sarahkstephensauthor) and read more of her writing on her website (www.sarahkstephens.com).

Printed in Great Britain
by Amazon

41361896R00163